I0708425

FORBIDDEN MISTRESS

FILTHY BILLIONAIRES

Evelyn Austin

SILVER GRIFFON ASSOCIATES
ORANGE, CA, USA

Silver Griffon Associates
P.O. Box 7383
Orange, CA 92863

Book Layout ©2023 BookDesignTemplates.com
Cover Art ©2023 Kristie Vanilla Lilly Designs Co.

Accidental Mistress / Evelyn Austin. – 1st ed.
ISBN 979-8-88908-017-6

www.EvelynAustin.com

CHAPTER 1
COCK-BLOCKED

I SHOULDN'T BE HERE.

It's been three years since I've been home, and Malibu is one of those classic beach towns that somehow, magically, always remains unchanged. Beautiful oceanside houses drenched in sunshine. I've always been comforted by that, but I'm a grad student living on the other side of the Los Angeles area now. And I've avoided this magical place. I don't know why—memories, I guess.

But I had to accept the invitation to my cousin Lexi's engagement party. It's a lavish affair, themed like a Mardi Gras masquerade. She's always had a flair for the dramatic. And since family is a priority, she wants us to all spend time together to get to know each other before her big wedding day.

I couldn't say *no* to that. She absolutely insisted I attend this big moment in her life, much as I might have wanted to turn down the invitation. As a plus, the party is being held at the ultra-exclusive beachside club, Exeter House. Well, not inside Exeter House proper, but in the public-facing restaurant, Isca Dumnoniorum. But it's as close as I'll ever get to Exeter House, and I'm anxious to be a part of the elite, even if for one night.

But what I really do *not* want is to bump into my stepbrother, Liam. It's been a year and I'm still avoiding him. The last time I saw him was at my dad's funeral. He didn't speak, or mingle, or interact with anyone at all—not even me. He was like a ghost, a dark figure hovering near the door, ready to sprint at any moment.

Later, I discovered why he was a specter at his own stepfather's funeral. Less than a month later, he assumed full ownership of my dad's multi-million dollar business. Having worked for my dad since his teens, he had a close interest in the business. But to deny me my 50 percent share was just cruel. As a result, I've been left with no money and no way to cover my tuition or rent. I can't even pay for a decent lawyer to fight for what's rightfully mine.

These days, when talking to my stepmom, Lori, I make a conscious effort to *not* ask about Liam. Occasionally, she mentions him—little scraps of information that I cling to and scrutinize afterward. From what I can tell, he's doing ridiculously well running my dad's company and making tons of money. He also has a girlfriend who just got hired as a runway model for fashion week in Paris. And he's doing keto now, apparently.

But me? I'm slightly depressed and perpetually broke. Passing my classes—barely. Eating ramen to keep from starving, and wondering how bald my tires can get before I'm forced to replace them.

I sigh, check my watch and glance around the room; people are enjoying themselves, apparently. Lori mentioned that Liam wouldn't be attending the party, thank God. Something about an award ceremony in New York. Quite honestly, after the words "Liam won't be flying in for the party" fell from her mouth, I stopped listening. I'm just relieved I won't have to dodge him all night.

I adjust my green and gold peacock mask, just as a passing waiter stops to offer me a glass of champagne. With a smile, I pluck a flute off the silver tray and take a sip. "Thanks."

"Cassie," comes a voice at my shoulder. It's my roommate, Avery. I turn to her, all golden-sweet angelic beauty, sparkling blue eyes behind her own feathery mask.

"Isn't this amazing?"

I sip my champagne and study the goings-on under my lashes while I plot how long I have to stay in order to not be rude. "Yeah, just great."

"So hey, there's someone here you should meet."

I throw her a skeptical look, and she laughs. "Not in that way. I mean I was standing in a group with Maddy and Evan and this guy was there too. Maddy introduced me. He's a corporate attorney."

I frown. "So?"

"He specializes in business succession."

I blink, and she turns to point him out to me. He's tall, dark haired, standing beside the bar wearing a green and gold mask with leaves all over it. "His name is Lucien. Go introduce yourself. I bet he could help you with your, uh, family issue."

My brow twitches up. For once, Avery has some real solid advice that looks promising. I love my roommate and we are good friends, but she grew up in a very protected environment and so often she seems not of this world.

"Thanks, I might just do that. Besides, I could use a little more champagne."

The newly engaged host and hostess are off socializing, and Lori is still on her way. LA traffic is brutal this time of day—even when trying to get from one end of Malibu to the other.

With Avery's encouragement, I make my way over to the bar, bumping Lucien's shoulder accidentally-on-purpose as I exchange my empty champagne flute for a full one.

I'm suddenly aware of his attention turning toward me. I glance at him and smile politely. Up close, I can tell that he's gorgeous, even behind the mask—tall, with dark hair, brown eyes, I can tell, even with a hidden face, that he's sexy as fuck. Call it intuition. He's got a glass of scotch or whiskey in his hand, the other hand tucked in his pocket.

If I flirt with him enough, maybe I'll get a date and some free legal advice out of him. Or if I'm lucky, something more?

I smile and sip my champagne. Even just standing there, he practically *exudes* confidence and wealth. It's the way he carries himself, like he owns the world and he's surveying his domain, sipping on his drink. I swallow and slowly shift my gaze back to the dance floor in front of me, hoping he didn't notice my prolonged stare.

"Do you dance?" he asks, his voice low and gravelly.

I blink. *Holy fuck* . Is he talking to me?

"I, um...no. I'm not nearly drunk enough for that."

He laughs a little under his breath and sets his drink down on the bar. We stand there for a moment in awkward silence before he turns to face me. My breath is caught in my lungs, and I take a sip of my champagne to cover up my discomfort.

His gaze flicks over me, from head to toe. "I like your costume."

I smile awkwardly and tug on the hem of my short white skirt. The top crosses over my chest, but because I'm on the curvier side, it creates some *serious* cleavage. An extra few pounds does have its advantages. "You don't think it's too revealing?"

He chuckles. "Oh, yes. But in a good way."

I glance over his mask. "Are you an elf or a woodland creature or something?"

"The Green Man," he says.

"Oh, cool." I nod politely like I know what that is.

He holds out his hand as if to shake mine. "My name is Lucien." His voice is a deep, accented baritone. He sounds British. And he has a sexy name, too. My panties are instantly wet. "What's your name?"

I blink at him. My name? Fuck, what *is* my name? My mind goes blank for a second. Then all at once, I remember. "Cassandra Fitzgerald." I clear my throat. "Cassie, actually. That's what most people call me."

"Cassandra," he repeats, my name rolling off his tongue like a wicked promise. "What do you say we go outside where it's quieter and talk?"

Yes.

"Um, I should wait for my stepmom. She's on her way, and if she doesn't find me standing here, she'll start blowing up my phone," I laugh. My *stepmom*? *Christ*, my game is so off.

Lucien steps closer to me, and his gaze rakes down my body again.

My nipples harden under his scrutiny, and I swallow. "Well, maybe I can go outside for a *few* minutes," I say.

The smile on his face is fucking gorgeous and makes my stomach flip a little. He reaches out and brushes his fingertips down my arm. "What I have in mind will take longer than a few minutes."

I laugh, my breath coming shallow and quick. Just as I open my mouth to say something cute and witty, I feel a presence behind me. Lucien's gaze shifts to something just beyond my shoulder.

Something tightens in my belly, and I get an uneasy feeling. *Liam*.

I smell him before I see him. A thick, delicious cloud of cologne envelops me, tugging at every female cell in my body. Oh, *yesss*. A signature scent, I think they call it. Dunhill Black. He's worn it for as long as I can remember.

"Mr. Force," Lucien says, grating out the name, annoyance thick in his tone. "Good evening."

I'm too afraid to turn around. I don't want to see him. If the beautiful marble floor could open up and swallow me whole, that would be ideal. But that's not going to happen, and if I just stand here, it's going to look suspicious. So I do the only thing I can do; I straighten my shoulders and slowly turn around until I'm half-facing Liam.

"Liam," I say, in feigned excitement. "Your mom said you wouldn't be here."

He's taller than I remember, broad-shouldered, with dark brown hair, and equally dark eyes behind a plain black mask. I swallow, remembering the last time his eyes were fixed on me from a distance, at my dad's funeral.

Liam's gaze flicks over me quickly, and it feels...intimate. Possessive. Without a word to me, he leans in and says something to Lucien that I can't hear. His words are swallowed by the music. I strain to catch a word or a phrase, but I can't hear anything.

Liam pulls back and slaps Lucien on the arm good-naturedly, turns, winks at me, and then disappears into the crowd without so much as a word to me.

I stare after him with narrowed eyes. *What the fuck?*

"What'd he say to you?" I ask Lucien.

With that sly smile, Lucien leans in and whispers in my ear. "I think it's best if we revisit this later. It was a pleasure, Cassandra." Then he slips a business card into my pocket and turns to leave.

Anger bubbles up from my chest. I didn't even get a chance to ask him *one* legal question! What the hell did Liam say to him? Whatever it was, it scared him away. What a fucking cock-blocker! I can't believe him.

I set down my champagne flute and go on the hunt for Liam. Any hesitation I had about seeing him again is completely eviscerated by what he just did. Swoop in, destroy my night, then leave without a word?

Asshole.

I find him on the far side of the room, standing by the Adonis ice sculpture. Fitting, very fitting. There are half a dozen women surrounding him, hanging on his every word. They must have read the article in *Forbes* , outing him as a self-made billionaire. That usually brings all the girls to the yard.

What they don't know is that he's a billionaire because of my dad's hard work. Hard work that Liam is passing off as his own.

As I weave my way toward him, I'm stopped several times by extended family members I haven't seen in ages—asking me about my work, my studies, what I'm doing now. Am I dating? All the typical questions.

I'm thankful for the mask, because it hides my growing irritation.

I'm trapped, listening to Aunt Liz's play-by-play account of her most recent diagnosis—shingles—when I see my stepmom walk through the door. Lori smiles as she hugs and kisses Lexi and is introduced to Lexi's fiancé, Ash.

"I'm so sorry, Aunt Liz," I interrupt. "I see Lori. I'll be right back."

One hundred percent not coming back to finish *that* conversation.

I make a beeline for Lori.

"Hey, honey," Lori says when she catches sight of me. "When did you get here? Just getting across town took me thirty minutes."

"I know," I say. "I've been stalking you on the Find My Peeps app."

Lori takes off her scarf and fans herself. "Where's the booze? I'm not making it through this without a cocktail."

"They're walking around with champagne," I say. "So, um, you told me Liam wasn't coming. What happened to that award thing he was going to?"

Her eyes light up. "Oh, is he here? He said he might make it after all, but he wasn't sure. He's always so busy, you know?"

"Yeah, I do know." I was counting on that.

Lori is already distracted, waving at someone across the room. She then takes off in that direction, leaving me alone by the entrance.

Fuck it. I should just head home. I've shown my face, I've smiled, I've said hello to the beautiful host and hostess. My duty as Lexi's cousin is done, right?

Should I say goodbye? I glance over at my cousin. She's deep in conversation with someone, so I decide not to bother her. If I slip out quietly, she won't know exactly when I left, right? I can text her later, thank her for a fabulous time, and yadda yadda yadda.

I pull my phone out and text my stepmom.

I'm leaving. Headache. Call you later.

I don't even wait for a reply before shoving my phone back into my purse and heading to the coat check. I hand the attendant my ticket and wait as she disappears into the coat room to find my thirty-dollar coat from one of those discount stores.

My phone dings. It's a text from Liam.

Running away, little sister?

Of course, it's him. Of course, he knows exactly where I am and what I'm doing. He can't resist. I grit my teeth and type out a reply.

You're an asshole.

His response comes three seconds later.

You're not wrong. Why are you leaving?

This guy is unbelievable. I type something out that I know will piss him off…

None of your business.

The attendant appears with my coat. But before I can reach for it, my phone dings again.

You've been drinking. My driver will take you home.

What a fucking control freak. I've had a half glass of champagne. I type out yet *another* response.

I'm a big girl. Leave me alone.

As soon as the text is sent, I turn my phone off and shove it into my purse. Honestly, if I continue the conversation, I might turn on my heel, and head right back into the party just to punch him in the face—or knee him in the nuts.

But I don't want to make a scene at Lexi's party, so I do the next best thing…I retreat.

Slipping my coat on, I walk outside to the valet station, handing the young attendant my ticket. He sprints off to fetch my sixteen-year-old blue, beat-up Honda. I tap my foot on the paving stones, impatiently waiting for my car to appear. It's been three minutes, and I'm practically twitching inside because I know, without a doubt, that Liam will eventually come looking for me.

He's always thrived on control. It's what makes him a brilliant businessman. But it's also what makes him super fucking annoying. And the fact that I've turned my phone off, that I'm not responding, is legit eating him alive right now. It's only a matter of seconds before he comes stalking out here, demanding I stay.

Thankfully, I'm one of the first to leave the party, so the attendant is quick. My car pulls around the corner, and I breathe a sigh of relief. Just as the attendant gets out of the car, the front door of Isca swings open, revealing a very angry Liam.

I pause, momentarily dazed. He really is beautiful, *unfortunately* . He's taken off his mask and it's clutched in his hand, so I get a full view of his face. I get why women throw themselves at him. Handsome. Wealthy. Confident. But he's a fucking monster beneath all that, and I just can't pretend he isn't.

"Cass!" he yells, stalking toward me.

I grab the keys from the attendant, palming him a measly two-dollar tip. "Thanks," I say, quickly sliding into the driver's seat.

When Liam is within ten steps of me, I slam the car door, turn on the engine and peel out of there, leaving that sexy monster in my rear-view mirror. As I speed away, I shove my hand out the window and flip him off.

Fuck you, asshole.

If I never see Liam again, it'll be too soon.

CHAPTER 2
ALONE

An hour later, I'm pushing through the front door of Hill House, the student residence I share with a dozen other young female students at the California Institute of Technology. Though I was only at the masquerade for a little over an hour, I could sleep for days.

Thankfully, all the other girls are still at the engagement party, so I have the entire house to myself, which is rare. Heading up to the room I share with Avery and Haley, I slink out of my little white dress and toss it aside. Then I grab a hair tie and knot my shoulder-length hair into a bun on top of my head. Lastly, I throw on a set of soft PJs.

Ah, that's so much better.

Heading to the kitchen, I whip open the fridge. It's empty. One jar of pickles, a bottle of mustard, and a half-gallon of milk that probably expired two weeks ago. Damnit. I should have loaded up on free appetizers as the party when I had the chance. My stomach growls at the thought. Closing the fridge, I push out a breath and pick up the mail I'd grabbed earlier. Most of it is junk mail, but there's also another late notice for my tuition.

Fuuuck .

My mind races through possibilities. I could ask Lori for money again. She's floated me before, but I've always paid her back. And right now, my bank account is negative six dollars. I can't even afford ramen noodles at this point. Eventually, I'll run out of gas, and then I'll *really* be fucked. No gas equals no work. Even bus fare costs money.

Pulling my phone out of my purse, I turn it back on, and the screen is instantly flooded with texts from Liam…

Answer me, Cass.
Where are you?
Don't leave because you're angry with me.
This is fucking bullshit.

The corners of my mouth curl upward. I have to admit, watching him slowly unravel is more than a little satisfying. Maybe that makes me a bitch, but he fucked me over, took money that was rightfully mine, and as a result, my life has been hell. So, yeah, I'm happy he's pissed.

Dialing my stepmom's number, I listen as the phone rings and rings. She's still at the party, so of course she doesn't pick up. At the tone, I leave her a brief message.

"Hey, Lori, it's Cassie. I was wondering if I could borrow fifty dollars until I get paid on Friday. Please give me a call back. Oh, and don't tell Liam I asked you. I'm sure he'll feel some kind of way about it."

I turn my phone back off and set it on the counter. Then I scrawl out a note to Haley and stick in in the place it on her grocery shelf. *IOU a can of soup.*

I open the can and pour it into a bowl, then shove the soup into the microwave. As I wait for it to heat up, I lean against the kitchen counter. Tapping my fingers on the counter, my mind wanders back to the party.

Fuck Liam.

What gives him the right to swoop in—for the first time in *years* —and scare off the hottest guy I've seen in months? Okay, years, if I'm being honest. I'm usually so buried in my school work, I don't have time to come up for air. This time, I was forced to actually be social, and it looked like I might actually get laid. I'm not usually a one-night-stand kinda girl, but fuck, I could have really used some D tonight.

Instead, I'm sitting in bed with my bowl of soup, watching *Survivor* reruns on Avery's TV.

And eventually, I fall asleep—still hungry, and completely alone...

CHAPTER 3
MYSTERY DELIVERY

"CASSIE, HEY. SOMETHING CAME FOR YOU."

I wake up to the sound of Avery's impatient voice. I sit up and glance at the clock on my nightstand. It's eleven in the morning. Oh, shit, I overslept. Thank God I don't have work today.

"What?" I ask, yawning.

"Heavens, you sleep like the dead. I've been trying to wake you up for five minutes." She has a square box cradled in the crook of her arm. I frown and blink at it. I have zero money to order anything online and I never get packages otherwise.

"I'm not expecting any deliveries." I raise my arms above my head and push my toes out in a full body stretch. "Must be a mistake."

"It's not. It has your name on it. Haley signed for the delivery."

I frown as she places the box on my bed. Slowly, I rise to sit up and turn to open it. Inside are two dozen perfect roses, clipped and arranged top-up, forming a carpet of crimson pedals. And the perfume is amazing, delicate, and fresh. They're gorgeous.

There's a card tucked into the side of the box. I open it up. There's a stylized *L* embossed on the front, but nothing else. Inside, the briefest of notes is scrawled in a man's handwriting.

Forgive me.

I stare down at it, trying to figure out who would have sent these. There's no indication who this came from, so I hunt down my phone and turn it on to call the shop that delivered the flowers. As soon as I do, three separate messages pop up, all from Lori.

Got your message. I'll send the money to your account.
Liam is asking about you. He wants to see you.
How about dinner tonight? I'll make your favorite.

Yeah, that's a hard pass. There's not enough lasagna in the world that can convince me to sit down at a dinner table with Liam Force. I shake my head. If she expects Liam and me to come together as one big happy family, she is deep in denial. I can't ignore the fact that he's taken my dad's legacy away from me. Shaking my head in disbelief, I type out a response to Lori.

Thanks, Lori. I appreciate it. I can't do dinner, though. I've got plans tonight.

It's a lie, of course, but she doesn't know that. Not that it will satisfy her. She'll text and call twenty more times, but my mind is made up. No way am I seeing Liam again. It's actually in Lori's best interest. Because if I see Liam, in person, sitting at our family dinner table, drinking my dad's whiskey, I'm going to fucking lose it.

A new text comes in.

Whatever this is between you and Liam is silly. Your dad wouldn't want this. Come have dinner.

Silly. Wow, talk about invalidation. Maybe it is silly to her, but she's not relying on the money from dad's company. She got the house, his pension, everything else—as she should have. No shade there. I just want what should have been mine, and Liam took that from me. So, yeah, I'm pissed.

I toss my phone on the bed. This shit is fucked up. I'm just annoyed that Lori is making this rift *my* fault instead of looking in her son's direction. Maybe she just can't imagine her baby boy doing something shady, but fuck, you don't become one of the richest men in the country while still in your twenties by playing nice and making friends. And apparently, that ruthlessness extends to family.

I turn my attention to the flowers. Who could they have come from? Oh, right, the flower shop. I quickly dial the number on the business card. Someone picks up on the first ring.

"Hi, this is Cassie Fitzgerald. I just got a delivery of flowers, but there was no name. Can you tell me who they came from?"

The woman on the other end is very nice, but after looking it up, then talking to her manager, she tells me the sender was anonymous. I hang up, more confused than ever. I study the card again. Why would the sender want to apologize, and yet be anonymous?

My mind is cast back to that hot guy at Isca last night, Lucien. It was clear he wanted more, but Liam had scared him off. His departure was rather abrupt—almost rude. Maybe this is his way of reaching out? Maybe he's afraid if he gives his name, my stepbrother will get wind of it? Admittedly, Liam can be fucking scary, especially in business. There are rumors about his ruthlessness. My situation is only one of *many* stories.

But how would Lucien have gotten my address? I guess that's no mystery either. That restaurant was filled with my family and childhood friends—any number of people could have given him my address. Shady? Yes. But industrious, to be sure.

Excitement bubbles up in my chest. The flowers are gorgeous and must have cost a ton of money. I scour the card for clues.

Forgive me.

I smile to myself. What a sweet gesture. He's gone to a lot of trouble to tell me he regrets his hasty departure last night. But how am I supposed to contact him?

I'm not gonna lie. The mystery is kinda thrilling. I could definitely use a little excitement in my life. Work and school. That's all I've got right now.

In the middle of my investigation and musings, the phone chimes. A text comes in from Liam.

Come to dinner tonight.

I bristle. Not a question, a command. I scoff at his boldness. I'm not one of his fucking employees or hangers-on. He can't just order me to do something, and I know that pisses him off. I furiously type out my response.

Last night you ambushed me. There's no way I'd ever choose to be in a room with you again unless it's a courtroom and my lawyer is ripping you to shreds. Have a nice life.

As soon as I hit send, a little shiver of fear rolls down my spine. I've known Liam since he was thirteen, and I'm one *thousand* percent certain that text will make him angry. And Liam isn't someone who lets shit lie. He never was. If he doesn't have control, he'll do everything in his power to get it. It's just a matter of when and how.

Don't poke the bear. Isn't that the saying? In this case, that's pretty solid advice. And yet...I can't help myself. *Not* seeing him is the only control I have right now, so I'll use it. And if that makes him retaliatory, then well, what more do I have to lose?

Today is one of the rare occasions that I don't have work or school, so I decide to go to the grocery store with the fifty dollars Lori lent me. I take a quick shower, throw on a baby tee and some yoga pants, and head downstairs to ask my housemates if they need me to grab anything at the store for them.

Haley is at the kitchen table, books open, highlighter in hand. "Oh, hey, Cassie."

"Hey, I'm headed to the store. Need anything?"

She ignores my question. "Were you at the party last night? I didn't see you."

"Yeah, I got there early and left early," I hedge. I don't really want to tell her why I left so abruptly. "It was a beautiful party, and Lexi looked deliriously happy."

"She wears love well," Avery smiles. "It really agrees with her. So...I saw your brother there, looking hot as fuck. I would have talked to him, but he was surrounded by women. How's he doing?"

"I wouldn't really know. We don't talk much." I shrug. Hopefully, that puts an end to it. But of course, knowing Haley, it doesn't.

"Wow, what a shame. He's sooooo fucking hot," she says again, emphasizing her words with a purse of her lips.

My lip curls. *Awkward*. The quicker I can change the subject, the better. "Lexi did look so beautiful, though. She and Ash are serious couple goals."

"Oh! Keith and his frat brothers are having a dayger next Saturday at the house. I told them we'd all be there," she says excitedly.

"I'll have to check my schedule at work. If I'm free, I'll be there," I reply.

"Cool," she says. "Nothing for me at the store, but thanks for asking."

With a nod, I save some gas by walking to the corner grocery store. I grab some chicken-flavored ramen, replacement soup, some milk and a few other things, then head back home.

Three days later, when I get home from work, Avery hands me a note on her own way out the door.

"No one was home earlier when they tried to deliver, so the delivery guy left this note on the front door," she says.

I frown. "Oh, thanks." I glance down at the note as Avery leaves. It's from a high-end department store. They wanted me to call to receive my delivery.

I pull out my phone and call the number on the card. The answering service informs me that they'll send someone over right away with my order. I didn't order anything, but I don't tell them that, obviously. Maybe it's something else from Lucien? My insides tingle with excitement from the thought. What could it be?

An hour later, my "order" arrives. It's a large box this time, with a smaller turquoise box perched on top. I thank the delivery guy, whom I *would* tip, if I had any cash to spare.

I take the packages upstairs and place them on my bed, ripping into the largest one. Resting on a cloud of tissue paper is another card with that same *L* monogram on it. I open it, and the note is just as succinct as the first.

I want to see you.

Okayyyy . I scrunch my brows and try to figure out how I'm supposed to contact him. Again, no name, no other information.

Setting the note down, I dive into the tissue paper and pull out a delicate black satin slip dress. It's so finely made, it feels like a silken cloud between my fingers. My father was well-off when he was alive, but even then, I've never owned something so exquisite. I move to the mirror to hold it up against me.

Haley walks into the bedroom and tosses her backpack down on her bed. "Whoa, what's all this?" She comes over and touches the fine satin dress. "Are you going to a party?"

I shrug. "Some guy I met at Lexi's engagement party has been sending me things. First those roses the other day. And today, he sent me this."

Haley picks up the note and reads it out loud. "'I want to see you.' Oooh-la-la, sexy and mysterious. I likey. What's his name?"

"Lucien." I pause. "Well, he's never actually signed anything so I'm assuming it's him. There's no name on the note or the packages."

She picks up the card from the bed and turns it over in her hands. "Well, there is an *L* there, so that makes sense. Looks like you and Lucien are going somewhere fancy." She picks up the little blue box. "What's this?"

I snatch it out of her hand. "I don't know. I haven't opened it yet."

"Well, then open it before I die of suspense! That's definitely a Tiffany's box. Not that my poor ass would know from firsthand experience, but at least let me live vicariously."

I laugh a little and open the small box. Inside is a smaller velvet jewelry box, with the *Tiffany & Co.* logo emblazoned on it.

"I told you!" Haley says excitedly. "Opennnnn it."

Inside the box is a gorgeous necklace. It has a white-gold chain and a platinum pendant that spreads wide like a *Y* of intricate Celtic knotwork. A large emerald rests in the center.

"*Wow* . This is stunning. Who is this guy?" Haley asks.

I quickly recount the story of meeting him at the party, our brief exchange before my stepbrother chased him off. I shrug and gesture. "I have no idea why he's sending me all these gifts." I stare down at the necklace, confused as fuck.

Haley grins wide. "Well, it's quite obvious he's into you. Snagging a rich dude seems to be catching around here. Maybe it's in the water or something? First Maddy, then Lexi. Now you. Damn, come to think of it, I'm thirsty."

I laugh but can't cover my sudden nervousness. I touch the delicate chain and pendant. "Who gives this kind of gift to someone you exchanged three words with at a party?"

"A rich guy who knows about your brother," Sam supplies. "You think he's trying to get in good with Liam or something?"

My mind is cast back to that short exchange between Liam and Lucien, right in front of me. "It's possible."

I stop and consider that for a second. I've often had to factor my stepbrother's reputation into every friendship I've had. Is the person interested in me, or my super successful, celebrity-like brother?

Lucien and I obviously had sparks before Liam came along and killed the vibe. So it had the opposite effect. Maybe he is just the guy to help me with the business succession issue. He seems…eager to spend time with me, anyway, and couldn't get away from Liam fast enough. Good enough for me.

"Huh. What are you going to do?"

I set the necklace down and look into Haley's green eyes. "I'm going to have some fun with Lucien. Maybe even get some legal advice from him about my situation. Bonus points if any or all of that pisses off my stepbrother."

Chapter 4
Sacked

THE NEXT DAY AT WORK, MY MANAGER PULLS ME INTO the back office and fires me. Well, okay, *fire* is a bit harsh. She's "let me go" because they just don't have the hours to give me. Which is strange, because in the last few weeks, we've been busier than ever.

After turning in my apron and filling out some paperwork, I'm near tears as I walk home. What the fuck am I going to do?

Aside from filing for unemployment, of course. My mind races. I'll need to update my resume and start putting out applications for other server jobs nearby. But all of that is going to take time. And living in a college town, jobs like that are hard to come by, at least in this area. I could look for a job in a neighboring city, but I'd rather not have to spend money on gas going to and from work if I can help it.

My shoulders sag in defeat as I realize that after my bills are paid, I'll only have twenty dollars in my account. And there's still that late tuition notice hanging over my head.

With a deep breath, I walk into the Hill House. One of my housemates, Sam is studying on the couch. She turns to see who's just come in. "Oh, hey Cassie, I thought you had to work. Is everything okay?"

I hadn't planned on telling anyone quite yet, but whatever. I swallow a lump in my throat. "I was let go."

She turns her whole body, shock registering on her face. "Oh no!"

Avery walks in with a bowl of cereal in her hand. "What? What happened?" She looks between Sam and me, all the while shoveling a spoonful of fruit loops into her face. "Did I miss something?

"Cassie just got fired," Sam supplies.

"*Let go* ," I correct. "And it's fine. I'll find something else."

My stomach sinks even as I say it and put on a brave face for my two friends. After a little more chit-chat, I head off their rapid-fire suggestions of where I'll be putting in applications by heading upstairs.

"I'll ask around for any open positions. There might be something on campus," Avery calls after me.

"Thanks!" I say without losing a step or turning around. I just want to curl up my bed, hide under the covers and scream into my pillow. I don't do that, though, because as soon as I get up to my room, I remember that Haley has the day off work, and a late class, so she still sleeping.

So instead of screaming into my pillow, I do the next best thing—I throw on some yoga pants and head over to the university gym. I spend some time on the elliptical, then join a Zumba class that starts up. It feels good to expend my energy in a constructive way. By the time the class is done, I'm exhausted.

The next day, I start pounding the pavement after class, looking for jobs in my area. I have some experience with working as a server. I dip into office buildings in search of a light office job but only end up leaving my CV in a handful of places with no promises of a callback.

As the days pass and stretch into a week, I can feel the anxiety start to creep up on me. Unemployment won't kick in for weeks yet, and even then, it's a fraction of what I can earn at a full-time job.

As I'm updating my job search spreadsheet, I start looking for retail jobs as well, though I'm aware that it's the wrong time of year. Jobs that are easy to pick up during the holiday season are ever-so-challenging to find in the early spring.

Without realizing what I'm doing, I also find myself Googling Lucien. He and his mysterious gifts are still on my mind. On the internet, I discover pictures of him from his law office and at local public events. Tall, dark-haired, brown eyes, handsome face, nice physique. He's even hotter without the Green Man mask and I start to fantasize about him and what he could want from his mysterious gifts.

I decide to stop playing coy and email him to set up an appointment and tell him about the case I want to build against Liam. I ask him if he does pro bono work, since I'd recently lost my job.

Hopefully he'll end up telling me what he's expecting to accomplish with his mystery deliveries.

While waiting to hear back from him or any prospective employers, I manage to wrangle up some dog-walking money from a couple of the professors who live nearby, but I'm still pretty broke. I grit my teeth at the thought of asking Lori for another loan. I'd do anything to avoid that. It's a pride thing. Even if I tell her not to mention it to Liam, I know she will. And

I don't want him to know my business. *Especially* how much I'm struggling.

After walking Professor Andrade's adorable corgi, Matilda, I enter Hill House one late afternoon. Avery, Sam and Haley are sitting on the couch, watching a Hallmark movie and munching on gluten-free snacks. Avery points to a table by the door. "Cassie, you got yet another delivery from your secret admirer! I signed for it."

There's a large envelope with my name on it. I blink, excited. Could this be in response to my email to Lucien?

Thanking Haley for accepting the delivery, I decide to take the envelope up to my room and open it up away from prying eyes.

Inside is a formal letter addressed to me using my legal name:

Dear Cassandra Fitzgerald,

We are pleased to offer you the following position.
Assistant Hospitality Hostess
Location: Obscura at Exeter House, Malibu, CA
Pay Rate: $150-$250/hour commensurate with experience. (Negotiable).
Hours: 10-15 per week (negotiable). Evenings. Flexible.

Should you choose to accept the position, please see the instructions on the attached sheet. We're thrilled to welcome to the Exeter House family!

Kind regards,
Miss Chloe Lawrence
Head of Hospitality, Obscura at Exeter House

I frown, mind racing. What the hell? I would remember applying for a job at Exeter House, for sure.

I've actually heard of Obscura before. My cousin, Lexi, went there a few times before getting together with her guy, Ash. And my former roommate, Gwen, was actually doing an article on the club several months ago, before she suddenly dropped everything and took a trip to Hawaii and came back with a handsome British royal.

Neither of them ever explained to me exactly *what* the club is. Just that it's *super* exclusive and attached to Exeter House.

My eyes scan the letter again, sticking on that "negotiable" hourly rate. *Damn.* I have experience in hospitality. Before the restaurant server job, I worked graveyard shift at a hotel reception desk. If I could score the higher end of that hourly rate, that could bring me upwards of twenty-five hundred dollars per *week.*

That's...life-changing money. I could pay my bills, and wouldn't have to be a connoisseur of every flavor of ramen available. I could pay my overdue tuition. But more importantly, I could hire a lawyer to take my stepbrother to the cleaners for my half of the company.

Did I say life-changing? I meant paradigm-changing. I meant rewriting the story where the underdog wins and kicks the bully to the curb.

My heart is racing as I lift the cover letter and look at the details...Obscura's address, where to enter the building and how, and when to report for work, plus contact info for this Chloe Lawrence person.

At the bottom is a handwritten note in the same sloppy writing as the other two cards I've received.

Heard you were in need of a new job. I took the liberty of suggesting your name for an opening at Obscura. Sending a car to pick you up at eight tonight. Wear the dress and the necklace.

-L

Finally, a signature! Of sorts. A smile spreads across my face at the realization that I was right—it must be Lucien, sending me these things.

But one question looms—how did he find out about me losing my job? I make a mental note to ask him the next time I see him.

Once the movie's over, downstairs, my roommates bound into the bedroom asking about the newest delivery. I blink and hand them the letter, still stunned and hoping they can maybe help me make sense of it.

Avery's eyes are huge. "Are you going to take the job?"

Haley scoffs at her. "Did you see how much they want to pay her? Of course she's going to take it. What kind of job is it, do you think?"

Avery points to the first page. "Well, it says right here it's for an assistant hospitality hostess, whatever that is."

Haley rolls her eyes. "Yeah, that's what I mean, what kind of job is it? Assistant hospitality hostess doesn't tell me anything. That could be anything from cleaning hotel rooms to…I dunno, serving drinks topless at a nudy bar?"

Avery—who exudes such pure innocence that we've sometimes referred to her as Snow White—looks scandalized. Her pale beauty only serves to reinforce the image. "You wouldn't serve drinks topless, would you, Cassie?"

I shrug. "For that kinda money? Why not?"

"But—" The worry is clear on Avery's face, in her big blue eyes.

By this time, Sam has wandered in to ask what all the fuss is about, has inspected the letter, reading it with a smile and a nod of approval.

"You're at least going to find out what it entails, right?"

I glance at the invitation in my hand. It does look really intriguing. "I don't know," I say. "Is it too good to be true? What if he's a serial killer or something?"

Avery laughs. "I'm the one who told you to go introduce yourself to him. I do know he's a very respected lawyer, if that helps. But you should definitely find out more info before you agree to anything."

Haley cuts in. "Besides, murderers don't bother to woo their victims by sending gifts. Serial Killer 101, don't leave a paper trail."

"See, this is what I meant by you watching way too many true crime shows," Sam tells Haley.

Haley throws her hands up. "What? It's useful information to have!"

Avery taps her chin with her forefinger, thinking. "Don't they do extensive background checks to even be a member of Exeter House? It's not likely that they'd let a serial killer in."

Sam points at Avery. "Yes, excellent point. Exeter House is a safe location. Three of our roommates live there now, at least part time. Maddy and Lexi are there most of the time and Gwen bounces between there and the UK. I guess you could ask your cousin, right? She might know Lucien well enough to vouch for him. Exeter House is huge, but the community is small. Maddy says everyone knows everyone else's business."

"Yeah." I suck in a sharp breath. "Maybe I'll give Lexi a call and see if she knows anything about this Lucien guy."

"What's his last name?" Sam asks. "I can Google him."

"I already looked him up and everything points to legit. I even emailed his work email asking if he takes pro bono since I don't have a job right now and can't pay him. I'm guessing this is his response. Maybe he felt sorry for me?" I laugh.

I know it's almost impossible for lawyers who belong to big expensive law firms to promise pro bono work because they have to cover the services of the research team, the assistant work and everything else that doesn't directly involve the lawyer.

"I could go with you tonight…while you check it all out." Haley suggests. "Safety in numbers, you know?"

I perk up a little and smile at her. "Really? You'd go with me?"

"Hell yeah," she half-laughs. "Hot trillionaires are hidden in every nook and cranny of that place. Might as well go on the hunt for one of my own! Maddy, Lexi *and* Gwen all found their guys there."

Sam rolls her eyes. "They didn't *find* them there. Okay, maybe Lexi did. But they just all happened to be members."

Haley waves her hand dismissively. "Same difference."

I hold up the invite. "Okay, well, a car will pick us up at eight! Now I'm getting excited."

All the stress and worry of meeting this mysterious stranger is melting away now that Haley is going with me. She's like my armor, my confidence. If we feel anything is the least bit sketchy, we'll bail.

As soon as the girls file out of the room to go to their group yoga, I pull out my phone and text my cousin, Lexi.

Hey, do you know a guy named Lucien at Exeter House? He recommended me to a Ms. Lawrence for a job at Obscura. Assistant hospitality hostess. I just want to make sure L is legit and that this job is on the up and up.

I go about my afternoon, taking a shower, shaving every bit of my body I possibly can—hey, I might score soon with an incredibly hot executive lawyer. When I check my phone again, I see two messages from Maddy in reply.

He's a high-level executive consultant and one of Ash's business associates. He's also an associate member of Exeter House, not fully fledged yet. All I know is that he's rich as fuck and a playboy, but not dangerous.

As for the job...Obscura is an adult members-only club. You know that, right? I've been a few times with Ash. You'll need an open mind as you'll see a lot of new things, believe me. But working for Chloe Lawrence seems like it could be a lot of fun. Not sure what that job will entail, but there are a lot of moving parts to Obscura. I'm guessing she'll have you at the coat and phone check room but that's just a guess. I can reach out to her to find out more details if you want.

I suck in a breath and let it out in a long sigh. Well, all of that information has put my mind at ease, at least. I type out my reply.

It's all good, by the time you hear back from her, I'll have had a chance to ask her myself but thank you for all that info. Very good to know. Love you, cuz!.

Exeter House caters to the uber-ultra elite. The *elite* of the elite. I mean, fuck, their tap water tastes like it's run through gold pipes. So, Avery is right, Exeter House wouldn't risk welcoming someone into their realm who is problematic—even if he isn't a fully fledged member yet.

By the time eight o'clock rolls around, both Haley and I are ready to go. We're standing in the small foyer at Hill House, clutching our sequined purses. I tug on the hem of my silky black dress.

"Do you think this is too short?" I ask the room.

Sam is staring out the front window, waiting for the car to pull up, but she glances back at me. "No, it looks lovely on you. Your guy has great taste."

"How'd he even know your size?" Haley asks.

"No idea. Wild guess, maybe?" I offer.

"That's one hell of a wild guess," Sam says. "Maybe he fucks so many women that he knows how to size them up?"

"Gross!" I scrunch my nose. "I *choose* to believe it's a lucky guess."

Lexi did say Lucien was a playboy, but I didn't tell them that. The last thing I need right now is anyone talking me out of going to Exeter House this evening. The choice is made. Haley and I are going. It'll be an adventure, right? Right.

The car pulls up right at three minutes to eight, and the driver gets out and comes to the door. Avery and I say our goodbyes to the rest of the girls and climb inside the luxurious black town car.

We're offered champagne, weirdly, which gives me pause, since I'm on my way, essentially, to a job interview. I don't accept any, but Haley sips at a flute during the hour-long ride to Malibu. We spend the time chatting about anything and everything, and for a time, I'm distracted from my nervousness.

When we arrive, we're driven around to a side entrance for Exeter House. There, we enter through the discreet doors of Obscura. It's already bustling, but a security guard outside seems to know who I am before I even inform him I'm here for a job. Strangely, his eyes linger on my necklace before he looks up into my face.

"You're here to talk to Ms. Lawrence, I believe," he says in a harsh New York City accent.

I nod, and we're shown in directly. Haley clasps my arm excitedly, and we are taken past the reception area and into a small office around the corner.

We barely have time to say a few words to each other before a petite and exquisitely dressed woman, her chestnut hair styled in an an elegant updo and a thin golden cat-eye mask enters the room. She's wearing a tight calf-length black dress, four-inch stilettos. She looks stunning. Her vibe is professional with a slight edge to it. I like her already.

The woman's gaze shifts between Haley and me. "Miss Fitzgerald?"

I raised my hand slightly, then lower it because I realize I look dorky, like I'm in class or something. "Yes. I, um, brought my friend, Haley Ortiz. I hope that's okay."

The woman nods once. "Miss Ortiz, you are most welcome. I am Ms. Lawrence, and I will be providing you with your employment documents. If you agree to the terms, we can sign and you'll do a shift tonight. Your host is expecting you."

"My—my host?" I stammer as Ms. Lawrence places several documents in front of me. I glance down, remembering my folded up resume in my purse. I was going to use it to negotiate up a better hourly rate, but my jaw drops when I see the figure on the papers in front of me. The pay rate has been filled in already. *Four hundred dollars an hour*. What...what the fuck? My mind races to do the math—*at ten hours per week, four weeks per month....*

"Hart is your host. Your job will be assisting him in one of the VIP rooms."

"Assisting? And um, what does that entail?" I'm suddenly realizing that my lack of curiosity and questions about Obscura has left me incredibly ignorant. Adult club? But...what is that exactly? And do all jobs at Exeter House pay this monumentally well? I spare a glance at Haley, and she's reading the same paperwork I am.

"You won't be asked to do anything you don't want to do. Consent is of the utmost importance here. You will not be touched unless you've given permission first."

I swallow. "Okay...and I keep my clothes on?"

She smiles and nods. "That is completely your choice, as well. No one may force you to remove your clothing or force you to perform sexual favors. You will, however, likely be seeing a lot. Obscura is an exclusive adult club, after all."

I nod. "Oh—okay. And if I decide the job isn't for me?"

Her smile is perfectly in place, never faltering. "You may resign at any time with two weeks' severance pay."

Oh! That's...beyond generous.

Ms. Lawrence points to the places where I should sign, then discreetly dismisses herself after receiving a text, saying she'll be back in a few minutes. I suspect it's a ploy to give me some privacy, so I can ask Haley's opinion.

Haley has been reading the entire document as I've been talking, and she tells me that everything looks standard. I nearly faint with relief, like I'd been holding my breath, afraid someone would tell me this is all a dream.

I frown. There has to be a catch to this, right? I've never gotten this lucky. Or maybe all the good luck ever due to me has been saved up for this one moment. Maybe I should buy a lottery ticket on the way home.

By the time Ms. Lawrence returns, all the flagged places have my signature on them and she collects the papers with a satisfied smile. "Welcome to the Obscura family, Ms. Fitzgerald. Have you given any thought to what your club pseudonym will be?"

I blink a few times. "Ah, my pseudonyn?"

Ms. Lawrence hands us each a mask. Mine is brownish and covered by faux fur and a little cute black nose on it, like a woodland animal. Haley's has gold glitter and white feathers. They cover roughly half our faces, from the nose up.

"Identities are fiercely protected and discretion is key at Obscura."

"Okay..."

"For now, we'll call you C, your first initial, but you'll have to come up with a more permanent one. Your host might be able to help you with that. But again, it's very important that you never take off your mask or disclose any personal information. Violation can be grounds for dismissal. Do you understand?"

I nod. Ms. Lawrence raises her brows in disapproval so I clear my throat and say, "I understand the terms."

She smiles again. "Very good. Well, if there are no other questions, I'll have you escorted to your shift. Ms. Ortiz, you won't be permitted into the VIP rooms unless invited by a member. However, you are free to enjoy the bar, the dancing, and the public rooms." She hands Haley what looks like a wooden coaster. "First two drinks are on me. Enjoy." She informs me that she'll be emailing me a handbook of the club rules that I must learn and tells me I can study up on them tonight after my first shift.

We're required to surrender our phones to the cloak room— as Lexi had said—before we can enter the club proper. We put on our masks, as instructed, and soon, Ms. Lawrence is leading us through the labyrinth of an exquisitely upscale and luxurious, if dimly lit, nightclub.

Once we move through the thick double doors, music hits us like a wall of sound. Okay, so far so good. Perfectly normal for a nightclub, right? We enter from a balcony area that looks out onto the sleek, black dance floor. Everyone here is masked and many are scantily clad. Everyone dressed to the nines.

We follow Ms. Lawrence down the staircase to the main floor. The décor is black and polished gold chrome, shiny black marble with gold veins running through them. Everything drips wealth and decadence. The bar, at the center of the large room, is circular, and nearby is a large sunken lounge with low tables, velvet couches cloaked in dimness. All along the walls, there are private booths with dark curtains, some pulled to create a mini-room of sorts.

The dance floor is well occupied, and above, holograms of couples in sexy embraces undulate against each other. Real life, scantily clad and masked go-go dancers, like Las Vegas showgirls, dance on caged, elevated platforms all around the dance floor.

Haley and I glance at each other, and I mouth the words, "What is this place?"

I swallow and reach out for Haley's hand. She threads her fingers through mine and squeezes. It's the only indication that she's just as nervous as I am.

Ms. Lawrence stands at the threshold of this new place and extends her arm. "Welcome to Obscura."

I hesitate, aware, somehow, that there's no turning back. The papers are signed.

"What is this place?" I ask Ms. Lawrence.

"Come and see for yourself," she says. "Your host is waiting for you."

CHAPTER 5
OBSCURA

I STUDY THE SPRAWL OF FLESH ALL AROUND ME. WHAT THE fuck have we walked into?

Holy shit. I feel a bit like Alice falling down the rabbit hole. I laugh at myself and that cliché thought, but in this instance, it's 100 percent accurate. If anyone we encounter asks us to eat a mushroom, or invites me to tea, we're out of here.

I spare a glance at Haley, and she just shrugs at me from behind her mask. She doesn't look freaked out, which bolsters me a little. With a nod, I let go of Haley's hand and continue to follow Ms. Lawrence up the stairs, and that's when the real adventure begins.

Up here, people are barely clothed. The live music echoes off the walls. It looks like some kind of high-end brothel.

"Um, excuse me?" I say. When Ms. Lawrence stops and turns around to face Haley and me, I continue, "Where will I be stationed?" She'd said something about a VIP room.

"Your host is just this way," she repeats, extending her arm, indicating a long, dark hallway.

Haley comes up behind me and whispers in my ear, "I think this is the part of the movie where we get murdered."

"Yeah, I'm getting the murder vibe, too," I reply, never taking my eyes off Ms. Lawrence.

Ms. Lawrence leads us up yet another staircase, her hips swaying gracefully with every step. A concierge waits at the top. Ms. Lawrence stops and turns to back to us. "Only members, employees and invited guests are allowed past this point." Her gaze shifts to me. "C, your host's room is beyond this hallway. But I will need to escort your friend back to the bar, as I mentioned before."

Haley nods, prepared for this. "Sure, yes. And thanks for the free drink coupons."

I glance at the area beyond the stairs. It's dark, but I can see a few people milling about. Nervousness congeals in my belly. What should I expect from this new and unusually high-paying job? I'm confident with the boundaries clearly set, as they've been listed by Ms. Lawrence.

I have to admit that I'm nearly ready to call this whole thing off and head back home when Ms. Lawrence speaks up. "You're perfectly safe. And I'm always here to always back you up."

There's a confidence in her voice that sets me at ease. I can't help but think about that money, too. It's more than tempting—it's essential. This place does look well-managed with plenty of staff walking around. If there's ever a point where I feel unsafe, then I'll just bail, as Ms. Lawrence reassured me I can.

I nod. "Okay." I turn to Haley. "How long do you think you'll stick around?"

Haley smiles. "I've got you. I can stay 'til you're done. Go. Have fun and make the big bucks."

I laugh. "Thanks. I'll try."

Without waiting for Ms. Lawrence, Haley turns on her heel and heads back downstairs on her own. I watch as she disappears, then I turn back to Ms. Lawrence, swallowing the anxiety creeping up my throat.

She smiles at me. "Right this way, C."

We pass the concierge station at the top of the stairs and head into a central seating area. Everything is classic luxury—rich velvet, and satin wallpaper, and dim lighting, dark suede furniture.

But juxtaposed with the elegance is a raw, sinful quality. Exhibit A—a woman walks by us wearing nothing but a collar and leash around her neck. It's so unexpected that I do a double-take. I'm not a prude by any means, but some warning would be cool, you know? Just a quick "Hey, you might see some naked people with collars on" would suffice.

Ms. Lawrence leads me down a dark hallway. Every door is shut, but I can hear some of what is happening within each room. A moan of pleasure. The lashing sounds of someone being whipped or paddled. Grunts. And the sound of skin slapping against skin.

Working in a sex club might prove more challenging than I thought it might. I take a deep breath and try to summon some strength and courage.

Ms. Lawrence stops at a door at the end of the hallway and turns to me. "You will be assigned to this room, and this room only. When you come for your shifts, this is where you will meet your host, Hart."

I nod to show my understanding, glancing at the glossy black door. There's no number on it or anything. "Oh, okay. Um…" I glance back down the hallway. "So just to be clear…I won't be expected to participate in any of the..." I search for the right word, "...activities. Correct?"

Ms. Lawrence nods. "That's correct. You will serve Hart as his assistant hostess. But no physical touch is required of you, both on the giving and receiving end. You'll be assisting him in his activities but not participating unless you state your verbal consent to do so without being coerced in any way."

I swallow, still a little doubtful. I mean this is a sex club, and I guess I technically work here now. I filled out all the paperwork. But the second someone touches me, I'm out the door. I don't need a job that badly.

"Is there any kind of dress code?" I ask.

"That is for your host to decide," she says.

I nod once. I have my boundaries, and I resolve to hold firm to those. No nudity, no touching and absolutely *nothing* degrading.

Turning back to the door, she knocks once. When there's no response, she opens the door, then steps aside, allowing me to walk past her, into the room. As I step over the threshold, I'm expecting…well, I don't know what I'm expecting exactly, but the room is empty, and I release the breath that had been trapped in my lungs.

Why am I so relieved?

"Have a seat. Hart should be here shortly. There's an in-house phone on the wall in case of any problem whatsoever." Ms. Lawrence says before leaving, clicking the door shut behind her.

I take a split second to glance around the dimly lit room. I'm in a bedroom, I guess. There's a beautiful wooden four-poster and curtained bed raised on a platform in the center of the room. Nearby there is a single chair and a large gilded mirror mounted on the ceiling. There's another mirror that spans the entire length of the back wall. On the adjacent wall, there's another door, a small marble sink, and a large mahogany wardrobe. All in all, for such a large room, it's fairly sparsely furnished. Elegant, but definitely minimal.

I'm standing there for several minutes before a door on the westward-facing wall opens and a dark figure steps inside the room with me. My breath catches in my throat, and on instinct, my entire body tenses up.

It's him. *Lucien* .

At the masquerade, he wore a Green Man mask. Today, he's wearing a full-face stag mask that covers his entire face, framed by antlers and all.

He's wearing black slacks, a black belt, dress shoes, and nothing else. His chest is bare, and *fuck,* he's beautiful, perfectly sculpted. He has a large tattoo covering his muscular shoulder, bicep, and part of his chest that depicts a stag with intricate Celtic knotwork as part of its face and antlers. It's incredibly detailed and beautiful.

Instinctively, and without immediately realizing what I'm doing, I touch the necklace that rests at the base of my throat, right where my collarbones meet. It's cold and heavy there and bears more than a passing resemblance to that tattoo.

I step forward, my heels clicking on the black marble floor. "Lucien?"

He says nothing. Just stares at me for a second, then undoes his buckle and unthreads it from his pants, pulling it free with a flourish.

Oh. Kay.

Oh, wait, Ms. Lawrence did say we had to use pseudonyms here. Maybe that's the reason he's being so weird, because I called him by his name instead of by his pseudonym?

I swallow, fear rushing through my veins. Ms. Lawrence said I wouldn't be expected to do anything physical, and I suddenly wonder if *he* got that memo. He's eyeing me like a lion sizes up a piece of fresh steak.

We stand for several seconds like that, staring at each other. My gaze is locked on him, heart hammering in fight-or-flight mode. Like predator and prey. I don't dare say anything else lest I put my foot in my mouth again. Just when I've convinced myself to bolt for the door, it opens of its own volition, and a gorgeous dark-haired woman walks through wearing a white bunny costume—complete with whiskered mask capped by floppy ears, white thigh-high stockings, a skimpy leotard, and white fuzzy heels. She's about the same height, build and coloring as me. Her curves are incredible, and she owns the space with all the confidence I wish I had.

She struts in and closes the door behind her, not even sparing me a glance. She's completely focused on the man dominating the room around him. As she passes me, I notice something in her hand. A black leather whip. Lucien—or rather, *Hart*—steps toward her, and the woman meets him halfway. He's facing me, and I can see her back as she kneels in front of him, holding out the whip on her open palms, like she's presenting him with a gift.

What. The. Fuck?

I watch, riveted to the scene as he takes the whip from her hands and commands, "Stand. Turn around," in that thick, British accent I remember from the masquerade.

Without a word, the woman does as instructed.

"Good girl," he says in a deep voice that slithers through my veins. "Now, bend over the bed."

Again, without a word, she ascends the two steps to the top of platform and lowers her torso onto the mattress, bending at the waist, so that her ass is exposed to him. He steps up to her and reaches down to smooth his hand over the smooth globes. "You were late," he says sternly.

Her quivering tone comes a second later, though I can't tell if it's from fear or anticipation. "I apologize, Master."

"You will be punished."

My own breath catches, and I suddenly feel super awkward, standing here, just watching this intimate scene unfold.

The woman nods, her face half-buried in the mattress.

"Tell me you understand," he says.

"Yes, Master," she says with a breathy voice. "I understand that I must be punished."

Reaching down, he unfastens her bodysuit at the crotch and rolls it up so that her sex is exposed. Then he readjusts his grip, pulls his arm back, and releases the whip with a sickening crack. I only know it connects with her skin because of her yelp and the angry red welt the braided leather leaves in its wake.

When he pulls back his arm again, ready to repeat the action, I can't help but gasp. He's seriously going to do it again? Wasn't once enough? His head whips up, and his steely gaze from behind the mask connects with mine.

Oh, shit.

I was probably supposed to remain silent, like a fly on the wall. But to be fair, I wasn't given any instruction on how to behave once I'm in this room. Taking a step back, then another, and another, my spiked heel bumps into the chair and I fall to the floor, squarely on my ass. It could have been worse, but the hard marble isn't exactly forgiving, and I groan.

Okay, so far, my first day on the job has been a hot mess…and I'm only five minutes in.

Before I can get to my feet, Hart is barreling toward me. I can't see much of his face, but his dark eyes are snapping in anger. Will I be punished next? That thought fills me with fear.

And something else…

I flinch as he reaches down, grips my upper arms and hauls me up. Everywhere his skin touches mine, it feels like sharp, electric jolts zipping through my body. I've never felt anything like it. Of course, I've also never been in a situation quite like this. I consider myself pretty adventurous, but this place is pushing it.

I'm a vanilla sex kind of girl. Lights off. Missionary, maybe the occasional cowgirl or doggy-style. It all ends the same way— an orgasm, and a good night's sleep. What's not to love? Why all the theatrics?

"Stay," he says gruffly, depositing me firmly in the chair. "Do *not* move, unless I've told you to do so."

I press my lips together and nod.

Releasing my arms, he turns and goes back to the woman waiting to be punished, and I'm not going to lie, I feel a little twinge of regret that his attention is being pulled away from me. Swallowing, I watch as he picks up the whip and delivers another blow. Then another, and another. Even as he's whipping her, though, his gaze never leaves mine. It's both awkward as fuck and, oddly, fascinating.

When it's done, the woman is whimpering. He pulls back and sets the whip down. Tears are streaming down the woman's face from under her mask—and I only know that because she sniffles, and I can see the tears trickling down her neck. But there's also a smile of deep satisfaction etched on her face, like something from within her has been released. *Exorcised.*

Hart gestures to me. "The lotion is in the wardrobe. Hand it to me."

Oh, *me* . This is my job, I guess. Fetcher of things. I jolt into action, skittering across the slick marble floor to the wardrobe. I pull the huge piece of furniture open, and a little light flickers on to illuminate the inside, which is fortunate because it is quite dark in here. On one side of the wardrobe, there are whips, paddles, ropes, blindfolds, dildos…every sex toy I could dream up. On the other side are lotions, salves, jellies, and all the after-care stuff. There's a ton of it. I grab one of the bottles of lotion, shut the thick doors, and walk it over to him. He takes it from my hand and begins messaging the sweet-smelling lotion into the woman's reddened skin.

As I walk back to my chair and sit down, I take note of her face. Even behind the mask, I can still see the pure ecstasy in her relaxed features, and for a second, I feel envious. All of this man's attention is on her, his anger, his pleasure, his devotion. I might find that deeply satisfying, too.

When he's done, he sets the lotion aside and gently pulls her body suit over her swollen bottom. Then, he pulls her into a standing position in front of him. "You've pleased me," he says affectionately. "Now, you may leave."

I can see the hesitancy in her stance, but she ultimately complies, walking stiffly out the door.

"You may leave as well," he says to me.

I clear my throat. "I, um, I was told I would be here for a full shift."

Normally, I wouldn't argue about being sent home, but I desperately need the money.

"You are no longer needed this evening, but you'll be paid the full amount. Return tomorrow, same time," he says in an even voice. Then, after a pause he adds, "We'll see how much more you can take."

Am I seeing things, or is there a little glint of amusement in his eyes when he says that last bit?

With a nod, I stand up and walk to the door. Should I thank him or say goodbye? Should I call him "master?" I decide not to say anything. I just flash him a tight smile and walk out. But his words follow me.

We'll see how much more you can take.

CHAPTER 6
VOYEUR

"So, ALL YOU HAD TO DO WAS WATCH AND HAND HIM some lotion?" Haley asks, her red brows arched high on her pale face.

We're on our way home, in the back seat of the town car that had been sent for us by Obscura—I'd guess, by Lucian—and I'm recounting the night to her.

"And yet you're still getting paid for the entire night? Wow, where do I sign up? Talk about a dream job." She laughs.

I chew my thumbnail, thinking. "Yeah, it was weird, though. He was engaging with the woman and yet he was staring at me the entire time. Like, looking *right* at me as he whipped her."

Haley shrugs. "That doesn't seem too weird. He was getting off on you watching. I once had a boyfriend ask me to not wash my feet, and then before sex, he would lick them clean with his tongue. It's the only way he could get off."

I scrunch my nose. "I don't see the appeal, but I get your point. To each his own."

"Yep. Maybe having someone watch is just Hart's thing."

The rest of the night goes by in a sort of blur. I scarf down a bowl of noodles and zone out to old reruns of *Seinfeld.* But all the while, in my mind's eye, Hart's gaze is piercing through me.

I can still see every detail of his body in my memory—his broad shoulders, his perfectly sculpted torso, the cut abs…and those eyes. I know we just met, but they feel so warm and familiar to me. It's so strange. Beyond the intensity of his gaze, there's a deep recognition I just can't shake.

I'd really hoped that tonight I'd be able to pick Lucien's brain about getting my dad's business back, but a sex club didn't seem like the time or place. In fact, we barely said two words to each other. I walk over to my desk and check my email to see if there's any reply from Lucien.

I have his phone number, too, from the card he gave me on the night of the masquerade. If he doesn't reply soon, I resolve to call his office. I want to be persistent without coming off as desperate, but now I just might be able to pay his bill—ironically with the money he's paying me to help out his kink at Obscura.

The following morning, I check my email again before heading off to class. Waiting in my inbox is an email from Lucien, and I hurriedly open it.

Dear Ms. Fitzgerald,

I would be pleased to meet with you regarding your business venture. Please set up an appointment with my assistant, Sara. I have included her contact information below.

Kind regards,
Lucien Hunter

I stare at the email for a second. The formality of it has me kind of taken aback. Ms. Fitzgerald? Kind regards? The email is short and professional and more than a little stiff? I just watched him whip a half-naked woman last night at a sex club, for God's sake. If that doesn't call for a little casual banter, then I don't know what does.

Weird.

I run into Haley on my way down to the kitchen, and I tell her what happened.

She shrugs. "Okay, maybe he just wants to keep business and pleasure separate. I'm guessing a lot of professionals do that."

I nod slowly, absorbing her theory. It does make sense, except… "Why not just tell me that, though?"

She flashes me an exasperated look. "He's a man. Men don't explain anything. To anyone. They just bumble around, expecting everyone else to fall in line."

I press my lips together. I have a feeling something is going on with her. "You okay?" I ask. "Something you want to chat about?"

She shakes her head and laughs. "No, I'm just saying…they're all the same. Dumb as rocks."

"Yeah. You're right." I nod. "I'll just go with it."

It wouldn't hurt to keep Hart and Lucien separate, I guess. It might make things easier in my own head, as well.

That night, I get ready for "work." So the silky black dress he sent me is apparently my "uniform." Black heels. Hair down. Minimal makeup—most of my face is hidden by a mask, anyway. And the necklace…the one that lies heavily across the base of my throat and eerily resembles his massive chest tattoo. I haven't been interacting with him, really, but he's clearly got an aesthetic. I wonder if he chose me because I look so much like the woman dressed in the bunny costume. I choose not to dwell on that thought.

Oh well, whatever. It's a job, and if I want to get paid, I'll just have to go with it.

A nice perk of this arrangement is that an Exeter House town car picks me up every evening and drops me off at home when I'm done, whenever that is. And we're talking about a pretty intense commute. Pasadena to Malibu is an hour's drive usually. As it did the day before, the car picks me up at eight.

After spending some time on my phone or watching traffic go by, I arrive at the same side entrance from Exeter House. I tie my mask on before leaving the car, and the driver comes around to open my door.

"Thank you—" I glance down at the name tag pinned to his uniform. "Andrew."

With a smile, he tips his hat. "My pleasure. The front desk has my cell number when you're ready to return home."

There's no judgment in his tone, and that's a relief. I'm not someone who usually does this—comes to a sex club every night—so when I see the kindness in Andrew's aged face, I relax a little. Nodding, I touch the Celtic necklace at the base of my throat and head inside. I have to drop my phone off, of course, and once I do that, I head upstairs to the members-only area. That's where I get lost. There are a series of dark corridors, and I think I remember walking down one of the east wings to Hart's playroom, but I can't be sure now. I was in a daze the last time I came here.

When I checked my phone last, it was ten after nine. I'm supposed to be "at my station" no later than nine-fifteen.

Shit, I'm going to be late.

If I am, will Hart punish me, like he punished that other woman?

Hot tingles sweep up my spine at the thought of him bending me over…and I shake myself. I need to find that room. I'm just going to have to check every hallway, or ask someone.

Out of the corner of my eye, I see Hart's white bunny.

Oh! She's walking briskly down one of the hallways, and I rush, weaving around a few people to catch up. At the end of the hallway, she stops and knocks on the door. A brusque "enter" comes from the other side, and she opens. I slip in right after her, and I'm relieved to see Hart standing in the middle of the room. It's definitely the right room. I'd be super embarrassed if she'd been visiting someone else.

Hart's eyes move from the bunny straight to me. His gaze is intense and assessing. I move over to the chair and to avoid falling on my ass again, I slowly lower myself into it. Once I'm seated, that intense gaze finally shifts away from me and back to the bunny. She approaches him, her gaze fixed on the floor. He takes her chin and lifts her face up, so she is looking into his eyes.

"Ms. Lawrence tells me you have been a good girl," he says coolly.

I can only see her from the back, so I have no idea what expression she's making, but she nods.

He drops her chin. "Do you want my cock?"

I suck in a breath, shocked by his frank question. The second the sound leaves my lips, his head snaps up, and he looks straight at me. Oh, shit. *Whoops* . Fly on the wall, remember? And honestly, why am I gasping like an innocent schoolgirl anyway? I've had sex before. I've watched porn. But I've never seen it play out in front of me, up-close and personal. The experience is a little shocking if I'm being honest.

The woman nods vigorously. "Yes, Master."

He takes a step back. "Get on your knees."

Everything he says is firm and almost robotic, without emotion, and I watch him with pure fascination.

He unfastens his belt and undoes his pants, his forearm flexing as he moves to take out his cock. But her head and bunny ears are in the way, so I can't see a damn thing. Threading his fingers through her long, brown hair, he guides her head forward, and she takes him in her mouth. I expect his head to fall back in ecstasy, but it doesn't. Instead, he lowers his head and his gaze catches mine. And holds it.

Holy. Fuck.

I swallow, watching as the woman's head moves and swivels around his cock, stroking him with her tongue. Heat moves through my veins, and my breasts start to tingle. His gaze is locked on me, and I can't help but feel like I'm the one sucking him off right now.

My mouth starts to water, and I shift in my chair. My panties are suddenly wet.

Minutes tick by, and I hear her moan around his cock, her body rocking forward and back as she quickens her pace. His hand closes into a fist around her hair, his eyes never leaving mine. And then, a deep groan reverberates through his chest, and he stills.

The woman pulls away, still on her knees, and waits for his instructions on what to do next.

He lifts his chin to me. "Washcloth," he snaps.

Oh, shit. Should I have had a washcloth ready? I was so entranced by what was happening in front of me, I didn't even think about it. I scramble off the chair and walk the long distance to the marble sink. There's a stack of plush white washcloths sitting in a basket. I pluck one up, wet it, then walk it over to him.

His cock is still on full display, and I take this chance to get a good look. I actually suck in a sharp breath as I drop the washcloth into his outstretched hand, my eyes never leaving his straining erection. Even after coming, he's still rock-hard. That's just...incredible.

I stand beside him, watching as he wipes himself off, then tosses the washcloth into a nearby lined wicker basket before tucking himself back into his pants and zipping up. While he buckles his belt, he looks over at me. I'm still standing there, like an idiot, watching his every movement.

"Go back to the chair and sit down," he says in that delicious accent.

It takes a second for his words to register in my head, but when they finally do, I nod and return to my designated spot. As I lower myself into the chair, I can't help but feel a little dejected. like I'm on the outside, looking in—which is exactly the case, in truth. Suddenly, I want to be the one kneeling in front of him, his cock sliding into my mouth. I lick my bottom lip, and I swear I hear him growl from across the room—or maybe that's just my imagination.

I shake myself a little. I'm not here to suck off a complete stranger. I'm here to do a job, get paid, and then go home. Simple. Easy. And hopefully, as the weeks progress, I can pick Lucien's brain, and get some advice about getting my dad's business back.

But that's it.

His attention is back on the woman. "You've pleased me," he says to her. "Stand."

She rises, back rigid, completely still. Waiting.

My breath is caught in my lungs, and every nerve in my body is on full alert. Somehow, my breasts feel heavy, and my nipples are overly sensitive as they brush against the fabric of my bra.

"Remove your clothes."

There isn't much to remove, but she strips off her fluffy heels, her bodysuit, and her thigh-high stockings until she stands completely naked, except for her mask. Her beautifully curved frame is on full display, but she's still turned away from me.

"On the bed."

I hold my breath. Oh, my God. What's going to happen? Again, I feel so awkward being here, watching them like a voyeur. But that's why I'm here, right? To watch.

CHAPTER 7
EXCLUSIVE TO HIM

HART'S SUBMISSIVE, THE WOMAN WHO UNTIL A MINUTE ago was wearing the bunny costume, crawls onto the bed, obeying his command to do so. She lies on her back, spreading her thighs. I can see everything from this vantage point, but I'm not focused on her. I'm focused on him. He steps up to the bed and reaches over to take her large breast in his hand, pinching her nipple between his forefinger and his thumb. She writhes a little, tilting her head back. And then, with his free hand, he toys with the curls between her thighs, stroking her flesh.

The woman lets out a little moan, and he looks up at me. Even as he slips a finger inside her, his gaze never leaves mine. I can almost *feel* his fingers inside *me,* pumping in and out smoothly, languidly, drawing out my pleasure. Then he adds his thumb, circling it around her clit, drawing another moan from deep in her chest.

My own clit throbs, and every cell in my body tingles. My hands are folded on my lap, and I clench them into fists, squeezing until my fingernails break the skin of my palms.

I desperately want to get up and leave, but I can't. I'm rooted to the spot, his sharp gaze holding me captive. I watch intently as he adds yet another finger, stretching her, and my own center pulses. I can imagine what his long fingers would feel like inside me, pushing in hard, then pulling out again, mimicking the would-be strokes of his cock.

His hand works her so hard, and so fast, her body moves with every thrust of his hand. Her mouth is open in a silent scream as her body is drenched in ecstasy—I imagine. I can *only* imagine, and it's agony. I haven't been fucked in so long. It's been since last spring, to be exact. And just once. And that guy had never met a clit, let alone a G-spot, in his life. He was hot as fuck, but such a selfish lover.

I straighten in my chair, using the seat to apply a little more pressure to my throbbing center. I wiggle a little, and that only manages to intensify the desire pumping through my veins. *Fuck.*

With expert skill, he continues to twist her nipple, then with his other hand still working her clit, he leans down and swirls his tongue around her other nipple, taking it between his teeth. *Ohmygawd.* That nearly launches me off my chair. Swallowing, I realize my own hand has crept up and I am now pinching my own nipple through my dress. The sharp pain radiates through me, offering a small twinge of relief.

But it's not enough. It's nowhere near enough.

Then Hart lifts his head and again catches my gaze. When he sees my hand resting on my breast, pinching my own nipple, his eyes narrow—or maybe he's smiling behind that mask? I can't tell. But it has elicited some kind of reaction from him, and I'm empowered by that knowledge.

It's so strange…I'm just supposed to be watching, not participating, but I feel like I'm the woman on the bed, being finger-fucked by Hart.

With a low, reverberating growl, he quickens his pace, his thumb working her clit violently. Seconds later, her thighs tighten around his hand, and she screams out, her arms flung outward, catching the comforter in her fists. Her head thrashes and her back arches as a climax crashes over her, and he keeps his fingers inside her until, finally, her body melts into the mattress, completely relaxed.

I can't help but feel bereft. The woman has gotten her happy ending, but I'm sitting here, more on fire than ever. With a frown, my eyes flick to study Hart. I wonder if this arrangement is a bit selfish on his part.

As he pulls away from her, I remember with a start that I have a job to do here. I launch from the chair and walk to the sink. I wet two washcloths—one for him, and one for her—and then hand them over to him. He cleans the woman off first, then wipes off his own hand, and tosses them toward the lined basket. When one of them doesn't quite make it and slides to the floor, I reach down to pick it up. His strong hand wraps around my elbow to stop me. Heat and electricity zip through me, and I'm frozen in place.

"You're not here for that," he says gruffly. "There's a cleaning crew."

"Oh." I straighten, taking a step back. He releases me reluctantly, and the second he does, I'm pierced by a split-second feeling of emptiness.

"You may help Willow dress," he orders.

Willow. So that's her name here. I wonder what my name should be? I don't really like the one Ms. Lawrence gave me, C. But until I figure that out, I guess that's all I've got to work with.

As I grab Willow's stockings and bodysuit off the floor, Hart turns toward the hidden door and leaves. Just…that's it. No goodbye or anything. I stare after him for a second, wondering what the hell he got out of that besides frustration, like me. No happy ending for him either, apparently.

I bring Willow her things. She's now sitting up on the bed, her skin flushed and looking like she's just been to heaven and back. I place the bodysuit on the bed and prepare one stocking, so all she has to do is step into it. I hold it out to her, and with a smile, she moves forward.

"Hey…" I start awkwardly. "I'm C, by the way. Kinda weird to say nice to meet you after…"

She laughs lightly as she slides off the bed. "After you've seen everything nature gave me? Sure."

I nod. As she stands, I notice the flash of light at the base of her throat. She is wearing a necklace similar to mine, with the same Celtic design on it and the same shape. It's the Celtic stag tattoo that appears on Hart's chest and shoulder. I wonder what it's supposed to mean?

Willow steadies herself against the bed post as she steps into the rolled stocking I hold out for her.

Before I have a chance to stay anything she laughs. "We have the same hairstyle. Bangs and all." I start rolling up the second stocking for her while she adjusts the first one on her curvy thigh. "Of course, mine's a wig."

I arch a brow. "Ah, mine's just me."

She nods. "I'm naturally blond, but Hart asked me to wear this wig, which I gladly do."

I hold out her second stocking to help her step into it. "So, um, how long have you two been together?" I ask, pulling the stocking up her leg.

"He's been my Dom for a year," she answers as she hikes the top of the second stocking up her thigh. "We met here at Obscura."

"Ah, okay. So, like, do you date each other outside of the club?" I don't want to offend her with my questions, but I'm burning with curiosity—particularly with anything to do with Hart.

"He prefers us to meet here." I hand her the bodysuit—I'm not putting that on for her. I do have limits. She thanks me and begins to shimmy into it.

"Does he have other subs?" I ask.

She lifts a brow. We are nearly the same height and build, but I think she's prettier than me, same hairstyle or not. She flicks a glance down my form as if similarly sizing me up. Maybe she's noticed the similarities as well. "Why? Are you interested?"

My eyes widen, and I shake my head vigorously. "Oh! No. I'm not into this scene at all. I was just…curious, you know. About him. And how things work in this world. I honestly don't have any interest in actually participating."

She smiles as if pleased with that answer, and she bends to fasten up her suit. "Hart only engages one sub at a time. Some of the guys here will have multiple subs, but Hart isn't interested in multiple women. Just me. It's the way I prefer it, too."

"Oh, cool." I glance around. "So, uh, I guess I'm done for the evening."

Willow slips her heels on. "You should enjoy the bar. They have some specialty cocktails that are really good. Try the pear martini."

I nod and smile at her. "I will, thanks." Haley also told me how good the cocktails were.

I mean, why not enjoy the place, right? I've been here for a total of forty minutes. I don't really need to rush home to my sitcom reruns. I might as well explore this new environment and learn a little.

When Willow leaves, I head down the main staircase and back into the club below. Lights pulse with the rhythm of the music, and half-naked bodies move to the beat. This place is much more upscale than any regular club I've been to. And it's got an edgier vibe, too. I get the feeling that almost anything goes here, as long as you have access to a room—or even a curtained booth.

I wend my way through the throng and make my way to the bar. There's one available stool and I take it. The bar is a good distance from the dance floor, so it's a bit quieter here, thank goodness. A bartender sidles up to me immediately. "What can I get you?"

"Pear martini, please," I say, prepared to pull my debit card out from my bra. I have exactly forty dollars in my account, but I'll get paid for this job soon, so I'm not going to sweat it.

The bartender's eyes fall to my necklace, and he nods. "You got it."

A minute later, he's back and sets the martini in front of me. It does look good. "Thanks. I'm just getting this one drink. What do I owe you?"

He waves me off. "It gets charged to your Master."

"Oh, but—"

Before I can correct him and tell him I don't have a Master, he's gone, already helping another customer. I take a sip of the sweet martini and think about what the bartender just said. Being owned by Hart, having him be my *Master* …that doesn't freak me out as much as it should. But the harsh realization that I'm *not* actually his settles like a rock in my chest.

I spin on my seat, turning outward to watch the goings-on as I sip my drink and people-watch. Someone slides into the now empty seat next to me.

"You look lonely," he says.

It takes me a second to realize he's talking to *me*.

I look up at him. He's wearing a black mask. "Oh, yeah, no. I'm just grabbing a drink before heading home for the night." He's sitting, but I can tell he's tall with a frame that leans toward athletic. He has dark hair, and green eyes, and even behind his mask, I can tell he's beautiful. He's wearing a half-mask, like the Phantom of the Opera. All he needs is a cape, and he'd be the spitting image.

"What's your name?" he asks, looking me over.

"Ca—oh, um, actually, I'm called C, for now." I say. "You?"

"Phantom," he answers.

"Oh, that's very on point," I laugh. "Very nice."

"Mmm, not the only thing that's very nice…" He reaches out and brushes a strand of hair away from my masked face. It's a bold move for someone who just met me, but I get the sense that bold is the name of the game here at Obscura. Real world rules don't seem to apply in this place. It's like a world between worlds.

I turn toward him a bit and smile, still on fire from the session with Willow and Hart, burning with the memory of how he touched her and made her scream. I still haven't quite recovered.

"Thanks," I say as his hand falls away from my face, moving to my arm. The blunt tip of his thumbnail moves up my arm, then back down again, feathery light.

He leans in and whispers in my ear. "I have a private room here. What are you into?"

I'm a little shocked by the suddenness of his suggestion—but, again, I'm in a sex club. Why am I surprised? I guess it's because I'm not usually in this kind of environment. Even regular clubs freak me out a little if I'm being honest.

I finish the rest of my drink, savoring the burn as it travels down my throat. I already feel a little dizzy. "Why don't we just go check out the dance floor?" I ask. I'd like to get to know this guy more. I'm definitely not ready for a private room with a stranger. Baby steps.

His mouth turns up in a smile. "As you wish."

Threading his fingers through mine, he tugs me off the stool, but before we can even make our way to the dance floor, a giant wall of muscle appears in front of us. My gaze climbs up, up, up, until I see the same mask I just spent the last forty minutes staring into.

Hart.

What the fuck?

He now has more clothes on than before, wearing a dark short-sleeved shirt that conforms tightly to his muscled biceps. He steps up to Phantom threateningly, his body language tense and stiff. I wonder for a second what the hell this is about. Why is he so angry?

"Hey, my guy," Phantom laughs. "What's the problem?"

Without saying anything, Hart reaches out and takes the pendant around my neck in his palm, showing it to Phantom. "Don't touch what's mine," he grates out.

Phantom releases my hand like I've suddenly sprouted thorns and backs up. "Sorry, man. I didn't see the necklace. It's a fucking cave in here."

I frown, not believing for a second that Phantom didn't see my necklace. It lays across the notch at the base of my throat, spread along the area where my collar bones meet and it's not small. And the emerald in the middle glitters and gleams even in the low light.

"Now you know," Hart growls in response.

"Yeah," Phantom says with one last glance at me—like he regrets having to let me go. "Sorry, man."

As Phantom turns and disappears into the crowd, Hart takes me by the upper arm and hauls me over to the entrance. Behind his mask, I can see the tension in his eyes. "Andrew is waiting to take you home."

I tug my arm out of his grip. I'm feeling emboldened by the martini. "I'm not ready to go home," I snap. I'm looking for a guy who can satisfy the hunger that Hart has awoken in me. I don't say that, obviously, but it's the truth if I'm being honest with myself. I don't even stop to reflect on how that makes me feel. Like a slut? A whore? I glance around. If that's the case, I'm in good company, and I don't feel bad about it. Maybe I should. But I don't.

He steps closer to me, and the scent of his cologne wraps around me like a blanket. I find myself leaning in. He hooks the crook of his finger under my chin and tips my head up, so I'm looking at his face. "You are going home. And, in the future, you will not allow other men to touch you," he says.

I blink slowly, the warmth of the martini working its way through my body. Despite Hart standing over me like an angry Lord of the Manor, I'm completely relaxed. My God, I'm such a lightweight. "That was not part of the agreement. In fact, I was given very few instructions."

"Then allow me to be clear." His British accent is somehow thicker—which I guess must happen when he's angry. "You will remain pure for me, little fawn. That's what this job requires."

Pure for him? What the fuck is that supposed to mean?

"I can't date at all or *anything*?" I ask, incredulous. Talk about controlling.

He releases my chin, then crosses his arms over his broad chest by way of answering.

"Yeah, I don't know if any job is worth that level of control in my life," I huff. Even if this is the easiest and the most well-paid job I've ever had, it can't be worth that, can it?

I can see his deep brown eyes narrow behind his mask. "Those are my terms, and they're non-negotiable."

I clamp my mouth shut and stare over his shoulder at the women dancing in the far distance. Music thumps in the background, causing the walls to vibrate. I consider his terms. This is a cushy job—a life-changing one that can dig me out of the financial hole I've been at the bottom of, and quickly, if I'm smart. I'd be an idiot to walk away from that. It's not like I've been dating anyone anyway.

"For how long?" I ask, without meeting his gaze.

He hesitates. "I'll be in town for three months to negotiate a business contract. After that, our arrangement is done."

Three months. I can make some cash, pay off my bills, save up, and that'll give me a little cushion while I hunt for another job.

I lift my chin and straighten my spine. "If I'm giving you exclusivity, then that'll cost you, obviously."

I might be desperate for the money, but he doesn't know that.

He widens his stance. "Negotiating, are we?"

I shrug one shoulder. "You want something I've got—my *purity.*"

Neither of us is under any illusion that I'm a virgin—but while I'm working for him, he wants me unsullied by other men. Cool. I can do that. But he'll have to show me the money.

He nods once. "Give me a number."

"Fifteen hundred *more* a month."

Without hesitation, he drops his arms and says, "Done."

I blink at him, mind already spinning a calculation of numbers, four hundred dollars per hour at ten hours per week at approximately twelve to fourteen weeks with an additional forty-five hundred... *Whoa* . That's upwards of sixty thousand dollars for three months.

I peer at him, wondering about the speed with which he agreed. Maybe I should have asked for more. *Damn.*

I push out a breath. "Okay. So then, you should send me the updated offer via email. I obviously need that in writing—the lawyer in you should appreciate that. Were there any other hidden stipulations you're planning to spring on me? Because depending on what they are, those will cost you, too."

I can almost feel his amusement on the other side of that mask, but his body language doesn't change at all. "You'll receive written notice of this new agreement within twenty-four hours."

I lift my arms awkwardly, then let them fall back at my sides, not sure what to say now. "Okay, then, uh, goodnight, I guess." And without even waiting for his response, I turn on my heel and grab my phone from the phone check area. Outside, the car's already waiting for me.

"Ms. Fitzgerald," Andrew says with a smile, standing beside the open car door.

"Hey, Andrew," I reply. "Just call me Cassie."

He nods once as I slip into the backseat. "Yes, ma'am."

Once I'm back at Hill House, I sneak up to my room and shut the door. Thankfully, I have the room to myself because Haley is working and Avery's at the library working late on a project. I plan to be fast asleep by the time they get back.

I love my roomies, but I'm just so exhausted, I'd rather decompress instead of relaying every sordid detail of tonight's events. Tomorrow, maybe. Stripping off my dress,and underwear, I hop into a quick hot shower, then put on my pajama set—little shorts and a tank top that has "woke up like this" emblazoned across the chest.

As I lie in bed staring up at the ceiling, I can't stop thinking about Hart. In my mind's eye, I can see him approaching Willow, but in my head it's *me*. Everything he did to her, he's doing to me. Sliding his hand up my bare thigh, his fingertips brushing against the folds of my center. I tremble a bit, and I realize my hand has crept down my pajama bottoms, under my panties. The pressure between my thighs that has been building for hours is only provided a small degree of relief from the pressure of my own fingers.

As I reconstruct the details of his masked face, the hills and valleys of his incredibly muscular body, I apply a little more pressure to my clit. Rubbing in a circular motion, I imagine his fingers inside me, pumping in and out, in and out. My own fingers slip inside my channel, and I match the pace and pressure that Hart used on Willow. I'm so wet, it's hard to maintain traction, but within seconds, electricity begins building in my veins.

I imagine his eyes locked on mine, and I come so hard, my toes curl. That delicious energy pumps through my body, heat spreading through me, snatching my breath away. I arch into my own hand, drawing out the intense sensation.

When the orgasm finally abates, I go and clean up, then get back into bed. I have a feeling I'm going to end up rubbing one out every night before work. Otherwise, it's inevitable that I'm eventually going to climb Hart like a fucking tree.

CHAPTER 8
LITTLE FAWN

THE NEXT MORNING, I WAKE UP TO THE NOTIFICATION that two thousand dollars has been deposited directly into my account from Deerfield Park, Inc. In addition, there's an email from Lucien's assistant, offering a day and time for us to meet at his office. He's all the way out in Beverly Hills, so it's going to be a trek and five million dollars in gas, but it'll be worth it. If I can get my share of my dad's company, then the time and distance to Lucien's office will be a small price to pay.

And honestly, I'm a little excited to be in a room one-on-one with Lucien. No masks. In the club, it's never just him and me. I wonder if he's just as powerful and commanding in the office as he is in the bedroom with Willow—and the way he was with me last night. Sara sets up an appointment for me to meet with Lucien tomorrow afternoon at three.

The rest of the day is a bit of a haze—I have two classes, and then spend the rest of the afternoon in a coffee shop, getting caught up on my assignments. I'm done by six, so I decide to get dressed and head over to Obscura early to look around a little. I call the club and get Andrew's cell number, then text him and ask him for a pickup in an hour.

Two hours later, I'm inside Obscura, prowling the lounge area. I arrive at eight o'clock, a full hour before my shift and turn in my phone, as usual. I have an hour to explore. The only bummer is that I can't take any of these guys into a dark corner and make out. But I can look. There's no rule against that, right?

I'm in my uniform—the little black dress, black heels, and the necklace, of course. But this time, I have my hair up in a high bun. And for tonight, I did some smoky eyes, which look really good with my mask. The eye cutouts are large enough to make it really spectacular—glittering rhinestones and all.

I grab a drink at the bar, then work my way over to the dance floor, watching people move and sway to the fast-paced rhythm. Everyone here looks so elegant in their skimpy outfits and elaborate masks—each mask as individual as the person. Ms. Lawrence gave me mine. It's pretty, but nothing fancy. It's just as well, I guess, because I don't even know what I'd pick to represent myself here. I don't even have an Obscura name yet.

Casually, I scan the crowd, looking for Hart's familiar stag mask. He'd be easy to spot. He's tall, commanding, and can possess an entire room. I'm convinced I'd spot him in seconds, even in a room like this.

By my second drink, I'm feeling a little more at ease, and I'm in the mood to dance. I can't let anyone touch me—because heaven forbid Hart see that—*but* I can dance for fuck's sake. He didn't say anything to me about not dancing.

I pound back the dregs of my second pear martini and hand my empty glass to a passing waitress. As I make my way onto the dance floor, I scan the crowd again, just in case. This part of the club doesn't feel like his scene, but I have to admit I'd actually like to see him. I try to shake off thoughts of him so I can enjoy the now thirty minutes of quasi-freedom I have left before I have to go up to the room and watch him put his hands and mouth all over another woman's body. It's beginning to feel more and more like a punishment than an easy job, incredible pay or not.

The music is bumping, and I'm really feeling the rhythm. I close my eyes and tilt my head up and give myself up to the music, my hips swaying. A few guys sidle up to me, but I either turn away or back up to make it obvious I'm not interested. A couple of guys catch sight of my necklace and can't get away from me fast enough, which is really handy, but also a little baffling. Maybe news of the incident last night with Phantom has spread.

I'm caught up in my own little world when I feel a pair of strong hands on my hips, tugging me against a very definite male form. I pause immediately and whip around to tell this motherfucker off. I agreed not to allow anyone to touch me—and one thing about me, I'm true to my word.

But the second I whip around, I realize it's the man himself. The lights overhead are pulsing, and I can't see a whole lot, but I can see the amusement in his eyes. I imagine he's smiling behind that mask. Well, that's good...at least he isn't angry.

His hands find my hips again. Technically, he shouldn't be touching me either, since those are the terms of our work agreement, but I'm not working right now and I've been craving his touch since the first moment I laid eyes on him so...who's complaining?

Hart dips his head to speak in my ear. "Every man in this place is hungry for you."

I smirk a little. "Every man except *one* , it seems."

I don't know why I'm teasing him. He's already got a thing going with Willow, obviously. I'm just the girl that's been hired to watch and let them play out their kink. I frown. His possessiveness confuses me. If he has a dedicated sub already, why worry about what I'm doing? It's clear he gets off on control, and maybe that's all this is between us—*control*, nothing sexual. Except...I don't get that vibe. There's definitely something sparking between us.

The way he looks at me...it's like he's with her, but he *wants* me. Am I imagining that? Maybe it's just wishful thinking on my part. Just me wanting to be desired by this over-the-top sexy-as-fuck guy.

I sigh if only to myself. In three months, it's not going to matter anyway. I'll have my money, and he'll have...whatever it is that he's after. Then, we'll both go our separate ways.

I brace a hand on his arm and go up on tip toes to shout-ask in his ear. "Where's Willow?"

He just shrugs. He doesn't look even vaguely interested in knowing where she is. Maybe the level of trust between them means he doesn't have to worry about it. She said they've been together for a year, which is a long-ass time. My longest relationship lasted about three months, before he just randomly ghosted me. I get that a lot. Guys will date me for anywhere from four to eight weeks, until they discover some defect in my personality, maybe, and they just...poof. They're gone without explanation. Not even a text or sticky note. Nothing. I'm starting to develop a complex about it, actually. And have no clue what a long term relationship would be like, because I've never had one.

Hart smooths his hand down my bare arm, then hooks his fingers with mine and pulls me off the dance floor, to a quieter spot with couches and low tables. A couple of couches are occupied with people making out, practically dry-humping right here in the public part of the club. My heart skips a beat. Is this what Hart has planned for us? Is he going to make out with me in front of everyone as a way of "claiming" me? I have to admit, that thought turns me on more than a little bit.

Of course, that would be so wrong, considering the Willow thing, but I don't really know whether their relationship is open or not. Maybe now would be a good time to ask.

As we sit down, he signals a waitress and speaks in low tones—ordering us drinks, I'm guessing. When she flits away, he turns and refocuses his attention on me. I cross my legs and fold my hands on my lap—all professionalism. Well, as professional as I can be in a sex club.

"What are you doing here?" he asks pointedly.

I scrunch my nose, confused. "What do you mean? I work here."

"Your shift starts at nine-fifteen."

I shrug one shoulder and look around, not meeting his eyes. "I came early. Are you telling me that's against the rules, too?"

He ignores my question. "*Why?*"

I glance back at him. No way I'm telling him the truth—that I was hoping to catch a glimpse of him before starting my shift. I don't know how to describe it, but the thirty minutes I get to see him at night isn't enough. It isn't nearly enough. I find myself thinking about him when I'm home. While I'm cooking, showering, doing homework. I think I might actually be going insane.

I push out a breath. "Does it matter? No one has touched me, so you don't have to worry about that."

He nods once, and I take the opportunity to pepper him with questions. The waitress sets our drinks down in front of us. A pear martini for me and a scotch for him. Hm, so he has been watching me. How else would he know what drink to order for me? Unless, he just told them to make whatever I'd been drinking before. I guess that's possible, too.

"So what's the deal with you and Willow? She said you've been dating for a year."

"We aren't *dating*," he snaps. "But yes, she's been my sub for a year."

Huh, that was…emphatic. "Oh, sorry. I'm just learning about all this. Are you two…exclusive?" The second the question comes out, I wonder if I sound a little too eager. Can I make my interest any more painfully obvious? Ugh, I need to chill.

"Why do you want to know that?" he says in that beautiful accent.

"Uhh. No reason really." Great save, Cassie. Ugh. "I just figured the more I understand, the better I can, you know, do my job." Which is wetting and handing him a washcloth. Oh, and just being present and watching while he fucks another girl. Honestly, anyone with a pulse could do my job.

His eyes narrow behind his mask. "I have not been with anyone else in a long while, but no, it's not exclusive. Why? Perhaps you're interested in being my sub."

Do I detect a hint of excitement in his voice?

No. I'm imagining what I want his tone to imply. He remains oddly neutral and even his language doesn't give him away.

I shrug and try to appear equally nonchalant. "Just interested in doing a good job."

He pulls a phone out of his pocket, and glances at the time.

"Hey! Why do you get a phone and no one else does?" I ask, annoyed.

I can hear the smile under his mask. "Being a founder has its advantages."

I glance around again, seeing this place with new eyes. "You helped found this place?"

He waves a hand absently. "This particular den of iniquity is Domino's brainchild. But Exeter House is a joint creation."

"Ah, okay. Any chance I can get my phone? What with me being employed by one of the founders and all…"

"Not a chance."

I shrug. "It was worth a shot."

He pounds back the rest of his drink and stands, holding his hand out to me. I haven't even touched my drink, but I've had too much already anyway. The last two martinis are still buzzing through me, making my head swim a little. I take his hand, and he pulls me up. As I stand, my face brushes up against his torso, and *fucking-A* , I could climb that hard wall of muscle right here and now. He smells so fucking good. Like soap and whiskey. Yay. More material for the mental spank bank. Or the rub-one-out bank, literally speaking.

I place my hand in his, and he tugs me toward the staircase and up to the members-only area. He's holding my hand and I'm totally geeked out by that. I can't help but think, this is how it would be if I were his. His strong hand curled around mine, leading me through the crowd. Everyone turns to look at us, and I wonder what they're thinking. They're probably so used to seeing him with Willow that they're confused.

He drops my hand when we reach the private room, just before he opens the door. Inside, Willow is already waiting patiently sitting on the edge of the bed buck naked. Her eyes light up when Hart walks through the door and approaches her. She doesn't even register my presence at all.

I take my regular seat. In such a short amount of time, this has all become a strange sort of routine.

As soon as I'm settled, Hart's eyes connect with mine. I swallow, feeling the connection like it's a physical touch.

He flicks his chin upward. "Come here, Little Fawn."

I pause. Is that my name now? *Little Fawn* . I don't quite know what to think of it or the implications, given he is one extremely sexy stag.

I rise from my seat and move to him.

"Ropes," he says.

With a nod, I head over to the wardrobe and open the door where I saw all the toys yesterday. There's a red rope hanging on the hook, and I grab it, then take it over to Hart. He accepts it and turns back toward Willow. I take that as my cue to head back to my seat, but he stops me. "*Stay* ," he says in that thundering voice.

I pause mid-step and turn back to him. I really hope he doesn't ask me to participate.

"On your stomach," he tells Willow.

Licking her lips, she flashes him a smile and lays down on her stomach, arms spread out. He leans over her, takes her wrists and ties them together, then ties each ankle to a bedpost so she's spread wide, completely open.

"Ball gag," he barks at me like a surgeon.

I step over and grab that, then hand it to him. It looks like a small belt with a red ball in the center. Her head is turned to the side. He places the ball in her mouth and secures the strap around her head, careful not to cinch it too tightly.

Wow, that does *not* look comfortable.

"Bring me the plug, and some lubricant," he says.

I walk over to the wardrobe again and look for something that resembles a plug. My eyes wander all manner of strange tools and objects, half of which I have no idea what their use is. I must've stood there too long because he says, "It looks like a rabbit tail."

Sure enough, there's a silver pointed egg-shaped thing with a white cotton tail secured to the top. I grab that and one of the tubes of lube.

I walk it over, hand it to him, and watch as he rubs lube on the silver part, then inserts it into her puckered hole. Just slips it right in there. She moans a little, but it sounds like she likes it. Now, it looks like she has a fluffy white bunny tail.

"I need the nine-inch," he says to me.

Honestly, if I didn't know he was talking about dildos, I'd think he was a surgeon. Back at the wardrobe, I scan the toys. There are several dildos, all of varying sizes, but the red one looks to be about nine inches long, so I grab that one and hand it to him.

While she's tied up, gagged, with a butt plug inserted, he brushes the tip of the dildo along the seam of her entrance. She squirms a little, moaning behind the ball gag. She lifts her ass a little in a silent plea for more. With a swift slap on the globe of her ass, Hart puts her in her place. It's not super aggressive, but it does leave a red hand mark on her skin.

"You will be patient," he growls. He pulls his shirt off, exposing all those beautiful muscles. And that gorgeous tattoo of Celtic knotwork...my eyes slide over it, fascinated anew.

Quietly, awkwardly, I move back to my chair and sit down. Willow is turned toward me, so I can see the pure agony on her face, even with the mask and ball gag. She closes her eyes tightly like she's trying to quiet the desire rushing through her body.

Yeah, sista, I know exactly how you feel.

My gaze moves to Hart. He's so fucking gorgeous. I just don't think I'll ever get over that. He's one of those men you see in magazines about fitness, or as a lead in a movie. It's hard to believe he's flesh and blood, standing right in front of me.

I watch as he spreads her ass cheeks wide with one hand, and with the other, slides the dildo into Willow's entrance slowly. I swear, I can almost feel the long shaft inside me. I shift in my hard wooden chair and cross my legs to quell the pulsing in my center. When the dildo is fully seated, he pauses, allowing her body to acclimate. After about three seconds, he pulls it out of her and pushes it back in, slow and steady. But all I can see is him. I watch the flex of his veined muscles as his arm moves, the grip of his long fingers on the cheeks of her ass.

I swallow and straighten my spine, which puts a little pressure on my clit. It doesn't help. I'm on fire, just watching him. His tempo quickens, pushing the dildo deeper and deeper. Willow is squirming beneath him, her eyes rolling back in ecstasy. And then he stops. He pulls the dildo out and sets it next to her on the bed.

Both Willow and I swallow hard.

What the hell is he going to do next?

I pray he just puts her out of her misery, because by extension, Willow is me. It feels like slow motion when he turns his head and pins me with that dark stare that spears me all the way to my bones. I'm biting my bottom lip, practically drawing blood with my blunt teeth. He stalks over to me and hauls me up off the chair. His masked face is inches from mine, his muscles bulging.

"You're distracting me," he says coldly.

I frown. Uh…I'm not sure what to say to that. Can he read minds? Can he tell I've been lusting after him this whole time?

"I'm–I'm just sitting here. Not doing anything."

His fingers tighten around my upper arm. "You're squirming."

"What? I can't move now, either?"

His eyes narrow, and his voice, when he speaks, sounds dangerous. "Do I need to get you off, too, Little Fawn? So you can fucking concentrate?"

Oh…*Yes, please*.

I just blink up at him, feeling a bit cheeky. "I can do that for myself, thanks."

I swear to God, the growl the rumbles in his chest is so fucking low, I fear he might actually do some damage to my arm. His restraint is incredible. He releases my arm and barks, "Sit down and remain still."

I plop back into my seat, feeling a little chastised. I didn't do anything wrong. I might have been a little squirmy, but so what? Jeez. If he wants someone who won't move at all, then he should get a fucking robot. I almost want to move *more* now, just to fuck with him. It's too bad I really need the money, or I'd do just that. But I can't risk getting fired. Unfortunately.

Sitting stock still, I watch as he slides the dildo back inside Willow and fucks her with it until she comes three times. Her voice echoes off the walls, even with the ball gag caught in her mouth—which is saying something. Once he's done, Hart takes a flip knife out of his pocket and cuts the ropes securing her wrists and legs. He removes her ball gag, and moves her mouth from side to side, stretching the muscles of her jaw.

"Leave the plug in," he tells Willow.

"Yes, Master." She scrambles off the bed, a little wobbly, and picks up her leotard from the floor, pulling it on in one fluid motion. She pulls the crotch of the leotard aside so the fluffy bulge of the butt plug is out. It doesn't look ideal comfort-wise, but she doesn't seem to care. She slips her heels on and teeters over to Hart.

But before she gets there, he turns his head toward her and says in a flat voice, "Leave us."

Willow throws a long, questioning glance at me, pressing her lips together in silent protest. But without a word, she does as she's told. Clearly she's not happy with this turn of events. And as for me, my heartbeat has ratcheted up a few notches imagining Hart renewing his offer to get me off. And if I'll have the strength to turn him down again.

I watch as Willow silently opens the door, steps out, and then shuts the door quietly behind her.

Hart and I are now alone. Again.

I rise from my seat and turn to follow her out. If he's still angry about the squirming, I really don't need to hear it again. I don't want to give him the chance to fire me, either. Or dangle that temptation of getting me off again.

Leaving seems the best course of action.

He lets me get as far as reaching for the door handle before he calls out. "Come here."

His voice is authoritative, commanding, and I feel compelled to obey. Turning on my heel, I walk back to him. When I stop, we're practically toe-to-toe, and I have to crane my neck to look up at him. I wish I could see what's underneath that mask. All I can glimpse are his eyes, but that's not really enough to get the full scope of his expression. I need to see the line of his jaw, the shape of his nose. His mouth.

"Yes?" I raise my chin pertly.

He pulls something out of his pocket. For a fifth of a second, I think it's the knife, and my heart jolts a little. But it's not. It's a tiny remote control of some kind. He holds it to the side and presses a button. The second he does, the lights go out. It's so dark, it's pitch black.

I suck in a breath. "Why'd you do that?"

I feel him move, but I can't see what he's doing. "I'm going to touch you," he says.

I swallow, wondering if his statement has anything to do with Obscura's rule about consent. It was in my contract that no one could touch me without permission. But he's not asking, is he?

I guess, if I wanted to object, this would be the time to do it. But I don't. I've been wanting him to touch me since the moment I laid eyes on him.

"O-okay," I say, but it comes out as more of an exhalation than a word.

And before I can even guess his next move, I feel his lips on mine. He has taken off his mask and is kissing me. That fact doesn't even register for a full thirty seconds. And the kiss isn't soft. It's not light. It's full of all the violence and passion that I feel as well. His tongue slips into my mouth and takes complete control, and my eyes drift closed, allowing myself to give into the sensation of him overpowering me.

His hand comes up to cup my head as he continues his possession. My God, but he can kiss. The flavor of him is so fucking amazing, I don't think I'll ever get enough. My arousal ratchets up so quickly, I could come from him kissing me alone.

In the darkness, I feel his free hand move up to my breast. He cups it in his large palm, pinching my nipple between his thumb and palm. The pain zips through me, trapping the breath in my lungs. How does he know exactly what I like? He seems to know how my body will respond before I do.

I can't help but question if he's this way with everyone, or just me? He seems to know Willow pretty well, but outside of their sexual encounters, they don't seem affectionate.

My body melts beneath his kiss and the mastery of his hands. Already, my knees feel weak, and my pulse is racing so fast behind my ribs, I'm genuinely concerned I might have a heart attack. Actually, I'm not that concerned. At least I'd die experiencing pleasure in the hands of this hot-as-fuck man.

His mouth leaves mine, and he whispers harshly in my ear, "Is that what you wanted, Little Fawn?"

Chapter 9
Maskless

I SWAY ON MY FEET, MY EYES SQUEEZED TIGHT, EVEN though the room is completely dark. Hart's insanely masculine scent surrounds me, and the heat of his body makes me feel…safe, somehow. I tilt my head back and wait for his lips to find my skin. When nothing happens, my eyes pop open.

"I asked you a question," he grinds out harshly. There's no warmth in his tone, no charm. It's almost…angry. Is he angry with me?

I lick my lips, unsure how to answer. Is this what I want? Do I even know? I mean, fantasy and reality are two different things, right? Now, confronted with Hart in the flesh, asking me what I want…yeah, that's an intensity I'm not sure I'm ready for. Or am I?

I blink into the darkness. My mind is swirling, and unreleased sexual tension is tightening in my core like a Gordian knot.

"I…"

Before I can get the words out, his hand raises up and curls around my neck, his thumb caressing the column of my throat. Then his mouth comes down on mine again, cutting off whatever it is I should have said. I've forgotten now, anyway.

He pulls back again with a growl deep in his throat and steps away from me. I hear the rustling of something nearby, then the light flicks back on. He's standing a few feet away with his mask on, arms crossed over his bare chest. He looks so damn powerful, I want to go to him and dissolve into a puddle at his feet. But his barriers are back up. That snapping energy between us has been capped, and we are employer and employee again.

Did I just fuck things up between us? And if so, should I be surprised? It's the story of my life. The question isn't *if* I can drive a man away, it's how quickly will it happen.

"I—"

He lifts his hand, cutting off my words.

"You will arrive at nine-fifteen for your shift, not a moment before. And you will leave the club when I dismiss you."

My eyebrows knit. *Fuck* , dude. This guy is a total killjoy. "Why can't I be here outside of my work hours? I–I'm not trying to be difficult," I rush to add. "I just don't understand why being here early is a bad thing."

He lowers his arms and approaches me again. He takes my chin in his hand. "I can't always be here to watch you, and I'd rather not take the chance."

I'm looking up into his beautiful brown eyes, snapping with that energy again. "Take a chance at *what?* "

This place is devious, to be sure, but there's security and staff everywhere. Nothing is going to happen here. Obscura runs an insanely tight ship. Anything that happens here is allowed to happen, period. I've only been here a few times, and that's already abundantly clear.

Unless….is he afraid some other man will lure me away? Like Phantom tried to do the other night? I guess it's possible. I'm here for the money, right? Some other sexy beast could offer me the same deal—watch him have sex for a generous hourly fee. If the money were more, I might be tempted. But I don't know, there's something about Hart that I find incredibly enticing, and I'm not sure that can be so easily replicated, even if the guy is hot.

His grip on my chin tightens, and he ignores my question. "Are my terms clear, Little Fawn?"

I swallow. "Yes."

Whatever. He doesn't want me having fun here, fine. I'll find someplace else on the nights I'm not working. Somewhere he can't watch me. There are a hundred different clubs in the L.A. area.

"My car will take you home," he says.

I twist my head out of his hold. "It's fine. I can call an Uber."

The less I rely on Hart, the better. I can already feel myself falling for him—though why that is, I have no idea. We've only ever had what amounts to a five-minute conversation. I wonder if I'll feel the same way when I see him as Lucien in his office tomorrow?

"I'll see you tomorrow," I say, then I turn and leave Hart standing in the room alone.

The next afternoon, I'm on my way to Beverly Hills. No car is sent for me this time, so I have to navigate the L.A. traffic myself, which is no easy feat. I left early, though, so I get to Lucien's office with time to spare. Parking is another nightmare, but I manage to find a tiny spot in the bowels of the parking garage of his office building.

As I climb out of my car, I grab my purse and run my sweaty palms down my black-and-white-striped skirt. Even though I've literally watched this guy getting sucked off, I want to look professional. So I dug out my best pieces from the very back of my closet. Honestly, I hadn't worn this outfit in so long, it was legit like an archeological dig. I was half-afraid it wouldn't fit. But it does, thank goodness. Months of a ramen-only diet will do that for a girl, if nothing else.

I head up to the seventh floor, per Sara's instructions. The elevator opens to an enormous lobby, all glass and marble, with a reception desk directly ahead. I approach and wait for the woman behind the desk to look up and notice me. When she finally does, a friendly smile spreads across her face. "Good afternoon," she says. "How may I help you?"

I swallow past the dryness in my throat. "My name is Cassandra Fitzgerald. I'm here to see Lucien Hunter. I have a three o'clock appointment."

"Please have a seat," she says. "While you wait, can I offer you some water, tea, or coffee?"

"Water would be great, thanks."

I take a seat, and the woman brings me a chilled bottle of fancy sparkling water. I practically swallow the entire bottle in one gulp—which is a mistake, because now I'm going to have to pee. And I'm so nervous butterflies are rioting in my stomach. So that makes me feel like I'm going to throw up. Why am I so anxious? I analyze that for a second. I think it's because this will be the first time I'll be seeing Lucien's face, completely mask free from either the Green Man or the stag. I tried Googling him, but there are no pictures of him online. Like, none. Just an Instagram account with scenic travel photos, which seems to be one of his hobbies. So this is the first time I'll see him as he is. In his real life. And I'm worried I'll be disappointed.

I shake myself mentally, reminding myself this isn't about what happens in Obscura. This meeting is about my father's legacy and snatching it back from my asshole stepbrother's tight grip. I have to focus on that. Anything that happens inside that office is separate from whatever happens inside Obscura. For my own sanity, I have to compartmentalize the two.

"Ms. Fitzgerald?"

I glance up, yanked out of my thoughts. "Yes?"

"Mr. Hunter will see you now."

The woman is standing a few feet away, ready to escort me to his office. The space is gorgeous. All windows with a ton of natural light—even in the long, winding hallways. She leads me down the main hall, past a huge conference room, to a door at the very end. Knocking once, she waits for the brusque, "Come in," and opens the door. She ushers me in, before backing out and closing the door behind her.

There's a man at the far side of the room, behind a large desk. His office is the size of the entire bottom floor of our house, no joke. There's a sitting area with black couches, a meeting area with a huge glass table and several chairs, and then there's his massive desk. Several expensive-looking sculptures are scattered around the room and exquisite art decorates the walls, giving the space a sophisticated feel.

But it's the man I'm entirely focused on. He's writing something on a legal pad. When he's done, he sets his pen aside and glances up. The moment his eyes meet mine, a sexy smile spreads across his face. Any fear I had of what Lucien may look like is quashed. He's classically beautiful with dark hair, dark eyes, a strong jaw, and lips I could kiss for days.

"Hello again," I say, stepping deeper into the room.

With that sexy smile plastered to his face, he stands and comes around the desk to greet me. Maybe it's the massive space or maybe it's just my faulty memory but he seems a bit shorter in this space than he does at Obscura. It's probably the antlers on the stag mask that give him the illusion of being taller.

Lucien reaches out and takes me by the upper arms. "Even more beautiful without the mask," he says.

I blush a little and look away, suddenly embarrassed by his attention. "Thanks. Not so bad yourself."

"I'm glad you came. Have a seat." He gestures to the empty armchair in front of his desk.

I sit down and fold my hands over my lap, and he takes his seat again. Leaning back, he steeples his hands, pressing the tips of his fingers against his lips. "So tell me more about this business your father owned."

I explain every detail I can remember about my dad's company, from its conception to what I know just before his death, while Lucien takes notes on a brand new legal pad. "My dad's death was sudden." I take a breath and swallow, even now feeling a slight stab of that same grief. "And he didn't share much about the ins and outs of day-to-day tasks with me. But my stepbrother worked closely with him, so obviously, he knows more."

Lucien nods completely focused on me. "This is the same stepbrother that took the company over when your dad died?"

"Yes. And I feel I'm owed at least a half share in his company. I got nothing at all."

Lucien lays down his pen and places his forearms on his desk, lacing his fingers together in front of him. "Okay, I'm going to need to see any wills, codicils or trust documents, anything your father may have in writing with regards to the succession of the company."

I bite my lip and stare back at him. "Uh, yeah, I don't have any of that. My stepmom or my stepbrother would have all that."

"Do you know who your father's attorney was?" he asks.

I shake my head. "No."

My glaring ignorance in the face of his questions is starting to embarrass me. Dad and Liam always took care of everything, and I just let it happen, as long as I had the money for school. I was in my own little world, wasn't I? In my defense, Dad rarely talked about work. Not to me, anyway.

Lucien nods, considering. "Okay, get that information from your stepmom, and then we can go from there. We really can't do anything until we see how everything was laid out. Once you retain me, I can put some investigation hours into it as well."

I smile, nodding. "Right. Yes, of course. Thank you for your help with this."

As he talks to me about legalities and what our possible plans of action might be, depending on various scenarios, I let my gaze wander over his clothed body. It's so crazy how different someone can look with clothes on—but his build, and the suggestion of muscles beneath his tailored suit, is familiar. And that accent. It's deeper when he's in his Hart persona, it seems. Maybe it's the lighting, the stuffy atmosphere? Anyone's going to look and sound different from a legal office to a secret sex club.

I wonder how he manages to switch that Hart persona off and on. Does he ever slip up? Obscura is a fantasy world, and dragging that into one's daily life could be dangerous, I'm guessing—especially since Obscura is supposed to be completely anonymous. So maybe that's part of it too, protecting one's anonymity by changing speech patterns and mannerisms.

Lucien smiles. "I'm glad you came to me about this. I'll do everything within my power to get what's owed to you, Ms. Fitzgerald."

I straighten in my chair. "I can't thank you enough for your help with everything. You've been incredibly generous. Maybe we could…go out sometime?"

Inside, I almost groan at myself. My God, I'm awful at this. It's no wonder I can't keep a boyfriend longer than a few weeks.

His brows twitch together briefly before he flashes me a wide smile. "My schedule is packed at the moment, but when it frees up a little, I can have Sara set something up."

I blink. His assistant handles his personal dating life, too? *Interesting* .

"That sounds great." I nod and smile politely. "I look forward to it."

***

By five o'clock that afternoon, I'm back home at Hill House and in my sweatpants. I have three hours before Andrew comes to pick me up for work. I left a message for my stepmom as soon as I got home, but I haven't even touched the pile of homework I need to have done by Friday. So I'm just chilling on my laptop, watching something when Avery walks into our bedroom.

"Hey, a couple of us are going to grab something to eat. You wanna come?"

I snap my laptop shut and sit up. "Nah, thanks. It's been a day already, and I still have work in a couple of hours."

Her eyes light up. "Oh, yeah." She flops onto her bed, facing me. "How'd it go with Lucien today? You met with him this afternoon, right?"

I shrug one shoulder. "It went well, I think. I need to get some paperwork together for him so he can look it over."

Avery pulls a face. "Okay, if it went well, then why are you making that face?"

I fold my legs crisscross and face her. "He was really nice and super knowledgeable, but I don't know…it was *weird* ."

She frowns. "What was weird about it?"

"I guess it's because I've seen this guy do some pretty intimate things to another woman, and then, today, he's just sitting across from me like none of that even happened, you know?"

Avery nods. "Well, I'm sure he has to keep all of that separate. Some people can do that—especially higher-ups like him. They have to keep their business and private lives separate. Isn't that the whole point of Obscura, anyway? Anonymity?"

I bite my lip. "Yeah, you're right. I was thinking the same thing earlier." I pluck a piece of lint off my comforter and roll it between my fingers. "I asked him if we could go out sometime, but I don't know, maybe I shouldn't have brought that up."

Avery looks at me like I've got two heads. "*Why not* ?"

"Because maybe it's not a good idea to co-mingle the Obscura stuff with real-life stuff. He might be good at keeping things separate, but I'm not."

She purses her lips, thinking. "Yeah, true. Plus, you really need this job. If something goes wrong on your date—not that it will, but just *if* —then you don't want to give him a reason to cut you loose, 'cause then there goes your payday."

"Yeah." I nod. "Exactly. We all know I'm shit when it comes to dating."

"Let's not go *that* far." Avery laughs. "That's a little dramatic."

I haven't really told her about my dating history. She only knows what she's seen since I've lived here at Hill House—a couple of guys here and there, never lasting more than a couple weeks. She doesn't know about the dozen guys before them. And just as well. It's embarrassing as fuck.

I sigh deeply. "Well, I guess we'll see. His assistant is supposed to get a hold of me when his schedule frees up. Maybe I'll make up an excuse why I can't go."

Avery rises to her feet and does a full body stretch, her long shiny blond hair flopping down her back. "Can I bring some pizza back for you?"

I smile. She's always so thoughtful. It's one of the reasons we all consider her the unofficial house mom. She's always looking out for each one of us.

"That would be great, thanks. If I'm gone by the time you get back, I'll eat it when I get home."

For the rest of the afternoon, I manage to get some work done on an assignment and fight hard not to think about Hart. It's always like this in the hours before I "clock in" at Obscura. All I can think about is Hart and those intense brown eyes. I can't focus on anything else.

As I'm getting ready for my shift, my phone pings. It might be Lucien, so I rush to check my screen. I let out a groan when I see Liam's name on the text. *Fuck* .

Mom says you need a copy of Dad's will and any documents related to the company. Why?

I scowl down at his text. *Why* ? Because I'm his daughter, fuckwad. I don't text that, because I need these papers from Liam and if I piss him off, then he might refuse to give them to me. Unfortunately, I'm at his mercy. For the moment.

What do you mean "why?" I'm his daughter. I need to see what's what .

Okay, so I wasn't super successful at keeping the sass out of my texting tone. But at least I didn't call him fuckwad to his face. So I'm calling that a win.

Why now? It's been a year.

I push out an angry breath. This fucking asshole.

I wasn't ready then. But I'm ready now. You can send them to my email. You already have the address.

I switch my phone off before he can reply. Of course, he doesn't want to give me the paperwork. It probably has my name emblazoned all over it. I doubt my dad left me *everything* , but he left me *something* , surely. Probably a substantial something, because I am his only biological child.

Shaking Liam from my thoughts, I go back to getting ready. I can't help but think about Hart and what he's doing right now. Is he already at Obscura? Does he hang out there after work? I decide I'm not going to wear my panties because, I don't know, I'm feeling a little rebellious tonight.

Will Hart notice?

CHAPTER 10
ANTICIPATION

WHEN ANDREW PICKS ME UP, I'M PRACTICALLY vibrating with excitement and squirming in my seat the entire drive to the club. I'm already anticipating what's going to happen between Hart and Willow. And I'm not going to lie, I'm half-wishing Hart decides to invite me into the mix. Just watching is its own kind of torture, and I wonder if that's intentional on his part. Why does he stare at me while he's toying with her? Is it a control thing? It just feels so fucking unfair. But I'm not being paid to think about what's fair, am I?

When I get to the club, I turn in my phone and head directly up to the private room. As I walk up the stairs to the members-only area, my heart thunders against my ribs. I can't even hear the club music thumping in the background. All I hear is the pounding of my own heart and the quick tempo of my breathing. I don't know why I'm so anxious today. Maybe it's because my emotions are getting all tangled up. Watching Hart perform is getting more and more intense, and each day, it's harder for me to just sit back and observe.

Tonight, as I walk into the dimly lit room, I'm shocked to see that Willow is already tied up on the bed. Well, someone got to work early. I'm a little annoyed by that actually, and I have no idea why. I guess the thought of them alone, doing something without me, makes me feel like the odd woman out. The third wheel. Which is silly. They've had this thing going on for a year now and for me it's been about a week.

Willow is completely nude with just her bunny mask on, her legs spread wide, knees bent, feet flat on the mattress. She's tied wrist-to-ankle on both sides, which keeps her in that position. There's no ball gag in her mouth this time, so she's just staring up at the ceiling, completely still. She doesn't even acknowledge me coming into the room, but to be fair, Hart probably instructed her to remain perfectly still. There's an antique-looking wash basin—with a bowl and pitcher—positioned right next to the bed.

I glance around the room, but Hart isn't in here. It's just me and Willow. And my chair is in a different spot this time. Instead of being at the foot of the bed, looking at all of the action straight on, the chair is positioned on the side, so I'm looking at the bed lengthwise.

I lower myself into the chair and take a deep breath that doesn't help at all. Lord. It's like opening Pandora's box of sex. What's going to come flying out today?

When Hart comes strolling out of the attached bathroom, the breath catches in my throat. He's completely naked, except for his mask, which is slightly different this time. It's the same stag mask, but it stops just below his nose, exposing his mouth and chiseled jawline.

My God, he's fucking gorgeous—somehow even more striking than this afternoon and it's not just because he's naked instead of in his buttoned-up suit. There's something...feral and savage about him. My gaze travels hungrily down his muscled abs, to the patch of dark hair between his strong thighs. He's semi-erect and his cock is huge, hanging heavily as he walks toward the bed. His gaze catches mine, and I swear to God, his cock swells to twice its size in seconds. The length and girth are…impressive to say the least.

My mouth waters and my throat is tight.

Oh. My. God.

I've seen his cock once before, but he was still wearing his pants then, and I wasn't able to appreciate the true size of him. Now, he's on full display, and he owns the room, strutting forward with complete confidence.

All sensation gathers around my throbbing center. I'm immediately wet, an instantaneous bodily response in reaction to his.

I shift in my seat and try to sit more upright, which puts a little pressure on my clit. I tried it last time, and it worked to a degree, but I have a sinking feeling that's not going to be enough this time.

To say nothing of the fact that my squirming seemed to anger him last time.

Fuck.

With his eyes still fixed on me, he approaches the foot of the bed. He reaches forward and pulls Willow down until her feet and ass are at the edge of the bed. Then he kneels, grips her thighs with both hands and touches his tongue to her center.

Jesus.

She moans loudly as he strokes her slit with his masterful tongue, dipping it inside briefly, before pulling back out and swirling it around her clit. Once she's well primed, he tugs her a fraction closer and buries his tongue inside her. From my vantage point, I can see it all clearly, and it unleashes a violent torrent of desire rushing through my veins.

Tugging the neckline to my dress down, I pinch the nipple of my exposed breast. I hardly even know I'm doing it. All I can see is Hart, gripping Willow's thighs, his muscles moving and flexing. I imagine his tongue stroking me instead, and I feel myself arching against the back of the chair, my toes curling.

All at once, Willow's muscles seize, and she cries out as a climax takes hold. Her hips lift off the mattress, and he continues his assault, drawing every last drop of pleasure from her body. After several long seconds, Willow relaxes, and Hart pulls away.

He walks over to the wash basin, pours some water from the pitcher, and washes his face with soap and a washcloth, then dabs it dry. He uncaps a bottle of water and downs half of it.

Meanwhile, Willow is breathless, watching Hart intently.

He picks up something from the edge of the basin table and rips it open. I can't see what it is, initially, but it immediately becomes clear when he places it on the tip of his cock, then rolls the latex down over his shaft. When he's done, he approaches Willow again, his sheathed cock jutting out, poised to penetrate her.

Reaching out, he grips her thighs again and pulls her forward, so the tip of his cock is nestled at her entrance. I let out a little squeak of anticipation, and his head whips to the side, his gaze colliding with mine. He pins me with that intense stare as he rocks his hips forward and slides his cock into Willow. She moans and thrashes her head from side to side, but he doesn't take any notice of her. Because his sole focus is completely on *me*

I watch his fingertips dig into her thighs as he rocks forward powerfully, then back again, his hips pistoning. Each stroke is so violent it rocks Willow's entire body, jolting her powerfully, his thighs slapping against hers.

And all the while, his stare pins me down. I can't breathe. I'm starting to sweat a little under my silky dress and…

My God.

I can't stand this anymore. I crave the feel of this man inside me. I need him to fuck me hard to climax.

As he relentlessly pounds Willow, I lean back, pull the skirt of my dress up and spread my thighs. He's still looking at me, still watching everything I do while he fucks her.

Well, you know what? Two can play at this twisted game.

Slipping one finger into my drenched channel, I can't help but release a groan. My own thumb finds my clit, and I apply some pressure, until that delicious heat starts building in my veins. Bracing myself with my free hand, I lift my hips a little, deepening the thrust of my fingers.

That's when it happens.

That's when he breaks.

Pulling out of Willow, he takes the wet washcloth he just used to wipe off his face and uses it to remove the condom, cleaning off quickly. Then without another moment's hesitation, he pivots to approach me. His cock is straining, the purple tip glistening. Reaching out, he pulls me up by the arm so I'm standing. His hands slip around me, both grabbing the globes of my ass and pulling me fast against him. I feel him at my entrance and I'm holding my breath.

I rock my hips toward him and stare into those brown eyes. And without another word, with his eyes scorching into mine, he impales me on his huge bare cock.

CHAPTER 11
THIS CHANGES THINGS

"OH, MY GOD," I GASP HOARSELY.

He's fucking massive. His cock stretches my channel to the point of pain. Hart picks me up and walks with me toward the nearest wall, slamming me against it. He uses the wall as leverage to push himself deeper into me. I cry out, but either he doesn't hear me, or he doesn't care, because he rocks his hips forward, even deeper without waiting to give me a chance to accept the size of him. It's frantic and a little out of control, like he can't get enough of me.

His blunt nails cut into my skin as he fucks me hard, deep and violent, each breath sawing from his lungs. I regret not being able to look at his face—but I lock gazes with him. His eyes are dark and seething with desire. The way he looks at me, like he wants to devour me whole, just stokes my own pleasure.

"You feel so fucking good. Fuck. I'm going to come inside you," he growls.

"Yes. Oh! My God," I breathe, tilting my head back against the wall.

The sensation of him being inside me, impaling me, pressing me between the hardness of the wall and the hard muscles of his body while he takes complete control, is the hottest thing a guy has ever done to me. With every forceful thrust, the breath is snatched from my lungs, until I'm left gasping—but hungry for more. More of him, more of this. I can't get enough.

"Fuck," he growls.

His thrusts become harder somehow, definitely fast and more shallow. Focused. I arch my back against the wall and bite my bottom lip to keep from crying out. It feels like my soul is about to burst from my body, and I'm trying to keep it contained. But I don't know how long I can stave off the inevitable. That pressure is building. That all-consuming electricity that zips through my veins is threatening to break free.

Positioned as we are, with me against the wall, he has to look up into my face. He tilts his head forward and takes my lips in a hard kiss. His tongue sweeps into my mouth with urgency, and he takes absolute control. His mouth claims mine with powerful mastery, and it drives me fucking crazy.

I brace my hands on his broad shoulders, and he shifts a little to push even deeper inside me. I gasp, sucking in a gulp of air. I don't think I can take much more of him. I'm going to literally come apart at the seams. But just when I think it's too much, my body begins to accommodate him, stretching to accept his huge shaft.

"Yes, mmm, so perfect. Your pussy was made for me, Little Fawn," he rasps against my lips. "I always knew you'd feel like heaven."

I can't even respond; I'm drowning in sensation.

I bring one hand up between our bodies, and pinch my nipple—hard.

I'm seconds away from climax when he pulls away—actually pulls out of me and sets my feet on the ground. A whimper escapes my throat as I watch him walk over to Willow. My heart is in my throat. Is he going to fuck her again, come inside her, instead of me? My body is still buzzing, desperate for release. I can't watch him fuck another woman. Not after what just happened between us.

Willow watches as he walks toward her, anticipation written all over her face. I have no idea how she felt about him fucking me, because she was silent the entire time. But she's definitely excited that he's going to finish what he started with her, I can see the excitement written all over her face.

I lean back against the wall, empty. I want to say something, but I don't dare. I just watch, frozen as Hart approaches Willow, then bends to loosen her restraints, freeing her wrists and ankles.

He spares her only one glance when he straightens, then looks away. "You are dismissed."

Willow gaze darts to me, then back to him. Her mouth works, like she's going to protest, but decides against it. With a pronounced pout and stiff movements, she climbs off the bed, grabs her robe, and scurries out of the room. With a last long glance at me, she leaves the room, shutting the door behind her.

I'm relieved but feeling a twinge of regret for Willow regardless. "That wasn't very nice," I tell Hart.

He turns back toward me. "Willow knows her place."

I glance down at his straining cock and swallow. "Does she?"

"Our terms have always been clear." He prowls toward me. Grabbing my ass, he picks me up and walks with me across the room, then places me on the bed. My shoes have fallen off at some point, and I have no underwear on, as he well knows.

Without hesitation, he takes the hem of my dress and pulls it over my head, tossing it aside.

His hungry gaze rakes over my body, his breath quickens, and his swollen cock twitches in anticipation.

A bead of moisture is gathered at the tip, and I lick my lips, consumed with the overwhelming need to taste it. Rising up onto my hands and knees on the mattress, I lean forward to take his cock in my mouth, but he stops me by grabbing my chin between his fingers.

"Ah, ah. Time enough for that later," he reprimands. "I've been waiting far too long to come inside that sweet pussy."

Pushing me flat on the mattress, he takes my hips in both hands and flips me over onto my stomach. He abruptly tugs my hips up, so that I'm in a sort of downward-facing dog position. With my face pressed to the mattress, my breath coming hard and fast, I wait. My ass is literally in the air, and I'm wet and ready for him. *So, so ready*.

Languidly, he pushes a finger between my folds, entering me.

"You are so beautiful, Little Fawn. I can't take my eyes off you."

I'm awash with sensation again. His fingers aren't any match for his thick shaft, but they'll do in a pinch. I lean back into his hand, silently begging for a faster tempo. As it is, he is slowly pushing his finger into me, then pulling back out, like he's exploring my body, learning how it responds to his touch.

Then he adds his thumb, brushing against my clit in a feather-light touch, and I'm already so keyed up, I nearly launch into orbit. Pressing my face into the mattress, I fist the comforter to keep from climaxing. I want him inside me. That's what I really want. That's what I need.

"I need your cock," I rasp.

"What was that?" he asks in a mocking tone.

"Please. I need you to fuck me."

This slow, deliberate exploration is going to kill me. Little sparks of pleasure zip through every cell of my body, and I'm so close to climax. So painfully close. All I need is for him to push me over that edge, into oblivion.

With a low chuckle, he removes his fingers from me, to be quickly replaced by the tip of his cock at my entrance. "Is this what you need, Little Fawn? My cock inside you again?"

"Yes," I choke out. "Please."

Gripping my hips tightly, he pushes himself into me, slowly, seating himself deeply once more. I gasp loudly in shock. From this angle, the feeling is intense, painful. He's much larger than any guy I've ever been with, and my body is struggling to adjust. But I love the intimacy of him inside me, that powerful feeling of connection.

When he's fully seated, he releases a groan from deep in his chest, and it sets my blood on fire. My body is buzzing, frantic with need. I need to climax *now*. I'm so desperate for it, I'll do just about anything.

He must be reading my mind. With us still connected, he reaches down, between my thighs, and rubs my clit with the tips of his fingers. At the same time, he thrusts forward forcefully, then pulls out, then pushes back in again, fucking me with the same rhythm of his fingers.

My eyes squeeze shut. I'm lost. That's all my body can take. As an intense climax consumes me, I cry out. He slows down slightly, but he's still thrusting, drawing out my orgasm. Then he bends over me, kissing my back, his finger continuing its assault on my clit. I feel him tense as his own climax claims him, his cock growing stiffer, larger inside me, then pulsing as he pours himself into me. His orgasm is drawn out, and by his hoarse breathing and the way his fingers dig deeply into my flesh, I can tell it's good for him. When it's over, he collapses next to me on the mattress, pulling me into the curve of his body.

We lie like that for a long while, and I listen as his breathing slowly begins to relax. The warmth of his body, and the sound of his breathing lulls me into an incredible sense of contentment, and I allow myself to sink into it.

After a few minutes, he rises up onto one elbow and glances down at me from behind his mask. My mask is still firmly in place as well, and honestly, I hardly notice it now. After only a week, I'm already used to wearing it.

Finally, he breaks the silence. "This changes things," he says.

Yeah, no kidding. But the question is how?

I flip onto my back so that I'm looking up at him, his body curved over me. "What will happen with Willow?" I ask tentatively, because I'm not going to compete with her. Despite what just happened, I'm only interested in being with a guy who has one woman—*me.*

If he wants to continue things with Willow, then I'll have to bow out. No shade. I mean, she was here first. But I just wouldn't be able to merely sit there and watch him fuck someone else now. It was hard enough to do before he fucked me. Watching him do it after, knowing what it feels like to be taken by him, would be impossible, and I won't put myself through that. No matter the money involved.

He pushes out a breath and brushes a strand of my hair away from my face. "She knew our arrangement was temporary."

Huh. A year's worth of temporary?

I swallow. "Just so we're clear, I'm only after something monogamous. If you're not into that, we can go our separate ways." But just the thought of him going his own way fills me with sadness. I just met this guy, and I'm already feeling a certain kind of way about him.

He stares down at me from behind his mask with hard eyes. I swallow. Regardless of how he answers, I'm fucked emotionally.

Chapter 12
Only You

H ART REACHES DOWN AND BRUSHES HIS THUMB ACROSS my bottom lip, watching me closely, like he's trying to decide how to answer. "While we're together," he says in that thick British accent, "it will only be you."

I think about that qualifier...*while we're together* . That sounds suspiciously temporary. But what can I really expect—a lifelong commitment? Just that thought is ridiculous. I don't even really know him, and he's only here for three months, anyway. But, I might as well enjoy him while I have him. I'll just have to be careful and guard my emotions.

And on that note, I'd better not lie here too long, lest I get too cozy.

Untangling myself from him, I slide off the bed. "Do you mind if I use your shower?"

"Be my guest," he says easily.

A bit self-consciously, I tiptoe across the marble floor to the bathroom on the far side of the room. I can feel him staring at my ass the entire way, and I get a little thrill from it. Obviously, he likes what he sees, or he wouldn't have jumped me like a horny stag.

Once inside the bathroom, I pull the door closed. It's huge actually. As large as the living room at Hill House. It has a shower, a separate tub, two vanities, all straight, harsh lines in a sleek modern style. There are plush towels, washcloths, robes, shampoos, soaps…anything you could possibly want. It's like a mini spa in here.

Glancing at the shower, I decide that I'd rather have a relaxing soak in the bath, so I turn the water on and sink into the pristine marble tub before it's even full. Removing my mask, I set it aside and sink back against the cold stone as the warm water surrounds me. My eyes drift closed. I imagine Hart has already dressed and headed out—maybe to go talk to Willow, who looked upset when she left. It means I get the suite to myself for a while.

I'm half-dozing when the water turns off abruptly. My eyes fly open, and I see Hart standing above me, a wry smile on his face beneath the bottom edge of his mask. "You could have drowned."

I blink up at him. "Were you worried about me?"

He's dimmed the lights in here while my eyes were close, but I can still see well enough and I definitely like what I see. He's still completely naked, and my eyes wander over him, intricate tattoo and all. How can someone be so beautiful? It's almost painful to look at him.

He chuckles, the sound coming from deep inside his chest. "I'm always worried about you."

I sit up a little and grab a washcloth and bar of soap that are laid out on the bamboo caddy straddling the end of the tub.

"Allow me." He takes both from my hands and dips them into the water, then begins lathering the washcloth.

With a smile, I lie back, watching him intently. "You can take your mask off," I say playfully. "It's just you and me now."

His mouth thins. "*No* . That's one rule I won't break." He sets down the soap and brushes the foamy washcloth across my breasts. My nipples are so sensitive, I suck in a little breath when the soft cloth makes contact. I'm still flush with my afterglow, but his touch is threatening to rekindle that fire inside me again.

I laugh a little to release the sudden tension. "But I've already seen you without it. Yesterday in your office." I reach over to pull the mask off his face, but he grabs my wrist, stopping me.

"I said *no* ," he barks sternly. His tone is infused with anger, and that fact—the fact that he's angry with me—makes my heart stutter to a halt.

He releases my wrist, and my mood sobers. I let my hand drop. "Why? What's the big deal?"

"Because that's what it means for you to be here. You obey me."

I blink, jaw slack with shock. I was literally staring at his unmasked face this afternoon in his office. We had a whole conversation and everything. He asked me out for a date this weekend, even. I don't understand what the issue is.

"Lucien..." I begin in a pleading tone.

He visibly stiffens, drawing back. "Don't call me that," he grinds out between clenched teeth. Then he rises to his feet and flicks the water off his hand. He turns to pull a towel off a nearby table and wraps it around his waist. While I'm sitting there, completely baffled, he walks to the door, turning just as he's about to walk out of the room. "I'll let Andrew know you're ready to return home. He'll be waiting out front. Don't linger."

And with that, he's gone. And I'm left speechless.

***

"When I said his name, he was genuinely upset," I say to Haley. We're sitting at the kitchen table, eating cheap Chinese food straight out of the little white boxes with our wooden chopsticks. I gesture with mine. "*Visibly* angry, even."

Haley gathers a heap of chow mein and shoves it into her mouth. "That's so fucking weird," she says between bites. "Maybe it's an Obscura thing? Like, taking off the mask, saying his name…those things would take him out of the fantasy?"

I tilt my head, considering. "Okay, then why not just say that? Why get all pissy with me?"

Haley shrugs one shoulder. "Maybe he feels like you should know that?" She throws up her hands before I can snap back at that. "I'm just throwing out theories."

I lean back in my chair and shake my head. "Yeah, I don't know. Maybe that is what it is—he doesn't want to shatter the fantasy. What else could it be?"

She acknowledges that with a swirly gesture of her chopsticks and a vigorous nod. "Yeah. Listen, it's weird all around. So is he going to continue to pay you?"

"Uh…" I scrunch my nose. "I actually don't know. I did tell him we'd have to be exclusive, and he agreed. But we didn't talk about money at all."

Haley pushes out a breath. "Well, let's hope he's still willing to be your sugar daddy."

I frown and pick at my kung pao chicken with my chopsticks. "Would that make it weird, though? Like, he's paying to have sex with me?" And if that's the case, then does that mean that I'm technically prostituting myself?

"Would you have sex with him regardless of the money?" she asks, shoving another clump of chow mein into her mouth.

I don't even need a second to think about the answer to that one. "Yeah, of course. He's hot as fuck."

She lifts her hands. "Well, there's your answer. Think of this as a sugar daddy situation. Or having a rich, temporary boyfriend. I'm damn jealous, by the way. I've been so busy with school that I haven't had a good roll in the hay in way too long."

"Yeah, I guess that's a good way to look at it." I sigh. "I'm not going to overthink it too much. But I do have another question—do I show up at Obscura tomorrow night, as scheduled?"

She takes a bite of her spring roll. "Has he contacted you, or told you not to go?"

I sip my root beer from the straw. Eating out is the only time I allow myself to have a bit of soda. Otherwise, it's just too sweet. "Nope. No call, no texts, no emails…nothing."

Haley shrugs again, in a there-you-go kind of way.

She's right. Whatever happened earlier tonight was weird, for sure, but not a deal breaker. At some point, I'll have to ask him what the fuck that was about. I really can't pretend everything is okay—that's just not my vibe. I'm a pretty direct person, usually.

Until I talk to him, though, I'm just going to play along. All this business with Hart is temporary anyway, right? In three months none of this will matter. I just need to keep telling myself that.

Haley glances at her phone. "Oh, shit. It's two a.m. I have a class at nine-fifteen in the morning. I better grab some sleep."

I sigh. "Yeah, same. I have a class at ten."

I'm not even a little bit tired, but we head up to our bedroom where Avery has already been asleep for hours. She's such a morning person.

I still have a pile of homework to do, but I need to try and get some sleep. I glance at my phone to see if there are any messages from my stepmom, but there's nothing. Just that last message from Liam, asking me why I want to see my dad's will. Fucking asshole. I literally can't stand him. I'll just have to go to my stepmom's house and ask her for the paperwork in person. Liam was in town for the engagement party, but he has almost certainly left town by now.

When I wake up the next morning and head downstairs to start the coffee, there's a knock at the door. I glance at my phone. It's eight in the morning. Who could be knocking at this hour?

Barefoot, I walk through the living room to the front door and peer through the peephole. It's a delivery person standing with a huge bouquet of flowers in one arm. I open the door with a smile. "Good morning."

"I have a delivery for Cassandra Fitzgerald," the young guy says.

Oh! I perk up. "That's me."

He shoves a clipboard at me, and I sign the delivery confirmation, then hand it back to him. I reach out to take the flowers, but he shakes his head. "There's more. I'll bring them in. Where would you like them?"

I direct him to the dining room table. He sets down the huge vase then spins and goes back out to the truck. It takes him twenty minutes to unload everything. Flowers upon flowers upon flowers fill our coffee table, dining room table, sideboards, kitchen table, counter…every available surface. Once everything is unloaded, the guy hands me a medium-sized square box and an envelope. I tear it open impatiently and read the contents.

Forgive me for last night .

No signature. But I know who it's from, and I'm not going to lie, looking around at the hundreds of flowers filling my living room, my heart melts a little—okay, *a lot.* I've never had a guy do something like this for me. It's unbearably sweet.

Setting the box down, I open it and dig through the layers of tissue paper, until I feel something. I pull it out and gasp. It's a gold mask, beautifully detailed with two twisting horns, and flowers framing the eyes.

It's a fawn. The female counterpart to Hart's mask.

I smile. It looks insanely expensive. When I hear someone coming down the stairs, I shove it back into the box. I don't really feel like explaining the significance of the mask. It's the proverbial "long story."

"Why does it smell like a flower shop in here?" Avery says, stomping down the stairs. When she reaches the living room, she gasps. "Oh, my God! Whose flowers are these?"

"They're for me," I say sheepishly. "They're from a guy I'm kinda sorta seeing."

"Holy cannoli, girl," she says, light eyebrows arching high on her forehead. "You really know how to pick 'em."

I laugh. "Yeah, I guess so. Maybe we should take some of these up to our bedroom? In fact, help me out and grab a couple vases, we'll put some flowers in everyone's room. Heaven knows there's way more here than just I can enjoy!"

By the time we are done putting vases in our room and the adjoining bathroom upstairs—and on the table at the top of the stairs, and in the deep windowsill that overlooks the backyard in our hallway—the others are waking up. They, too, get to share the wealth, to their amazed surprise.

A short while later, Haley and I are sharing the bathroom to get ready. She's just finished brushing her teeth when I reach into my drawer to pull out my birth control pills. When I go to pop out the next pill, I take a look at the day of the week on the label.

"What day is it today?" I double-check with Haley, who has just rinsed out her mouth and is wiping her face dry on a towel.

"Friday, why?"

"Fuck." I blink.

She glances down at the pills and sees that I'm several days off. "Wow, did you, ah, start that pack late?"

I sigh. "No, but I'm awful with these. I miss days all the time and have to admit I've been a little lax lately because, you know, it's not like I've been getting any."

"'Til Hart fucked your brains out last night." She giggles conspiratorially.

I glare at her and make a shushing motion. The door is open and Avery is probably nearby. I don't want to scandalize our poor naive roommate about the dirty, dirty stuff I did with Hart last night. Although I have to admit that I find it hard to think about anything else today. Just thinking about meeting him tonight at Obscura gets my heart racing, even at this hour and before I've consumed a sufficient amount of coffee.

"You know what, I've messed up before, too. Just double up for the next couple days 'til you catch up."

"Really? That's all I have to do?"

Haley makes a waving motion. "It's very forgiving. The pill is 98 percent effective. You only did the deed once last night and you're catching up on the pill. You should be fine."

I sigh, my shoulders relaxing. "Good. Will do." I pop out two pills and quickly down them with a swallow of water. Two more days and I'll be caught up. I make sure to remind myself not to be so lax again. If Hart fucks me tonight without a condom, then I have to make sure these puppies work.

And there's that zing of anticipation again, with the thought of Hart's body on top of mine tonight. I wonder what filthy things he'll have in store for us?

I'm wet just thinking about it.

Chapter 13
Melt Down

Later that day, I head over to my stepmom's house. I have a key, so as usual, I just let myself in. I have one of my gift flower vases in one arm. Hart sent so many flowers, I have more than a few to spare, and I know how much she loves fresh-cut flowers.

"Lori?" I call out, walking through the living room to the kitchen. I put the flowers on the kitchen counter, but I notice a filled vase already on her breakfast table. Who is sending her flowers? I pluck the card from the pink bouquet.

Just because. Love you.
   -Liam

I have to restrain myself from tossing the card across the room. He's probably just buttering his mom up so she doesn't side with me. Not that she would anyway. She has a huge, monster-truck-sized blind spot when it comes to Liam. In her eyes, he's a huge success and he can do no wrong. Understandable, if gross, in my opinion. He is her little boy after all. And she relied on him heavily after she fled England and her abusive marriage to Liam's father. For a few years, when they came back to the US, it was just the two of them until she met and fell in love with my dad.

Remembering all of these things doesn't change the fact that whenever I talk to her about him, I have to bite my tongue so hard that it hurts for days.

"Oh, hey, hon!" Lori says, strolling into the kitchen. "I didn't hear you come in." She kisses me on the cheek, and spots the flowers I brought her. "Wow, two bouquets today. You two kids are so sweet."

Well, one of us is sweet. The other one is a manipulative bastard. But instead of saying that, I put another set of teeth marks in my tongue.

"So, um, I was wanting to take a look in Dad's office upstairs. Is that okay?" If there's any paperwork regarding the company, I'm guessing it'd be there. It's a good place to start, anyway.

"What are you looking for?" she asks casually.

Oh, my God. Does she not remember the message I left yesterday? I love her to death, but she's so scattered.

"I need the paperwork for Dad's company, remember?" I ask, trying so unbelievably hard not to sound as annoyed as I feel.

She shakes her head. "Oh, Liam has all that. He went through everything right after your dad died."

Fucking-A. I bet he did. *The bastard* .

I nod and shove all my anger deep, deep down. If I show any frustration whatsoever, she'll accuse me of being too uptight, too excitable. She'll ask me if I've talked to my doctor about going on medication. Or spoken to the therapist about grief counseling in the wake of my dad's death. It'll be a whole thing, and it will have gotten me nowhere in terms of what I actually need—the fucking paperwork. I need to get my hands on it before my next business appointment with Lucien.

I clear my throat. "Can you ask Liam for me? I just need a copy. He can keep the originals."

"I already mentioned it. I asked him to reach out to you. Didn't he do that?"

I take a deep breath and slowly let it go. "He texted me, yes."

She pulls a face. "So why don't you call him back? He says it's really hard to get hold of you. It'd be nice for me if you two could just put all of this anger aside. I know I probably sound like a broken record, but I hate being in the middle of whatever this is."

I press my lips together and just ignore her response. She doesn't get it, and she'll never get it, so it's not worth discussing. "Do you know who dad's attorney was? His last name starts with an *M*, I think. And his office is in Orange County." Though where in Orange County, I have no idea.

She just shakes her head. "I was in such a daze when your dad died that I really leaned heavily on your brother for all that. I can't remember his name either. I'm sorry."

My eyes narrow suspiciously. It's very likely she does remember, but she wants to force me to connect with Liam about this. I love Lori to bits, but she's practically obsessed with the idea of us being one big happy family again, especially since my dad's been gone.

I can't blame her. We were happy once. All those years ago. I push out a breath and flash her a tight smile. In her defense, in his later years, Dad became an all-out workaholic and a bit of a control freak, and seldom involved her in his business, much like he did for me. He was terribly old-fashioned like that, and it frustrated me to no end. Though, to be honest, I was never as interested in the running of the business as Liam was. The hard sciences, specifically chemistry, were always my greatest love.

"Okay. No worries. So, can I take a look in Dad's office, just in case?" I ask.

Maybe there's a stray sticky note with information I can use, or something. It's worth a shot.

She shrugs. "Sure, hon. I've got lunch with a couple of my book club ladies, so just lock the door when you leave." She gives me another peck on the cheek, then heads out.

As it turns out, there's nothing in Dad's office, as I suspected. Liam is an asshole, but he's not dumb. He took everything of importance. *Fuuuck*. I'm going to have to find another way.

That night, I'm wearing my usual black dress, the gleaming stag necklace and black lace panties with a matching bra. They're my best pair of underwear, and with a little giddiness in the pit of my stomach, I have a feeling Hart will be seeing them tonight. With my brand-new gold fawn mask in place, I walk into Obscura.

"Fawn," Ms. Lawrence says. I blink at the new form of address and realize that Hart must have informed her of my new persona. "How good to see you tonight. Your mask is beautiful."

I smile at her. "Thank you."

Fawn. I appreciate the theme Hart and I have going. The stag and his fawn. Couple goals, right?

As it's Friday, the club is pretty busy tonight, but I don't even stop to grab a drink. I just head straight up the main staircase to the members-only area. My heart is beating like crazy in anticipation of seeing Hart again. Things didn't end well last night, but the flowers have more than made up for the few minutes of awkwardness.

When I reach the hallway leading to Hart's room, I see a bunch of people gathered in front of the door to our regular room. Someone is screaming, a woman. Her high-pitched shriek cuts above the din of the club music below. I turn to the nearest person, who happens to be a man dressed like a dog, complete with mask, collar and dangling tags. He's being led on a leash.

I lift my chin to indicate the ruckus. "What's happening?"

He shrugs. "One of the subs is going apeshit."

Oh, no. It couldn't be Willow, right? I mean, that's crazy. Last night, when Hart turned his attention to me, she was completely silent on the bed. If she were going to go crazy, wouldn't that have been the moment?

I press my lips together and nod. "Thanks."

I guess I could wait until the crowd thins out, but I'm eager to see Hart and I don't want to be late for him, honestly. Whatever is happening probably has nothing to do with me. So I forge a path down the hallway, pushing my way through the crowd. When I get to Hart's door, my heart drops. It's Willow, and she's fighting three security guys, screaming at the top of her lungs.

"This is my Dom's room! You can't keep me out," she practically spits at the guy standing guard in front of her. His face is completely impassive. "Call him now. Tell him I'm here."

I push my way to the front of the group, and she catches sight of me. I can see her face change behind her bunny mask as she takes in my gilt fawn mask—the female version of Hart's stag mask. Every ounce of fight in her is immediately focused on me.

Well, *shit*.

"*You*," she spits, lunging at me. "You're the reason he shut me out."

She darts toward me so quickly the security guards can't restrain her before she gets to me. With one hand around my throat, she half-falls into me, and the crowd parts like the Red Sea. I stumble backward into the wall, and now she's practically on top of me.

"You won't take him away from me," she cries, and I see the torment in her eyes. If she weren't currently trying to choke me out, I might actually feel bad for her.

With everything in me, I shove her mask forcefully against her face, until she has no choice but to release my throat. I stand up a little straighter and brace myself for her to lunge again. This time, someone pulls Willow's elbow from behind, yanking her violently away from me. At first, I assume it's one of the security guys, but once she's flung a fair distance away, my line of vision clears and I see antlers framing a stag mask. *Hart*.

Somehow, he's forceful without being cruel. It's a delicate balance, but I can see the pure, undiluted anger seething behind his mask and in his stiff body language. He is completely focused on Willow. With one hand gripping her wrist, he touches the tip of his finger to the underside of her chin and tilts her head up.

"I will not tolerate this disobedience," he tells her in a stern voice. Her breathing visibly quickens. Excitement flashes in her eyes, and I feel my own flash of jealous rage, but I ball my hands into fists and manage to keep it tamped down.

Hart drops her chin, then addresses one of the guards. "Take her downstairs to the Blue Room. I'll be down in a moment."

All three guards usher Willow down the hallway, and she goes willingly. But not without one last, smug glance at me. We both know Hart's brand of punishment, and it's a punishment we both crave. Fuck this shit. I will *not* share him with another woman. But she was here first, so obviously the problem is me. Maybe it'd just be easier for everyone if I just gracefully bow out. I honestly don't want to be the reason for someone's mental breakdown. Who needs that kind of drama? Definitely not me. With Liam back in town and this whole fight over the family company succession, I've got enough drama of my own, thanks.

With nothing left to see, the crowd dissolves. Hart approaches me. I can see the line of his jaw, and it's clenched tight. His eyes rove over me, and he reaches out to touch my neck. I flinch, taking a step back.

"Did she hurt you?" he asks, his voice thick with concern.

I shake my head and glance down at my feet. It takes me a second to gather my thoughts, and when I do, I meet his intense gaze. "This is all a little too much for me. Maybe we should—"

"*Don't* ," he says forcefully, interrupting me. He unlocks the room door and pushes it open. "Come inside. We'll discuss it."

I pull a deep breath into my lungs and stare at the door for a hot second. If I step over that threshold, I'm going to let him fuck me. As much as I want to think of myself as a bad bitch who isn't that weak, I know, deep down, I have a soft spot for Hart and his fathomless dark eyes.

Fuck my life .

Chapter 14
Possession

With a hard swallow, I step into the room. Hart follows, shutting and bolting the door behind him. We're completely alone. The chaos of the world is on the other side of that door, but in here, we're protected. Alone. Enveloped in our little sanctuary.

I turn to face him. He's wearing a black T-shirt that hugs his biceps, black slacks, black boots, and his stag half-mask—the one that ends just below his nose, exposing his mouth. Heat instantly engulfs me. I know what that means. He intends to use his mouth today—and I can't help but wonder what he has planned.

"What could you possibly have to say? This obviously isn't going to work."

He steps up to me. "You don't tell me what works between us and what doesn't," he says quietly, but forcefully. "I know your needs. It is for you to trust me."

I clench my jaw and fold my arms over my chest. "M'kay, but one of my needs is to not be choked out by your *ex-sub*." I use air quotes on those last two words, because who knows if she's actually his ex? And there's spice in my tone. I can't help it. What just happened wasn't cool. Not even a little.

I can see the tension in his shoulders. He's wound tight, and I have no idea what will happen when he finally snaps. He has that dangerous energy about him. I make a note to tread carefully.

"She will be dealt with."

I sigh and look away. "Yeah, I don't know. Maybe Willow is right. Maybe I have no right being here. You've been her Dom for a year. Of course, she's pissed about me and you. Who wouldn't be?"

He takes me by the arms, and I don't even try to flinch away from him. I don't have the energy.

"Willow always knew our arrangement was transactional, no emotions. We were not in a relationship. I was quite clear about that."

I sigh. "Unfortunately, I don't think she got that memo. She was wrecked. I—" I shake my head. I don't want to be the person responsible for causing that kind of heartache.

"I'll speak with her. Later." His hands slide down my arms, then move to my hips and around to my ass. He splays his fingers possessively there and tugs me into him. "Right now, all I'm thinking about is you."

The low timbre of his voice vibrates through me, instantly igniting my desire. I swallow and try to keep my head. "Considering this mess with Willow, maybe we should lay down terms."

He laughs a little under his breath. "What terms are needed? I've made you mine…for three months."

I glance up at him from under my lashes. "Am I your submissive?"

He drops his hands and steps back, now completely serious. "You aren't just my sub," he says. "But you must understand, I need a certain level of control in any of my relationships. That is non-negotiable for me."

I nod, absorbing his words. "And what choices will I have in the...things we do?"

His lip curls up into a half smile, and fuck, I just melt inside. "You always have a choice, Little Fawn. But you may not like the consequences for those choices."

Well, as long as there's a choice, I'm not sure how bad it could be. Granted, I'm pretty new to this world. I inhale deeply and push the breath out slowly. Three months. That's a blip in time. If the relationship doesn't work, it doesn't work, right? No pressure.

"So, um, I'm guessing I'll need to quit the job officially."

He must hear the worry in my voice, because he pulls me into another embrace. "I'll take care of everything," he says. "Leave it to me."

I don't know if he's talking about all the termination paperwork or...what, but I just decide to let it go for now. Now isn't the time. It's already been a day. I just want to relish the feel of his arms around me.

I sink against his solid chest, and his strong arms envelop me. It's so strange how safe I feel with Hart already. I've only just met him, and yet, he feels as familiar as my own heartbeat. It's an incredible feeling—one that I never thought I'd feel for someone else.

After a few seconds, he pulls away. He eyes me from head to toe and then folds his arms across his broad chest. "On the bed."

I step out of my heels, then hesitate, unsure. As if impatient, he steps up and pulls my black dress off me in a swift, deliberate motion. He sucks in a breath, then he takes me in, standing before him in the dim light with only my black lacy bra and panties. Then, without a word, he reaches around and unhooks my bra, pulling it off me and dropping it to the ground. My panties soon join the pile.

"On the bed," he repeats. "You will not like the consequences if you make me repeat myself a third time."

With slow, tentative steps, I crawl up onto the bed. His eyes never leave me, but he manages to pull his shirt off over his head—and over his antlered mask. He must have lots of practice with that here. Then he unbuckles his belt and unthreads it from his pants. He holds it out in front of him, one end in each hand. "Roll onto your stomach, Fawn."

Licking my bottom lip, I do as he asks, flipping onto my stomach on the mattress. The silky fabric of the comforter is cool on my skin, but I still feel feverishly hot. A breath later, he grips my hips and pulls me up into a downward-dog position, my ass in the air. With a sharp crack, he snaps the belt behind me. A shiver rolls down my spine. I've never been whipped before, and I wonder how badly it will hurt.

His large hand brushes over my ass. "I can't wait to come in this pretty little pussy. But not yet..."

I swallow and nod, my head turned to the side.

He pulls his hand back and swings the belt, which lands squarely on my my ass. I jolt a little, but the pain is minimal. It's more of a surprise than anything.

"Do you want my cock?"

"I..." The words are caught in my throat in the wake of the pain. When I speak again, my voice is breathless, desperate. "Yes."

He leans over me and whispers harshly in my ear. "Let me tell you how much I want to use you tonight. I'll take my pleasure from you and ride you hard. And every time you come, you'll scream out for me."

Every time you come . Tingles ripple throughout my entire body at the thought. I want him to make me come. Over and over again. I want to feel the weight of his hard body on top of me. I want the feel of his cock impaling me, stretching me so wide it hurts. I want to take every inch of him.

I tremble with need and arch my back, encouraging him to enter me. Instead, he bends and touches his lips to my pussy before using a finger to trace along the seam of my sex and open me to his attention. His tongue slowly inside my channel licking with a slow, torturous rhythm. When he pulls away, I let out a little whimper, but he doesn't leave me neglected for long. A second later, his tongue plunges between my wet folds. I gasp at the sensation of his mouth on me. The intensely focused pressure is almost more than I can handle—and then the tip of his tongue pushes inside me, and I nearly go into orbit.

On instinct, I lurch forward, but his hands are on my hips, holding me in place. His blunt fingernails dig into my thighs as he buries his face in my pussy. The feeling is unbelievably intense, too intense, as he licks the length of my slit, around my clit, before pushing his tongue inside again. I writhe beneath his expert tongue, pushing myself harder against him. A torrent of sensations ripple through me, and I'm engulfed in pure, undiluted need. It's dragging me beneath dark waves, drowning me in sensation.

Panting, I struggle for breath as he continues drinking from me. My climax begins building, hovering like a specter lurking in the shadows, poised and ready to snatch the breath from my lungs. I don't want to come yet, not alone. I want him with me, bathing my channel with his come.

Desire is running rampant inside me, and I'm filled with the need for more. So much more than just his tongue. I need every last inch of this man's cock inside me. I whimper but don't voice what I want. He's taken control, as is his preference. And he won't give that up easily.

As though he'd been reading my thoughts, he lifts his head, then takes hold of my hips and flips me onto my back so that I'm looking up at him. Reaching behind my head, he unties the ribbon holding my mask on and pulls it free, allowing my mask to fall from my face. I lick my bottom lip and reach up to do the same to his mask, but he catches my wrist, stopping me.

"Ah-ah," he teases in that deep, deep baritone. "That's against the rules."

I'm ashamed to admit it, but I pout a little. "That's not fair. You can see my face."

He dips his head to swirl his tongue around my nipple. Electricity and fire swirl around the exact point where his mouth connects to my flesh and I gulp.

"This isn't about what's fair," he says darkly, moving to my other breast. He sucks that nipple, then bites down, and I gasp as pain rips through me. His mouth is setting fire to my blood, like a match to kerosene. "This is about me fucking you so hard you won't want any other man touching you."

Yeah, we're already halfway there.

I already have a hard time imagining another man mastering my body with the skill and precision that Hart does. It seems unfathomable, honestly.

I rub my hands over his muscular shoulders, down his arms, to the ropes of muscle at his torso. Then bringing my hand around, I reach between our bodies and take his velvety smooth shaft in my hand. He arches over me, hissing as I work him with long, hard strokes.

"I can already tell you will be my undoing," he says harshly against my breast. His tongue darts out and curls around my nipple again, which only heats the raging fire in my blood. "You are ten different kinds of trouble for me."

My lips curl up into a smile. "I'm learning," I tease. "I have a pretty good teacher."

Before Hart, vanilla sex was fine for me. Little did I know that there was something more thrilling out there, something deeply satisfying. And here at Obscura, when it comes to everything that's possible, we've barely scratched the surface. I want what he had with Willow. More, actually. I want to kneel at his feet while he stands over me, wielding a riding crop and commanding me to take his cock in my mouth. I want him holding my hands behind my back, hands squeezing tight while he takes me from behind. I want to call him Master.

I find it hard to imagine ever going back to the regular, boring guys I used to date and their three-second joy rides. That thought is a little terrifying, because this thing with Hart has already been established as temporary. How will I ever find anyone so attuned to my body?

Hart reaches down and takes hold of my wrist, gently removing my hand from his cock. Then he pins my wrist above my head and rolls onto me, nudging my legs apart.

"Open wide for me, Fawn." He sucks in a breath, positioning the head of his cock at my entrance. Dipping his head, his lips skim the column of my throat, brushing lightly before his teeth sink firmly into my skin. I gasp as the pain seers me, flaming my already white-hot desire.

With a guttural growl, he thrusts his hips forward, surging into me. He buries his thick shaft so deep in my channel, I scream out. I'm still not used to his size, and instead of giving me time to adjust to him, he begins a relentless rhythm, pulling out the moment he's seated as far as he can go. The pain is exquisite, all encompassing, radiating to every cell in my body.

"Oh, my God," I scream. "Holy shit." But nothing can break that unwavering tempo.

I pull my knees farther apart as he pumps into me, his hips working like a fucking jackhammer. Then he lifts up onto his forearms, continuing to work his hips as he stares down at me with a gaze that is hard and intense. I love being filled by this man. I can't even explain it, but for the first time, I feel completely filled, and that feeling is so damn intoxicating.

"Look at me, Fawn," he commands between gritted teeth, the grip on my wrist now so tight it's almost painful. He speaks with a hoarse voice but a commanding tone that expects rather than commands my obedience. "I'm commanding your body to pleasure me, but I want more than that. I want your thoughts, your devotion, your *soul*. Take my cock and take my come and know who really possesses you, body, mind and soul."

I meet his gaze, and that connection is electric. I can't tear my eyes away from his.

"You do," I whisper, never wavering from his gaze.

His eyes close as he continues to pump into me with quick, long strokes, sinking in the entire way before quickly pulling back and repeating. He shudders. "Your tight little pussy feels so good. I don't think I can get enough. *Fuck* ."

I run my teeth along his shoulder, arching up with each thrust as he rocks against me. His hips piston into me with powerful, violent strokes, and I'm fucking here for it. The urgency of each thrust just pulls me deeper into his dark web, and I can't help but open myself more to him—because I feel that same urgency deep in my bones. I need this. I need him on top of me, inside me, all around me.

That familiar bliss starts coiling inside me, first between my legs, then slowly spreading white hot tendrils all over my body. It's only a matter of time before it encompasses me entirely, and I can't fucking wait. I need it so badly, and that need pulls at me like an addiction.

I arch up to him as my body begins to tense, preparing for what I can already tell is going to be an incredible orgasm, when suddenly, he pulls out of me completely.

Chapter 15
Abandoned

I REACH FOR HART, BUT HE'S ALREADY STANDING, STARING down at me. His erect cock juts straight up toward the ceiling, and his chest is rising and falling quickly, hands clenched into fists at his sides.

I gasp with the loss. "Why did you stop? Hart—" I plead. My God, I was so fucking close.

Without answering, he reaches out and flips me onto my stomach. Then he pulls my legs up, so I'm ass-up again. Then he threads his hand through my hair, tugging my head back. He kisses me like that, roughly, his energy hot, dripping with anger.

"I owe you no answer," he grates.

With a quick, sharp hit, he slaps my ass. The sharp sting jolts me, and I nearly jump a mile. It's only his tight grip on my long hair that keeps me stationary. I groan, but that doesn't stop him. Another hard smack on my ass. Then another. And another. It's an onslaught I'm not prepared for.

Soon, I'm screaming, my throat raw. Pain rocks through my entire body, and tears stream down my face. But I don't want him to see me as weak. I try burying my face in the mattress, but he won't allow it, yanking my head back by the hair. In a brief reprieve, he arches over me, and pulling my head back even farther, he traces the path of my tears with the tip of his tongue. His breath is coming fast, but I can't tell if it's from excitement or the exertion of hitting me.

It's too much. The pain is right on that edge of feeling too consuming. My entire backside is on fire. When he pulls back as if he's going to hit me again, I flinch.

"Stop," I yell.

I don't have to tell him twice. He's off me in seconds, releasing me and pulling away. I flip over onto my back, taking care to prop myself to reduce contact with my bottom. My ass cheeks are burning, and it stings when my skin touches the silky comforter. Tears are still streaming down my face as I look up at him, standing as still as a statue. Breath is sawing from his lungs, his hands clenched tightly at his sides, like he's restraining himself, barely in control.

Whatever the fuck that was, I sure as hell wasn't ready for it.

His cock is straining, red and angry, pointing as if reaching for me. I still want it so bad, but I'm afraid he might take things to a level I can't handle. I'm pretty much already there now.

For a few seconds, he stands stock still. Then, without a word, walks over to the wardrobe, pulls the doors open and returns to me with a bottle of lotion in his hand. His jaw is still clenched in anger. When he steps up to me, I flinch. That only seems to make him angrier. He curses, then curls his large hand around my upper arm and brusquely flips me back onto my stomach. Before I can even protest, he's smoothing coconut-scented lotion all over my ass. It feels cool against my skin, and I sink into the mattress, thoroughly enjoying the firm pressure he uses to massage the lotion into my heated skin.

He does all of this in silence. All I can hear is his heavy breath and my own sniffles as silent tears continue to flow. Once he's done, he sets the lotion aside and pulls on his pants, then tugs his shirt over his head. I'm half-turned on the bed, watching him thread his belt back through his pants with short, clipped movements, the veins on his forearms bulging.

"Have I done something wrong?" I ask, tears pricking the backs of my eyes. I won't cry in front of him. I refuse to do that, but that doesn't stop the stab of pain in my chest.

"I need to speak with Willow," he says flatly. There's no emotion in his voice, nothing to give me an indication of how he's feeling.

His mentioning Willow is like another stab to the heart. Has he realized she's better suited to him sexually? She could take a whipping, and she'd eat it up. She'd never tell him to stop. During my observations, she'd never asked him to stop, and in fact, the more violent his behavior, the more pleasure she seemed to derive from it. She'd take everything he would give her in silence and the outright obedience he craves.

That's obviously the kind of woman he needs. Not me, Ms. Plain Vanilla. I can tell he's practically vibrating with unpent need, his huge erection easily visible even under his pants. Do I really want him going to Willow in that condition?

I swallow, and when I speak, my voice is small. "What will you tell her?"

His voice is stiff like he's trying to keep a handle on his anger. "I need to set clear boundaries with her."

It's on the tip of my tongue to ask him what those boundaries will be because I'm dying to know. He's already said he won't fuck her while he's fucking me, but what does that mean, exactly? Is he just going to tell her to lay low until my three months with him are done, then they can resume their arrangement?

I hate not knowing. But asking him when he's in this state doesn't seem like a good idea. Maybe I can bring it up tomorrow, after he's had a chance to cool down.

Sitting on the edge of the bed, he pulls on his socks and shoes, then stands and stares down at me for a second. He takes a step forward and kisses me on the forehead. "I'll text you," he says quietly, then walks out.

I sit in the middle of the bed, naked, dumbfounded, and wondering what the fuck just happened. The sinking feeling in my gut tells me this might not just be until tomorrow. He could be dismissing me forever.

And as time stretches on after I pack up and leave Obscura, I think my gut feeling that night was right.

***

"He just left you sitting there?" Haley asks, horrified. "Are you fucking serious?"

"Yup," I say, still in a bit of a daze. It's been two days, and just as I feared, he hasn't texted me. But when I woke up this morning, I had an additional three thousand dollars in my account. Guilt money? Or maybe it's his final send-off? There was no note attached, no email or text explaining the money.

Nothing.

Haley shakes her head. "Wow, fuck that guy."

I lean back against my bed pillows. I've been trying to take an afternoon nap, and when Haley came in to grab something, she caught me staring up at the ceiling. Now we're each lying in our beds, talking. I push out a breath. I have this sinking feeling in my chest, a dark knot of uncertainty, and I can't fucking stand it.

"I think I'm just going to pop up at Obscura tonight. I mean, he owes me an explanation, at the very least, right?"

Haley fiddles with a loose string on her comforter. "Yeah. Totally. But…I don't know, do you think it's safe? Hart sounds like he might be a bit dangerous."

He's dangerous, all right. Just not in the way she thinks. I shake my head. "He stopped the second I told him to."

It's true that there's an air of danger about him, but somehow, I know instinctively that he would never truly hurt me. Maybe that makes me naive, or idealistic, but I've learned in the past to trust my gut feelings.

Haley is now fiddling with her hair, making a little side braid of reddish-brown hair just above her ear. "You don't think he dropped you in favor of Willow, do you?"

I shoot her a wry look. It's the only thing I've been thinking about, pretty much non-stop, since he walked out of his suite at Obscura to go "establish boundaries" with her. The lack of reassuring text from him has only compounded that feeling.

"You should probably confront him, then. It might be good to get some closure."

At that moment, my phone chimes, and I jump. Is it Hart? I turn the phone face up, but as soon as I see the notification, my mood drops. It's from Liam.

Stop harassing my assistant.

With a sound of disgust, I throw my phone to the end of my bed.

"What? What's wrong? Was that Hart?" Haley asks.

"No. It's my douchebag stepbrother," I spit. "I called his assistant yesterday to try and find out who my dad's lawyer was. I figured it was probably the same person who worked on all the company stuff. Clearly Liam got wind of the fact that I called her—even though I *explicitly* told her not to mention it to him. Traitor."

"Well, he's the one who signs her paychecks," Haley says. "So she wasn't actually being a traitor."

I scowl at her, half-joking but also half-annoyed by her sound logic. "Whose side are you on?"

She holds her hands up. "Your side, always."

I sigh and reach over to scoop up my discarded phone. "What time is it? If I'm going to Obscura, I need to start getting ready."

Andrew won't be picking me up, obviously, so I'll need to find my own way over to Obscura. But thanks to Hart's generous deposit into my bank account, paying for gas or an Uber won't be an issue.

It's just the frustration of dealing with traffic that's the bummer. I've been spoiled by having a private driver pick me up and drop me off every night. I already miss Andrew.

I get ready in record time, shower, do my hair and makeup. But today I decide to wear a dress that's a little more in-line with the mask Hart gave to me. It's a dress I bought for a Vegas weekend a couple years ago—off-white, shimmery, with a wrap-around skirt, cinched with a gold loop, and strips of fabric that cross over my breasts. The slit up the thigh is my favorite part. It's sexy and shows a lot of skin, but paired with the mask, it gives goddess vibes that I'm 100 percent here for. I have to borrow a pair of gold strappy heels from Sam—the girl with the endless shoe collection—but they really pull the whole thing together. And, of course, I have my necklace. I never took it off, actually.

Grabbing a long jacket out of my closet, I head over to Obscura in an Uber. It takes practically a decade to get there. Even on a week day, at eight o'clock at night, there's a fuck-ton of traffic going through LA. When I finally arrive, I say goodbye to my Uber driver and head into the club.

I'm stopped just inside the entrance by Ms. Lawrence. "Fawn," she says with a smile. "We weren't expecting you tonight. Can I ask one of the waitresses to get you a drink?"

Lord . Did Hart tell her to manage me if I showed up?

Regardless of my suspicions, I plaster a smile on my face. "I'm not really here to socialize. I'm here to see Hart."

Her beautifully shaped lips turn downward, into a frown. "He isn't here tonight. In fact, we haven't had the pleasure of hosting him since Friday."

I frown, realizing that was the night he stormed off to talk to Willow, leaving me naked on the bed.

I push out a breath, disappointed. I've come all this way to see him, sure that he would be here. "Do you know how I can reach him?"

"Why not come in and have a drink? I'll see what I can do."

I nod and, as always, turn my phone in at the check room, straighten my mask, and make my way down to the bar. This isn't such a bad idea after all. The last two times I wandered the rooms of Obscura on my own recognizance, he materialized out of nowhere to dictate to me that I shouldn't be here without him.

My heart thumps painfully as I look around, hoping for that same result tonight. I'm so confused. I honestly don't know what we are anymore, or were to begin with, for that matter.

I'm not at the bar ten minutes, sipping my pear martini, when a young man approaches me. He hands me a note in an envelope and stands at a polite distance while I read it.

John will escort you to my penthouse. Be prompt.

The handwriting is large and blocky and doesn't even remotely resemble the handwriting on the cards delivered to my house—I can only assume they were written by an attendant at Exeter House.

The good-looking guy wearing a simple black half-mask and tattoos snaking up his neck has been lingering nearby, awaiting my next move. John, I assume?

I nod at him, and he leads the way silently to a flight of stairs and then a door that must lead to Exeter House. He punches in a key code, and the door pops open. He guides me through the beautiful marble hallways with gold fixtures. I've been inside Exeter House only briefly to visit my cousin Lexi once and for Maddy's New Year's party earlier this year. My eyes wander over all the fine fixtures, the elegant marble and chrome. I could definitely get used to this.

After navigating several hallways and one elevator, my guide deposits me on the top floor, on an expensive-looking doorstep. I look for a penthouse number, or anything that could indicate where I am, but it's just a glossy black door. I glance at my guide, but he just smiles and tells me to have a good evening.

Turning back to the door, I take my mask off and suck in a deep breath, trying to gather the courage to knock. Butterflies riot in my stomach, and I feel vaguely nauseous. Just as I lift my hand to knock on the door, it opens. Standing on threshold is

Hart, looking fine as fuck. He has his mask on, prepared for my arrival.

He's wearing a white button-down shirt, sleeves rolled up, exposing his forearms. The collar is unbuttoned, revealing a portion of his tattoo and the dark hair on his chest. My mouth waters just remembering what his skin tastes like under my tongue. I bit him a few days ago, and I'd give anything to sink my teeth into him again.

He holds the door open with one hand, the other hand in his pocket, but he doesn't say anything.

I clear my throat and toy with the ribbon of my mask. "Hi…um. Can we talk?"

His gaze rakes over me slowly, taking in my risque dress and borrowed gold shoes. I shiver under the heat of his gaze. I swear I hear a deep rumble in his chest, like a feral sound of approval. But he says nothing. In fact, there's such a long moment of inaction, I wonder if he's going to turn me away. I'm about to say "never mind" and walk away, when he opens the door wider. "Come in."

CHAPTER 16
HIS LAIR

I BRUSH PAST HIM INTO A HUGE FOYER. IT LOOKS LIKE THE lobby of a hotel, with a short hallway that opens up into a rotunda. There's a round granite table in the center of the space with a huge glass vase of freshly cut long stem lilies on top. Just beyond the table is an entryway leading into the living room—and beyond that, a large window overlooking the ocean. It's unreal. It's crazy that people actually live like this.

He shuts the door, and I turn to face him. "You haven't texted me in days."

The second the words leave my mouth, I wish I could reel them back in. They make me sound desperate, like spurned high school desperate, like I've been staring at my phone, waiting for him to text me. Truthfully, that's exactly what happened, but he doesn't need to know that. I push out a breath. Whatever. So he knows I've been waiting—who cares? It was a dick move to leave me hanging for days.

He shoves his other hand in his pocket. "I thought we could both use some distance."

I cross my arms over my chest. "I never said I needed that."

He glances down at the ground and shakes his head. "I needed it," he says firmly.

My heart sinks. "Oh." I shrug. "Okay, well, I guess that's it then. You could have let me know."

That gets a response out of him. "No." He steps forward, so close to me that I think he might kiss me if he didn't have the full face mask on. "That's not it. I needed time to think, Cassandra. To get some things straight in my head."

When I inhale, the scent of him engulfs me, and I fight the urge to sink against his chest. I frown and prod gently. "What things?"

"Now isn't a good time," he answers.

Before I can even reply, I hear a screech. A *familiar* screech. To my left is a set of double doors leading to what looks like the kitchen. In the middle of the doorway is a young woman, same height and build as me, but with short blond hair slicked back from her face. She's all too familiar, though I've never seen her face until now: Willow. The second I see her, my heart seizes in my chest.

"Oh, *hell*, no." Willow folds her arms tightly across her chest. "What is *she* doing here?"

She's not wearing a mask, and she's wearing regular clothes— a graphic T-shirt, patterned leggings, and socks, but no shoes. Did she spend the night here? Is she the reason he hasn't been texting me? Is she the reason this isn't a good time to talk?

I try really hard to keep my composure, but I'm sure everything I'm feeling is written all over my face. Lori has always said I'm an open book, incapable of hiding my true feelings. But I have to remind myself that Hart isn't mine. We fucked twice. And as shitty as this whole situation is, it's my fault for allowing myself to get attached.

"Willow," Hart warns in that deep, commanding Dom voice. "You will wait for me in the kitchen."

She snaps her mouth shut and glares at me. Honestly, can I blame her? Given the situation, I'd hate me too, probably.

"It looks like you have a lot to deal with." I spin on my heel. "I should leave."

But he stops me, wrapping his large hand around my elbow. He's wound so tight, I can see the tension in his shoulders, and biceps. They bulge as he tugs me against him.

"You aren't leaving," he says through gritted teeth.

I swallow, looking up into his eyes. "You said you needed space..." I glance over his shoulder toward the kitchen. "...and now I see why. I'm giving you that space."

He shakes his head slowly. "You're trapped in the stag's lair now, Fawn. You came to me, and now you have to see this through."

I open my mouth to argue, but he tightens his grip and hauls me into a doorway to the left, opposite the kitchen, down a short hallway and into a bedroom.

"Wait here," he bites out, snapping the door shut.

I stand in the middle of the room and wonder what the fuck just happened. I've been shoved aside so he can speak with Willow, and that has stinging jealousy slithering through me. She's obviously more important. Otherwise, why is she here, obviously settled enough to take off her shoes, while I've been waiting for his call for two days? His priorities are clear.

God, I feel like an idiot. Here I am, chasing yet another guy. A guy that isn't even free for me to chase. I press my cool hands to my hot cheeks, heart thumping, wondering what I should do. Leave the penthouse? Cut things off with Hart permanently?

Sure, the money has been a godsend, but it's not worth all this drama. Over the past week, I've barely had time to concentrate on anything else.

No, no. Better to do this head-on. When he comes back, we'll talk, so I'm not ghosting him, like he ghosted me. Then, I'll go on my merry way.

Just the thought sends a sharp pain through my chest. I'll probably cry for a week straight. But at least I'll have closure. That's…something.

And obviously I'll have to find another consultant to help me get my dad's company back. Maybe he can recommend another attorney I can talk to?

To distract myself from the wait for him to return, I turn on my heel and look around at the room. It's large, of course, decorated in pure white linens and natural wood grains. It's simple, elegant, and a lot more airy than I would have guessed for someone as complex and mysterious as Hart. This is actually more along the lines of something I would pick for myself.

I'm guessing a female interior decorator dressed the room, and Hart just went along with whatever she suggested. But by far the most stunning feature of the room is the floor-to-ceiling glass door that opens out onto a balcony overlooking the Pacific Ocean. It's dark, but the moon is hanging low in the sky and it casts a long golden glow on the surface of the water. It's startlingly beautiful.

After admiring the view for far too long, I turn my attention back to the room itself. As the decor is sparse, there isn't anything personal on the nightstands. And short of going through the drawers, I'm given no clues as to who Hart is as a person. In fact, his office in Beverley Hills is more personalized than this space, and I find that really odd. Wouldn't his home say something about him personally? The only clue is the artwork hanging on the walls—gorgeous but somber oceanscapes. They're exquisite, but the mood is lonely. Melancholy, even.

I'm looking up the artist on my phone when Hart walks in, still masked. Without a word, he snaps the door shut and switches the light off. The room is drenched in darkness, except for the pale white glow of the moon. But that is soon blotted out by the automatic blinds that lower to close off the window. Now, I barely distinguish shadows, the most prominent of which is Hart's large frame stalking toward me.

I'm rooted to the spot.

Finally, I find my voice. "What happened with Willow?" I ask.

When he reaches me, there's a movement, and I know he's pulling off his mask and tossing it aside. It's too dark to make out the distinguishing features of his face and I'm itching to flip the light switch on, but still, I don't move. I've seen his face before, and we're not inside Obscura, but maybe he still needs to keep that material separation between us? I don't really know.

He says nothing as he dips his head and takes my mouth in a kiss. There's an urgency in the way he pulls me close and devours me. His tongue pushes into my mouth, and every thought I had about Willow immediately evaporates. It's been a few long, agonizing days since he has touched me, and I'm desperate for the feel of his skin on mine.

His hand comes up to cup the back of my head, his fingers threading through my hair—always that subtle bid for control. It's ever-present with Hart, but this time, I'm willing to submit to him. Without taking his lips off mine, he growls, "You look so fucking hot tonight."

I smile against his lips. I'm a little more curvy than the average woman, and I don't always feel confident in my body. But I can tell Hart loves my curves. He's always touching my shapely hips and my large breasts. Sometimes, I feel like he's worshiping my body—inflicting pain, invoking desire, gifting me with release. His relationship with my body is intense, for sure.

Breaking away suddenly, he steps back. I can hear his breath coming hard and fast, like he's on the brink of losing control. "I need to fuck you, Cassandra. If you don't want that, leave now. Leave while I can still let you go."

I'm equally as breathless when I reply, "And if I don't leave?"

He shakes his head, his frame still cast in shadow. "Then I can't account for what I might do."

CHAPTER 17
DARKNESS AND VIOLENCE

I BLINK, SHOCKED BY HIS WORDS. NO ACCOUNTING FOR what he might do?

"What do you mean?" I ask, half-afraid of what his answer will be.

I hear him push out a breath. "I don't want to hurt you, Little Fawn. But I crave dark things."

My heartbeat races from fear and…something else. I was afraid he'd say something like this and have a feeling the spanking he gave me days ago is only the tip of the iceberg. But I can't deny the fact that I need him inside me. He ignites my desire like no other man I've ever encountered. So, I need to ask him, find out just how dark his desires run. I need to know the worst of it, so I can make my choice.

"What dark things?" I ask, my voice trembling. I hate that he can probably hear the fear, but I can't help it. Like I said, open book.

"I crave violence and your ultimate submission."

The submission, I knew. I'd seen it with Willow. But violence? "Like, what kind of violence?"

It's a full thirty seconds of heavy silence before he responds. "Choking. Whipping. Bondage...cutting."

I swallow. "Have you actually ever hurt anyone?"

I need to know how deep this goes.

I feel the motion of him shaking his head. But there's still hesitation. I can tell this is difficult for him to admit. Not because he's ashamed—I mean, he's probably been doing this in Obscura with different subs for years—but because he's afraid it'll be too much for me and I'll run. And honestly, I just might. I haven't made that decision yet.

"No," he says. "My subs have all been into it."

Subs, plural? A stab of jealousy slices through me again. These subs were obviously more suited to whatever he needs sexually. I honestly doubt I can be that for him, especially given my lack of experience.

"Okay, then why would you choose me? I'm not into any of that and obviously not what you're looking for." I don't even try to keep the hurt out of my voice. Why is he even entertaining a three-month fling with me if my usual thing is vanilla?

His shadow moves toward me, and I feel his strong hand smooth down my bare arm. "You are *everything* I want," he whispers, his voice urgent.

Tears prick at the backs of my eyes, because I believe him. I can hear the sincerity in his tone. I take a deep breath. "I'm not saying I'm not interested in a little pain, but too much too quickly is obviously going to be a problem. And I'm not your sub. This world is new to me. You need to ease me into it, help me."

He takes my chin between his fingers and pulls my face toward his. His warm breath is feather-light on my lips. "You are so fucking magnificent." I can hear the relief in his voice, and it makes me smile. I was being truthful. The exchange of power, pain and submission is intriguing to me, and so far, I've mostly liked what I've encountered. But I need to go slow.

He kisses me again, and when his lips meet mine, I can feel every ounce of desire pour out of him, and into me. His tongue invades my mouth forcefully as he drinks me in, his hands moving over my dress, unhooking every clasp, pulling the fabric off my body. I'm not wearing a bra, and after I step out of my heels, my panties are quickly discarded.

"Get on the bed," he orders.

I can see the outline of the bed, and I walk over to it. The blankets smell like Hart, and I inhale deeply as I lay out on the cool fabric of the comforter. I hear a rustling in the shadows as Hart shucks his clothing. God, I wish I could see him right now. The ropes of muscle lining his abdomen, the dark hair dusting his chest. He's so beautiful it's almost a sin to turn off the light so I can't appreciate him. Even in the dim light, I could just sit and stare at him for days.

I'm brought out of my fantasizing when a drawer opens and closes. Hart is handling something metallic, and my heartbeat kicks up about ten notches. His shadow approaches the bed, and I tense a little. But when he touches me, it's gentle. His hand smooths up my leg, to my thigh, to my knee. The mattress dips as he joins me on the bed. He's on his knees, looming over me.

"Let's start by working on your obedience."

I bite my bottom lip. "Okay."

"First rule," he says. "You may only speak when given explicit permission."

I frown, absorbing that. Do I acknowledge that? That would mean speaking, so I opt to say nothing.

"Second, I will push your boundaries and take you to the heights of pleasure, but it's imperative that you trust me." His voice heavy, serious and husky with anticipation. I can tell the thought of what he wants to do to me excites him in a way he can't disguise. "Do you trust me, Little Fawn?"

His words—and the way he says them—send heat pulsing through my body. No man has ever been so focused on my pleasure—only in how much pleasure they can take from me. Hart's unwavering attention on me is so foreign I don't quite know what to do with it. But I do trust him, trust that he already knows my body and its capacities better than even I do.

Though it's silly to do, I nod in response.

"Speak, Cassandra."

"Y–yes," I say, my voice raspy. "I trust you."

A rumble of approval erupts from deep in his chest, and he presses the back of his fingers against my cheek. "Good girl."

With a hand still on my knee, he pulls my thighs wide. Cool air washes over my center and makes me shiver. I can still see the outline of his frame as he sinks between my thighs. I feel his nose brush down the inside of my thigh. "Now, where did we leave off?" he asks. He continues moving downward, until he reaches my entrance. His tongue darts out to taste me. "Mmm, I've been thinking about this for days." His accent is so thick I can hardly understand him. "I'm fucking obsessed with the taste of you."

I lift my hips a little to encourage his tongue. I want it inside me. I've also been obsessed with the thought of this for days. I need him so bad, I can practically taste it. My heartbeat is throbbing in my clit, my throat, my fingertips. I can barely suck in enough breath.

Just being here with him, naked, on his bed, is more than I can really handle. His head is between my legs, lavishing attention on my sex and sending me quickly into oblivion. This need he's stoking is all-consuming so that I can't focus on anything else, just the obsession of wanting to rub out an orgasm, just to get it out of the way.

As his tongue runs along the seam of my entrance, my hand finds my clit, and I start rubbing. Hot pleasure races through my blood. Oh, yeah. Now that's where it's at.

He laughs, the deep rumble vibrating against my center. Then, without missing a beat, he catches my wrist in his large hand and pulls it away. "You are a greedy little fawn. But you'll just have to wait. You won't come until my cock is buried *deep* inside you." He emphasizes the word *deep* , and I clench my jaw to keep from whimpering. I need him now, but I know begging him will get me nowhere, so I press my head back into the mattress and just focus on the feel of his mouth devouring me.

His tongue finds my aching, pulsing clit, and he takes it in his mouth and sucks gently. My legs stiffen. My. God. I can't take it. It's too much. Then the edge of his teeth graze the sensitive little pearl, and I nearly launch off the bed. He holds me firmly in place, pinning me down. And then, *God* , his tongue pushes inside me while he's still sucking, and I can't help it, I release a long, anguished moan.

"Oh!" My body twitches, and I pant. "My God, *please* ."

All of the sudden, he's gone, pulling away from me completely. It's reminiscent of two days ago, when I asked him to stop, and he just left. I realize my mistake right away—I spoke when he told me not to. Fear streaks through me with icy fingers.

His dark, ominous tone confirms it. "I told you not to speak. There are consequences for disobedience. I'm generous enough to give you one warning only, and this is it."

Oh, shit.

I nod briskly, desperate for him to come back. My body is on fire, sweet little tingles zipping through my center. I need him. I need him now. My legs are still wide open as he lowers himself back onto the bed. This time, it's his fingers that find my center.

"You are so fucking wet for me," he rasps. "This sweet little pussy is ripe for my cock."

One long finger pushes into me, and I swallow a gasp. Yes. This is what I need. I silently pray he'll finger me to climax. I need it so bad. He uses his thumb to apply pressure to my clit as his finger pumps in and out, in and out. My eyes squeeze shut and my chest rises off the mattress. My entire body is wound so tight, I fear I might snap. And not in a fun way, but a mental-health-crisis kind of way. Can people go clinically insane from edging? And how long did he intend to make it last?

He adds two fingers, then three. When he has me right where he wants me, he pulls his fingers out of me and encircles my waist with his arm, pulling me up to a sitting position. He leans back on his haunches, and pulls me farther, until I'm up on my knees. Already, my thighs are screaming with the tension of supporting my weight.

"Straddle me," he commands, guiding my thighs to envelop his. I hover there for a second, the impressive girth of his cock nudging my entrance. His large hands move up my back, holding me there to support me. We're face-to-face, and I can hear each ragged breath from his mouth, feel its warmth skate across my skin. I can only see the very vague outline of his head and body. "That's it," he says approvingly. "Now, lower yourself onto me, Little Fawn. Take every inch of my cock."

Using his shoulders as leverage, I slowly lower myself, until his cock is seated deeply inside me. From this angle, he feels impossibly large, stretching me so wide, I'm breathless and a little teary-eyed. The pain is almost too much, but I clench my jaw and push past it. I don't move, waiting for my body to adjust. Seconds later, the pain melts into incomprehensible pleasure, and my muscles begin to relax. I tilt my head back. He's still supporting me, taking the brunt of our combined weight, allowing me to move freely.

"Good girl." He speaks in that tight voice, accent thick once more, like it gets when he's really excited. He kisses my shoulder. "You took all of me in and you feel so good. So hot and wet and tight wrapped around me. Now, move, or I can't be held responsible for what I'll do."

I smile, loving the fact that he's so insane with need for me that he fears he may lose control. A part of me wants to see that— but I'm not sure I'm ready. So, I do as I'm told, and gently lift myself up slightly, then back down again. Over and over, until I find a rhythm I like. He helps me by lifting my ass, supporting my weight as I ride him.

Inside me, Hart feels incredible, and somehow, so right. Like he was always mean to be a part of me—not just physically, but emotionally. It's such a strange thought… I just met this man, and he's clearly fighting some demons. But the two of us together…I never knew it could be like this, so intimate and close. A part of me fears I'll never know this kind of intense passion ever again.

As though he's been reading my thoughts, he whispers, "You are so fucking perfect for me. I always knew you would be."

Always ? It's a strange way to express it, given how short a time we've known each other, but I don't linger on the thought. My body is too keyed up to focus on anything other than the feel of him inside me.

My thighs are cinched around his waist tightly as I rock against him, my rhythm growing frantic. I'm on the brink of climax, and my body is so greedy for it. "I'm going to come," I breathe, shuddering.

His blunt fingertips dig into my hips, my ass cheeks as he forcibly slows my pace. "Not yet, Little Fawn. We're going to go slow down, draw things out, enjoy each other's bodies."

No . My God. I can't take it.

My core is pulsing, preparing for that peak and flush of dopamine, but when he slows our pace, the pressure on my clit gently recedes. Lifting my ass, he nearly pulls himself all the way out of me, stopping just before the head of his cock comes free. Then he slams me down again forcefully, all the way to the hilt. Then he repeats the action, forcing my pussy to stroke the entire length of his cock. I want to cry out as he stirs me up inside, the tip of his cock hitting me in just the right spot—over and over.

Every movement shoots white-hot pleasure to my core, and it's the only sensation I'm aware of. All I can feel, see, smell, or hear is *him* .

And I can't take any more.

Every muscle in my body tightens. I throw my head back and let go as my body gives in to the pleasure. Wave after wave of pure liquid ecstasy crashes over me as he forces me to continue riding his cock. He's grunting and panting now, fucking me deep as he takes his own pleasure. My channel tightens and pulses around his iron shaft, and my orgasm radiates to every cell in my body.

"*Fuck* , Cassandra," he growls, driving himself impossibly deep. He's sweating now, and I can feel him tremble beneath my hands. "Take my come. Take it all."

I release a moan as he goes completely still, pumping his hot come into me. It goes on forever, it seems. His body tense, his arms holding me tightly in place as he finishes, still thrusting gently until he's drained of every last drop of come.

With an explosion of breath, his head droops to rest on my shoulder, and I can hear his breathing slowly return to normal. Lifting his head, he kisses me on the lips. "You are mine now," he whispers against my lips. "How in fucking hell will I ever be able to let you go?"

"It's funny," I say between kisses. "I was just thinking the same thing."

But this is all temporary... Yeah, I'm not so sure how I feel about that now. The way things are between us really doesn't feel temporary.

CHAPTER 18
PAMPERED

THE NEXT MORNING, THE SOUND OF WAVES CRASHING coaxes me awake. With a jolt, I bolt upright and glance at the spot next to me. It's empty, of course. I run my hand over the indent in the pillow. He slept here, at least. I know that because, for most of the night, we were tangled up in each other. The last thing I remember before drifting off to sleep is the puff of his warm breath on my cheek, the feel of a strong arm holding me fast against his hard body.

Last night, I felt...*loved* . I know it's crazy. Hart doesn't seem like the kind of guy who would love anyone or anything—other than sex and money, maybe. But there was an undeniable connection between us last night, and I'm not sure what that means for us, if anything.

Stretching, I sit up and climb out of bed. I'm completely naked, but it doesn't matter—which is saying something for me. Normally, I'd rush to find something to cover myself up with. Somewhere along the way, I got the message that curves are a bad thing. But Hart worshiped every dip and valley of my body last night, and I saw myself through his eyes. He thinks I'm beautiful, just as I am.

As I walk barefoot toward the bathroom, I notice coffee and a croissant on the table next to his reading chair, along with a barely legible note. What is it with guys? Both my dad and Liam have horrible handwriting as well.

Breakfast for my favorite woodland creature. I have meetings all day, but I'll be home by dark. I've informed the front desk that you will be using my account. Celeste is your personal concierge, and she is at your disposal.

Until tonight, H

There's a phone number scribbled at the bottom of the note, but there are two numbers I can't quite make out.

I purse my lips. I have two classes today, but I'm absolutely ditching. A full day exploring the famous Exeter House on Hart's dime? Yeah, I'm here for it. In fact…I grab my phone and text Haley. Why not share it with a friend?

While I'm waiting for Haley to respond, I step into the bathroom—and I'm instantly overwhelmed. It looks like a damn resort spa in here. It's huge, first of all, and the floor and countertops glisten with a gray stone or tile that makes it look modern and sleek. But the bathtub…the bathtub. It's a large freestanding tub positioned in front of a set of French doors that open up onto a balcony.

This is a whole new level of wealth that I've never been exposed to before. I grew up with a dad who had money and never wanted for anything—though things seemed tougher in the later years. But even with my privileged childhood, I could never even envision this kind of luxury.

I glance at the separate shower and decide against using it. Instead, I fill the tub, grab my lukewarm coffee and croissant, and enjoy them while soaking in the tub with the amazing view. The window isn't facing the ocean, but we're so close to the beach that I can hear the waves crashing. It's like real-life ASMR. It's incredible, and if I lived here, this would absolutely be my morning routine. Coffee and pastry in the tub, listening to the ocean. *Heaven* .

I'm all pruny when I finally decide to get out of the tub, which has an internal heater to keep the water warm, by the way. After drying off, I grab my phone and see a reply from Haley. She has class in an hour, but she's going to head over once she's done. Girls' day. I'm so excited.

Okay, so. Clothes. I arrived last night wearing a skimpy wrap dress. I can't exactly wear that while walking around Exeter House. It's clear the people here have their dark and kinky secrets, but on the outside, it's very upper crust. Very polished. Which means I'll need something else to wear.

Picking up Hart's note, I try calling the number he left. It takes me two tries to get the right number, but when I finally do, Celeste's cheery voice comes through. "Good morning, Ms. Fitzgerald. How can I be of assistance?"

"Um, yeah. I was wondering if you could grab some clothes for me?"

I know Exeter House has boutique designer clothing stores downstairs. It's a fully functioning community. A delightful and heavenly combination of shopping mall, spa, hair salon, restaurants, clubs. In a way, you wouldn't ever have to leave if you don't want to.

"Absolutely," she chirps.

I give her my size and the styles I'm looking for, and she promises to have the clothes for me within the hour. When I hang up, I smile to myself. Amazing. I could really get used to this.

Forty-five minutes later, Celeste is at the door. I'm barefoot, and wearing one of the plush white robes I found in the bathroom cabinet.

"Good morning!" She smiles like we've been besties forever. I already love her.

"Hey, thanks for helping me out on such short notice. I really appreciate it."

I open the door wider, and Celeste walks in with several garment bags slung over her arm. She's followed by a bellboy, who is pushing a cart full of more clothes, all dangling from hangars. Once the cart is wheeled in, Celeste turns to the bellboy. "Thank you, Thomas."

The young kid, no older than eighteen, nods awkwardly and leaves.

Celeste is quite young with sleek brown hair and wide green eyes. Stunning. She's wearing a white blouse, black slacks and a pair of red heels. She looks fabulous, so I guess I lucked out. She's the perfect person to pick out my outfit for the day.

Celeste claps her hands together. "So," she says excitedly. "Let's get started. I brought a variety of styles, depending on your particular tastes."

I show Celeste into the bedroom, and she glances around in awe. "I've always wanted to see this penthouse. It's beautiful."

"You've never been inside?" I ask, surprised. I dip into the closet to put one of the dresses on.

"Nope. Mr…" She hesitates. "Your host is usually out of town, and when he is here, he normally keeps to himself."

I don't know why it matters in the long run, but the fact that he doesn't have a stream of girls coming and going from his penthouse fills me with relief. He does seem more introverted in real life. But the fact is, Willow was here when I arrived. And she looked pretty damn comfortable. So he obviously has some women here. At least occasionally.

I come out of the closet and pivot for Celeste. "What do you think?" I ask.

The dress is a simple, champagne-colored with a low but tasteful neckline. It's perfect for going to lunch with the girls, or even just walking around Exeter House.

"I love it!" she says. "And…" She holds a finger up as she dips into the rotunda, where the cart is parked. When she reenters the room, she's holding a cloth bag with the name Jimmy Choo on the front. "I took the liberty of picking out shoes. I hope you don't mind."

"Oh, my God, no. Thank you. How did you know my size?" I ask.

"Your host gave us your dimensions this morning," she answers.

I open my mouth to respond, but I'm stunned silent. He gave them my dimensions? How? Did he measure me while I slept? Or…wait, he probably glanced at the tag sewed into the seam of my dress. And my shoes aren't terribly expensive. The size is still on the sticker on the inside sole. I'd meant to peel it off, but never got around to it.

"Well, I guess there are benefits to dating a type A personality," I laugh.

I pick out a few more things from the pile of clothes she brought. She had the foresight to bring some lacy black lingerie, which is awesome, because I don't own anything fancier than the black lace bra and panties I wore last night. And the underthings are so gorgeous. It's been a very long time since I've had the opportunity to buy something so beautiful and so impractical. None of my boyfriends ever gave a flying fuck about what I was wearing in the bedroom. All they wanted was to get me naked, tits and ass. Most of them took five minutes, and they were good to go. Hart's lovemaking was so different. Yes, it was more dominating, but the way he took his time. The way he savored the experience and slowed me down to savor it too…He takes his time with me, in no rush to finish it. I get the sense that he's attuned to my body on a level that borders on obsessive. It's just completely different from what I've ever known before.

That's the dream, right? Too bad this is all so temporary.

As Celeste and I are hanging my new clothes in the near-empty bedroom closet, I take the opportunity to pick Celeste's brain a little.

"So, um, how well do you know…my host?" I've noticed he takes special care not to use his real name. She's had to catch herself a couple of times. I wonder if that's a privacy thing within Exeter House, or if Hart specifically asked the staff not to mention it. I have a feeling it's the latter, but why is anyone's guess. He has a layer of mystery surrounding him that I find intriguing.

Celeste shrugs as she places my shoes on the built-in shoe rack. Hart has three pairs of shoes, so there's plenty of room. "Not well, actually. He's owned the penthouse for years, but he only moved in about a year ago. He travels frequently to the UK. I think he may actually live there most of the year."

I nod slowly, taking it all in. Given the sterility of his penthouse, that makes sense. He has no personal items here whatsoever, aside from some toiletries, a few sex toys in the dresser—yes, I looked—and some clothes in the closet. No medication. No pictures. No paperwork. Though, to be fair, I've only looked in the bedroom. I haven't explored the rest of the penthouse yet.

As soon as Celeste leaves, I change back into my robe and glance at my phone. There's a text from Haley, telling me she's stuck in a group meeting, and there's a text from Hart. He must have programmed his number in my phone before leaving this morning. I don't have a lock screen because they're annoying, and I hate the extra step of having to unlock it.

I'm in a very important meeting, but I can't stop thinking about your lips.

Smiling, I type out my reply.

If you were here now, these lips could be wrapped around your cock.

Then I take a picture of myself making a kissy face and hit send. Is that mean? Yeah. He's in a meeting, and it's not nice to tempt him, but I'm half-hoping he'll take the bait and come home early. I'm on a mission to see him while the sun is still out.

Be careful what you promise.

Oh, that sounds like a delicious threat. Does that mean he's coming home? God, I hope so. Haley will be on her way soon, but I could send her to the spa, and then I could escape for a half hour, right? She'd be the first to tell me to *get it.*

A second later, a photo comes through. It's a shot of his crotch. His swollen cock is straining against the fabric of his gray slacks. His shaft is so long, it rests against his thigh. I suck in a sharp breath.

Goddamn .

I'm hot all of a sudden, and I decide to tease him a bit more.

Laying down on the bed, I expose my large breasts from the front of my robe, and take a video of me pinching my pink nipples. I release a deep moan as the pain zips through me. It's only a shot of my body, not my face—because I know better than to send a pic with my face in it. But hopefully this gets him nice and primed for later.

Setting my phone down, I lean back on the bed and drift off to sleep. A while later, I'm jolted awake by my phone ringing. I was sleeping so deeply, it takes me a moment to realize what the sound is.

I feel around for my phone, and when I finally find it, I glance at the screen and groan. It's Liam.

Ugh, whatever. He can leave a message.

The phone stops ringing, and I breathe a sigh of relief. He's the last person I want to talk to right now. I'm having an amazing day and waiting for a stunning man to come home and fuck me unconscious.

I rub my eyes and stare at the ceiling. But just for a moment because…that grating trill of my phone ringing fills the room again.

My. God. Liam, get a life. Before I can think better of it, I answer.

"Someone had better be dying," I say with an annoyed huff.

"Mom is in the hospital," he says. I hear the fear in his voice, and that freaks me out more than anything. Liam is never scared. He's the model of power and confidence. If he's freaked out, then it must be *really* bad.

CHAPTER 19
CRISIS

I SIT UPRIGHT, SHOCK REVERBERATING THROUGH ME. "Where? What happened?"

"I don't know. I was notified at work. I'm headed to the hospital now."

"Okay, I'm on my way." He gives me the hospital name, and we hang up. I despise Liam right now, but if Lori needs me, then I'm there.

I call down to the front desk and ask for my usual driver, Andrew. Thankfully, he's available. I throw on one of the casual-ish dresses Celeste brought me and a pair of strappy heels. I'd wear jeans and tennis shoes if I could, but this is all I have at hand. Throwing my hair up into a ponytail, I grab my purse and head downstairs to wait for Andrew to pull the car around to the front of Exeter House. I don't have to wait long. Within fifteen minutes, we're on the freeway, headed toward the UCLA medical center in Santa Monica.

I pull my phone out to look for any updates from Liam. There's nothing. But it occurs to me that I'd better text Hart and let him know what's going on.

Hey. My stepmom is in the hospital and I'm headed there now. I'll call you later when I know what's going on.

After I hit send, I stare down at my phone, waiting for his immediate reply. I hold my breath, realizing suddenly that I need his reassurance, that I need to know he's in this with me—at least peripherally. Lori has been a fixture in my life since I was ten years old. And since I have *zero* relationship with my biological mother, I've leaned on my stepmom for just about everything. She *is* my mom, really.

And if anything happens to her...*no* , I shake away the thought, eyes prickling with tears. I can't go there—especially since I don't have any real details yet.

Hart hasn't responded by the time I arrive at the hospital. Andrew comes around to open the car door for me. As I step out, I place my hand on his. "Thank you, Andrew. I really appreciate your getting me here so quickly."

"Any time. I'll stick around, so I can take you back to Exeter House or home when you're ready."

"Oh, no, you don't have to do that," I say apologetically. "I have no idea how much time it will take. It could be a long wait. I'll just take an Uber or something."

With a stiff nod, he says, "You have my number. If I'm not out on another call, I'll come get you in a heartbeat."

I flash him a tight smile. "Will do. Thanks again, Andrew."

I rush into the lobby of the hospital, check in at the reception desk and that's when I'm informed that she's in ICU. My stomach drops and the receptionist directs me to the separate ICU reception on the third floor. I rush to the elevator, then down a maze of hallways, until I check in at ICU, inform them that I'm her daughter and am escorted to her room.

Even before I walk through the door, I can hear machines beeping, and it takes me straight back to my dad's death a year ago. I suddenly feel nauseous with the memories of that deep and sudden grief. Somehow, I manage to bite back the bile rising up in my throat. I can't allow myself to get emotional. Lori needs me, and come Hell or high water, I'm going to be present for her.

With all the strength I have, I walk through the open door to the drawn curtain beyond. As I round the corner, I see Liam first. He's sitting in a chair, forearms resting on his thighs, his face resting in his hands. Everything in me drops.

Oh, *fuck.*

ICU? Liam looking like he's already in mourning? This is bad. Really, really bad. Not both parents one year apart. I can't take that sort of cruel blow.

I steel myself and approach Lori. She's lying on the bed at a slight incline, her eyes closed. There's all kinds of intimidating-looking equipment hooked up to her. Monitors are beeping, lights are flashing on and off. My heart seizes.

I swallow. "What's going on? How is she?"

Liam lifts his head, and I can see the relief on his face that I'm here. He looks worn, haggard. "I'm waiting on the doctor."

I suck in a breath and nod. He points to a chair beside him, and I slowly sink down into it, flashing him a sidelong glance and acknowledging that something between us feels weird, different.

Honestly, being this close to Liam is doing things to me. He's always been beautiful—ever since we were kids—but he seems even more striking now, even with the obvious worry written all over his features. He's wearing a white button-down shirt, sleeves rolled up to his elbows, his suit jacket slung over the end of the hospital bed.

Taking a deep breath, I stand up and hit the call button for a nurse. When someone on the other end responds, I reply into the speaker forcing politeness to cover for my annoyance at being left in the dark this long. "Hi, um, my mom just got admitted, and we have no idea what's going on. Do you know when the doctor will be available to talk to us?"

I try to stay calm as I speak, though I feel like I'm going to lose my shit any second.

"The doctor is on his way up to you now. Sit tight. Just a few minutes."

My heart sinks, because the way he says it, with sympathy in his tone, gives me the impression that the news is dire. Tears prick at the back of my eyes, but I manage to keep them at bay as I sink back down next to Liam.

"Thank you for coming," Liam murmurs.

I can't fight the scowl and push out a harsh breath. "I might hate you, Liam, but Lori is still the only mom I know. Of course I'd be here."

He lets out a long sigh and leans back against his chair. I can tell he's about to crawl out of his own skin. Liam has always *hated* uncertainty. I'm guessing that's why he's developed such a control complex. And all this waiting, this uncertainty, must be unbearable for him. My heart softens toward him *just a fraction*. A barely detectable fraction.

As we wait in silence, I glance at my phone to see if Hart has responded to my earlier text. Nothing. I set my phone aside with a heavy sigh.

"Waiting for someone to call?" Liam asks, suspicion in his tone.

"Is that really any of your business?" I snap back. Now is not the time to argue, but seriously, he could just keep his nose out of it. I don't need him trying to cock-block me again.

He smirks a little. "You're my little sister. Of course it's my business."

I close my eyes briefly and clench my jaw to keep from saying something I'll regret. Now is not the time. We're here for Lori, not to bicker. She's all that matters right now.

At that moment, a doctor walks, saving me from having to respond to Liam.

"Good afternoon," the doctor says. He has Lori's chart in his hand, and he flips through a couple of the pages, then tucks it under his arm. "Your mother was brought to the emergency room this morning with a head injury. She had called 911, but by the time paramedics arrived, she was non-responsive. We're running tests, but our biggest concern, at this point, is bleeding on the brain."

A wave of nausea hits me. *Brain bleed*? That's bad. Very bad.

"How was she injured?" Liam stands to face the doctor and begin questioning him like he's negotiating a business deal, all of that previous uncertainty evaporated.

"We don't know. The dispatcher wasn't able to get that information from her."

"Is she in a coma?" I ask, afraid of the answer. But there has to be a reason she's not awake.

"It's a medically induced coma." The doctor turns to me. "We're keeping her sedated until we can figure out what's happening in her brain."

Liam asks a few more questions which the doctor fields until, finally, Liam nods. "Thank you, doctor."

When the doctor leaves, Liam turns to me. "You can head home, if you want. I'll stay with Mom and keep you updated."

I fold my arms across my chest and glare at him through narrowed eyes. "Nice try. I'm going to grab us some snacks. I'll be right back. Call me if she wakes up."

If I'm going to be dealing with Liam for the next couple hours, I'll need carbs. And sugar. A piece of cake or cookies would be ideal, but I'll have to see what they have in the vending machines. I take my time hunting out my snacks, and when I return a half hour later, Liam is deep in contemplation.

I toss him a bag of barbecue-flavored potato chips, which I know are his favorite. He flashes me a half smile and says, "Thanks." But I can tell he's worried and distracted.

"She's going to be fine," I say, sitting back in my chair beside him. "Lori is nothing if not stubborn."

"Yeah," he says, setting the chips aside. "I just can't help feeling like I should have been around more." He glances at me, his gaze biting into me. "Life is too short."

I know the meaning behind those words. He's referring to the sudden and very shocking loss of my dad—and his, too, really. Liam has had very little contact with his bio dad in the UK since moving here. In addition, the man was abusive so I don't imagine that's a relationship he really wants to repair. When Liam and his mom came to live with us, he had just turned thirteen. We got along surprisingly well in those days, considering our differences.

But things got weird not long before he decided to go off to college at Oxford, seldom returning home even for holidays. And when he was here, he was sullen, distant and quiet. The epitome of brooding. Right after finishing his university studies, he went to work for my dad's company on the East Coast and came back even less frequently than before.

Somewhere along the line, he became a stranger to me. And by the time my dad died, he was the ruthless businessman who swooped in and took all the leavings for himself.

Regardless of those negative thoughts, as I look over at him right now, I find myself transfixed by his gaze. Heat trickles down my spine, and I have the sudden urge to lean in and inhale his scent.

What the fuck ? Why? I hate this guy, right? His selfishness is next level. Who takes the fair share of a company away from someone—a family member, no less?

But, I don't know…there must be something about our current joint trauma that makes me see him a little differently. Or remember the old days. Or hope that under that cold-blooded businessman exterior is the boy I once knew so well I considered him my best friend.

It occurs to me that a situation like this, where we are sitting quietly and just chatting, might be the perfect time to bring up my dad's trust documents. My eyes wander to the motionless Lori lying on the bed. Given the situation, bringing up all that mess right now feels wrong. Maybe once she's on the mend, we can talk. As easy as it would be, I can't sink to his level. Unlike him, I'm not a horrible person, and it's not in my nature to take advantage of a situation.

But I'm not going to play nice forever…

CHAPTER 20
NOSTALGIA

THE NEXT FEW DAYS PASS IN A BLUR WHILE LORI undergoes several tests. I'm able to peel away for a few hours to pack a bag, notify my advisor and professors about the family emergency, and inform my roommates about what's going on. They are all amazing and supportive, arranging to have my lectures recorded and sending meals to Liam and me at the hospital.

They are the absolute best.

I also inform Hart about the reason why I vanished from his house and hadn't been responding to his texts. His reply makes me hold my phone to my chest and almost swoon like a Victorian damsel.

Fuck. I'm so sorry. Take the next few weeks—all the time you need. I won't be going to Obscura without you.

I'll put Andrew at your service, driving you to and from the hospital. What else can I do for you?

I want to crawl through the phone and kiss him. What I would give to be tucked away in his penthouse right now, curled up on his bed, smelling his pillows. But there's no way I can leave Lori's side. Not until I'm absolutely certain she's okay.

I type in my reply, smiling for the first time in almost a full day.

Thank you so much. You are so sweet. All of that is more than enough.

When his reply comes back, I read it, feeling a rush and realizing that I might just have heart-eyes.

I will be thinking of my little fawn every moment you're not with me, but I want you to focus on your family right now. You're never obligated to reach out unless you need me.

Wow. This guy is so amazing it's like he's not even real. It's like he's a dream man not quite made reality because of the face he keeps hidden behind his mask.

I send him a red heart emoji in reply and hit the road because I've already been too long away from the hospital and there has been no real news about Lori.

The drive from Pasadena to Santa Monica is tedious enough that I look forward to taking Hart up on his offer in the next few days.

As for Liam, well…we've come to an unofficial—but temporary—cease fire given our united front with Lori. Our fear of losing her far outweighs the bitterness between us. For now at least.

Tonight, when I arrive at the hospital, Liam is already there. In theory, while they'd taken Mom down for a CT scan, he was supposed to leave, same as me, to go grab what he needed. But he's still in the same clothes and the two-day-old scruff on his chiseled jaw is only making him look more devastatingly handsome than ever.

As I usually do when noticing how attractive my stepbrother is, I avert my eyes and remind myself not to think about it.

"I didn't want to chance her coming back from her tests to an empty room," he says by way of explanation about why he didn't leave. But honestly, he looks depleted, exhausted and uncomfortable, still wearing his suit from yesterday. The sadness and worry is all over his face. Our eyes meet. "We can't lose her, too. It would just be too cruel..."

I put my hand on his solid shoulder and give a reassuring squeeze. "We won't talk like that. We're not losing her. I'm here now, go take a shower, eat some food. Come back tomorrow morning if you want. I'll be here all night."

Honestly, I'm making that suggestion as much for me as for him. It's all so jumbled up right now, my feelings toward him. I'm still angry at what he did, but his love and devotion to his mom is so disarming. It gives him a vulnerability that I haven't seen in a very long time. Not from him.

It only takes a little more convincing to get Liam to leave, and then I take to the recliner they brought in and spread out a bit, getting comfortable.

Two hours later, Liam returns, showered, changed into casual clothes—sweats and a T-shirt which fit him all too well for me not to notice. In one hand he has a bag of Lori's things, and in the other he has a bag of fast food. The food he plops on the table beside me.

"You still like the honey mustard dressing on the crispy chicken sandwich?" he murmurs quietly.

I blink, amazed that he still remembers that. When he'd first gotten his license to drive, we'd made more than a few late-night fast food runs. This sandwich was always my favorite. I haven't eaten one in years.

I pop out of the recliner and dig through the bag he's brought for Lori. And there they are, a pair of fuzzy socks. Lori is constantly complaining about cold feet, and I'd mentioned that yesterday. He grabbed her socks. Without a word, I pull them out of the bag, unroll them, and carefully put them on her feet.

When I turn around, I catch Liam looking at me with the oddest expression on his face. I blink and tilt my head at him. "What?"

"Your food's getting cold." He looks away then, almost self-consciously. Instead, I look inside the bag and see a photo frame. *What's this?*

I pull it out of the bag, amazed when I recognize it. "Shit...where did you find this? I haven't seen this in years."

It's a family picture of the four of us. My dad, Lori, Liam, and me on our first family vacation about a year after they'd gotten married. We're standing under the towering granite cliffs and a massive waterfall in Yosemite National Park. We all look so happy, our arms all around one another. My eyes drift to my dad's smiling face, his arm around Liam's shoulders. His fourteen-year-old stepson almost the same height as him.

Daddy. I miss him so much.

"It was in Dad's office. Thought it might...help." He gives another self-conscious shrug, then reaches into the food bag, pulls out an onion ring and pops it into his mouth.

My eyes widen even as my mouth waters. "I haven't had their sweet Hawaiian batter onion rings in years. Give me some!"

He laughs. "Get your own." Then he hands me a grease-stained brown bag that, indeed, contains my own order of the delectable creations, and we dig in. Our lightheartedness lasts about thirty seconds after we finish eating, then our existence is punctuated once more by beeping machines and the slow, steady breathing of our mom.

I set the picture on the table beside her bed at eye level. "It will be the first thing she sees when she wakes up," I say quietly with an almost trembling voice.

Liam has gathered up the trash and is walking toward the door to dispose of it. He turns to me. "Take the recliner, Cass. You got hardly any sleep last night."

I stretch, my arms over my head. "You're heading out?" I'm hopeful but also a little dismayed. There are mixed feelings again.

He shakes his head. "I'll take the chair."

As I settle in, my eyes wander over to the wooden chair. It doesn't look the least bit comfortable. But I don't dwell on that thought for very long because it takes me less than five minutes—before he's even returned from depositing the garbage—to fall fast asleep.

There's early light peeking through the window when I'm lured awake by the sound of people talking in low tones. I'm enveloped in Liam's smell. It's a musky scent that strangely reminds me of Hart. It's sagey and masculine somehow and makes me feel safe. I shift and realize that Liam's jacket is draped over me. He must have given it to me at some point.

Sitting up, I wince and grab my shoulder. A deep ache radiates down my arm. I must have slept on it weird. Taking

Liam's jacket off me, I toss it over the back of his chair. The faster I get out from under his smell, the better. I can already feel the fire in my veins reigniting. I *hate* that he has that effect on my body.

Thankfully, Liam isn't in the room, but I can hear him just outside, in the hallway, talking to someone.

With a yawn, I stand up and walk over to Lori's bed. She's still unconscious, and I grab her cool hand. Liam walks back into the room, and I notice a lightness in the way he's walking. The slight shift is probably just apparent to me, but I've known him for so long that I know all his tells.

"Good news?" I ask.

He flashes me that devastating smile. "Her scans all came back normal. They're going to start weaning her off the sedatives. She may be awake by this time tomorrow."

Oh, thank God.

A wave of relief floods me, and the tears start falling. I'm not even fully aware of them until Liam walks over and pulls me against his chest. In a moment of weakness, I sink into him and let the tears come. Every anxious and frenzied thought I've dammed up for the past forty-eight hours comes draining out like a flood I can't stop, and for a few minutes, I don't even try.

"It's going to be okay," he says in that deep baritone, and I don't know, I guess it snaps me out of my daze.

Stiffening, I bring my hands up to press on his chest, separating us. I take a step back and wipe the tears from my eyes. I can't believe I allowed him to comfort me—the man that stole *everything* from me. I live in poverty because of him. Well, at least until Hart came along.

I suck in a steadying breath. "I'm going to get some fresh air."

Liam takes a step back, but I can tell it takes everything in him to do it. He doesn't want to let me go, and that realization is so fucking confusing. There's always been a lingering *something* between us, especially as teenagers. Maybe all this nostalgia has brought back a hint of that? I shake my head, unwilling to process what any of that means.

We're practically strangers now.

The next day, I'm done with my one class that day when it's still mid-morning. Liam urged me to go, and frankly, the tension between us has been growing so thick, you could hack it with a chainsaw. But I'm unwilling to let it chase me away from Lori's side for long. So it's just been something we've been dealing with without dealing. The proverbial elephant in the room.

Andrew drops me straight from class to the hospital, and I'm there by 10:30 a.m. When I get up to Lori's room, it's filled with the doctor and three nurses.

The doctor turns to say something to Liam, who comes toward me, quietly ushering me from the room and ducking just outside, in the hallway.

He looks hopeful, but I can sense his tension.

"What's going on?" I ask.

"Mom's waking up."

CHAPTER 21
GROWNUPS

THE DOCTORS HAVE ASKED US TO GO TO THE WAITING room while they monitor the procedure for waking Lori up. Instead, I opt to head down to the hospital cafeteria in the basement. Maddeningly, Liam follows me down.

Before we enter to find a booth, however, I hang back to pull out my phone and send a quick text off to Hart. I've been filling him in once a day on what's going on. He usually doesn't get back to me until later in the evenings.

When I look up from my screen, I see that Liam has stopped and is standing near the end of the food line with his arms folded over his chest, staring at me.

I heave a sigh.

"What was *that*?" he asks when I catch up to him and pull out a tray for myself.

I walk past him, scooting my tray along the rails and taking in the selections while rolling my eyes at my stepbrother. "I was texting a friend."

"The same *friend* you've been texting constantly from the hospital room?" The suspicion and innuendo in his tone immediately piss me off. He gets zero say in who I text, or when.

"Yeah," I say, very obviously annoyed. I reach out and grab a wrapped tuna salad sandwich.

He opts for a garden salad and turns his head to me once more. "A male or female friend?"

I throw him some serious side-eye while grabbing an iced coffee. "A none-of-your-business friend."

"Obviously *more* than a friend or you wouldn't be so defensive."

I turn toward him, folding my arms across my chest. "How's your runway model, by the way? The one you were pictured with in Italy?"

"No idea. Haven't talked to her in almost two months."

I arch a brow. "Another one bites the dust, huh? That's too bad." But I make it clear in my voice that the words are completely void of any real sympathy. I turn back, grab the rest of my food and hurry to the cashier.

Frustratingly, Liam is right behind me and insists on covering both our meals, pulling out his triple-diamond platinum rich-man club card or whatever it is. I watch the transaction balefully, seething with renewed resentment over his easy wealth.

I may have come into a nice bundle with this cozy arrangement I have with Hart, but it's with no thanks to my own stepbrother, that's for sure.

"So you're blissfully single these days?" I ask almost nonchalantly once we're sitting at a booth. I pull off the wrapping on my sandwich and pull it apart. I don't know why I care really, but I'm deeply curious about Liam's private life and Google-stalking him isn't as satisfying when I have him here in the flesh. Might as well grill him.

"I never said that." He spears his fork into his salad with a little more force than is needed and it clinks loudly.

My eyes widen. He seems weirdly tense.

"So you aren't single?" I ask.

His dark eyes come up to lock with mine, oddly intense. "I'm seeing someone."

I blink, stung by that information for some reason. Whoever this someone is must mean something to have him acting so on edge. And that makes me feel…weird. I take a breath. Should I keep needling?

My curiosity, as always, gets the best of me. "Someone out here? Are hearts breaking all over the West Coast now that William Force is off the market?" I'm out for blood when I pull out his full name. He hates being called William.

Instead of answering right away, he tears his eyes away and returns his attention to his salad. "Why do you want to know? Didn't you just tell me it was none of my business who you were texting?"

I narrow my eyes a little as he avoids my gaze. "Just a little harmless sisterly curiosity. But I guess, if she means that much to you, no harm done. Be sure to invite me to the wedding—and here I always thought I'd be the one to get married first."

A strange look crosses his face, almost a bitterness. He shakes his head. "I'm not–"

Just then, his phone chimes with a text message. He picks up the phone to look at the screen, and as he does, I wonder what he would have said because he looks so…almost *sad,* defeated. I frown. He never lets his emotions show like that. And who is this woman, anyway? It seems serious. Those are some real emotions he's fighting—and failing—to keep hidden.

He sets aside his plate and slides out of the booth. "Mom's awake."

I push my food aside but grab my drink and follow him out of the cafeteria. He's walking so fast that it's hard to catch up with his long strides. Clearly, he's pissed at whatever I said.

He halts at the elevator bank and punches the button. I catch up to him then. Just before the doors open, I reach out and put my hand on his solid upper arm. Under his golf shirt, his bicep bulges, and it's all I can do to keep from squeezing it. Fuck, he's too hot for his own good.

"Hey, I didn't mean to upset you. I was just joking around."

Liam keeps his eyes on the elevator door and subtly but deliberately shrugs off my hand. "Well, *don't*. It's not a subject I want to get into." I open my mouth to say more when he adds, almost under his breath. "With *you*, least of all."

I hold my hands up in surrender. "Fair enough."

The elevator arrives, and it's a tense ride back up to Lori's floor. When the doors open, he lets out a long breath as if he's been holding it. "Let's just get through this and get along for Mom's sake. Can you do that, Cass? Please? We can be grownups, right?"

He says it with such intensity that I'm taken aback. I blink, staring. "Yeah, sure. I can do that."

When we step over the threshold, one nurse is standing at Lori's bedside, taking close note of the monitors. She turns to Liam, smiling. Lori's eyes are cracked open. She looks pale and weak but most definitely awake. Liam instantly moves to her bedside and takes her hand. "Hey, Mom. We're here..."

She licks her lips and says she's thirsty. The nurse informs us that she can only have ice chips, but if she continues to do as well as she's doing now, she'll be moved out of ICU and into a regular hospital room this time tomorrow.

I can see the relief on Liam's face as he patiently answers her questions, and he asks his own to find out what exactly happened to put her in the hospital. She tells us she was in the kitchen when she felt faint and collapsed. She doesn't remember calling the ambulance, but thank goodness she did.

She's always had trouble remembering to eat, and I wonder out loud, "The doctor did say your blood sugar was low when you came in. Did you forget to eat?"

"I–I'm not sure. It's all so fuzzy. Maybe."

I nod slowly, convinced that must have been the issue. All her other tests came back normal, thankfully.

We sit there with her for a few hours, just talking. At one point, she's holding each of our hands in one of her own, and she sighs, a dreamy look on her face. "This isn't quite the way I wanted to bring you two together, but I'm so glad we can all be together now. Wouldn't your dad be so happy to see us all like this?"

Her voice trembles a little bit, and the silence once her voice fades away could be cut with a knife. I blink, suddenly fighting tears, and to my astonishment, a brief moment of unfettered grief can be seen in Liam's eyes as well.

I squeeze Lori's hand before releasing it and asking her to give me a list of everything she wants me to bring her from home.

Liam is still there sitting with Lori when I decide it's time for me to go and try to catch up on my studies. Lori reassures me that she's fine and that I shouldn't miss any more school on her account.

"We'll see…" I say noncommittally as I bend to kiss her on the cheek.

Liam insists on walking me out to the front where the car and Andrew await. But strangely, he shies away once he catches sight of the car.

"Thanks for the truce, Cass. I think it will be good…for Mom."

I nod. "Yep, exactly. I'm doing it *for Lori* ," I emphasize as I peel away from him and stride down the front walkway toward the car. Andrew gets out once he spots me and moves to open the back door. But when I turn around to get the last glimpse of Liam, he's already gone.

CHAPTER 22
GIVING IN

OVER THE NEXT FEW WEEKS, I MANAGE TO ATTEND every single one of my classes and spend chunks of time, usually in the afternoon, with Lori. I choose the afternoons because that's usually when Liam is checking in with his office and catching up on whatever it is that quillionaires spend their time doing. Or maybe he's just spending time with his mysterious lady love, whoever she is.

While at the hospital, I pass the time watching TV or playing cards with Lori or, if she's napping, flirt-texting with Hart, when he can reply. He's told me he's still waiting for when I'm ready to start up again at Obscura, and my body feels more than ready.

In spite of my willingness to blow off steam with Hart, however, my nights are mostly dedicated to my studies or checking in with my besties at Hill House. But I count the days until I can be with Hart again. Just the thought of him gets me hot and heavy, and I can't get to sleep without rubbing one out and fantasizing about him.

Seeing Liam here and there in passing isn't helping, either. The attraction I feel toward my stepbrother is stronger than ever, and I find myself having to fight extra hard to remember why I should hate him. But with my full bank account—and Hart has generously kept my pay coming even though I haven't been doing my "job" at Obscura—I'm finding it harder and harder to make this about money.

So I make the focus of my anger about my birthright and my dad's legacy instead. That helps.

After several weeks in the hospital and some rehabilitation, occupational and physical therapy and dietary training to go with her new diagnosis of hypoglycemia, Lori has been given a release date for next week. The light is finally at the end of the tunnel, and I can breathe a sigh of relief. For herself, Lori is wanting out of the hospital *yesterday* and taking every opportunity to leave her room to get fresh air and a little exercise.

Today, I've stayed longer than I usually do because Lori has begged for more time outside. As we return from a sojourn in the courtyard, me wheeling her in the wheelchair per hospital policy, we arrive just in time for her dinner to be delivered.

One of the dietary aides wheels in a cart stacked with trays of food. She smiles at us as she pulls a tray out and sets it on Lori's little table.

"Turkey, mashed potatoes and gravy, Ms. Fitzgerald. Just like you ordered."

Liam has already arrived and is sitting with the book they've been reading together. Time for me to make my exit.

But Lori makes a sound of protest when I bend to grab my bag. "It's Friday, Cassie. Can't you stay a little longer? Please?"

I straighten and make the mistake of meeting her gaze. Her eyes are pleading, and there's very little I can refuse her these days.

"I guess I can hang around a bit longer."

Andrew's shift ends soon so I text him to go ahead and leave and thank him. I'll splurge and take an Uber home tonight.

Liam stands from the recliner and gestures for me to take it. He doesn't have to tell me twice. He moves to the wooden chair, and for the next hour, as Lori eats and finishes up her dinner, Liam reads to us from *Great Expectations* , and I find myself getting lost in the sound of his deep, masculine baritone.

That voice of his…the only thing sexier is Hart who's got the voice *and* the cultured British accent to boot. Crazily enough, my mind wanders as Liam continues to narrate the adventures of Pip and Estella, and I find myself comparing my stepbrother to Hart. Hart wins in every way, of course. But it's crazy how similar they are.

Maybe I have a type? I definitely have a type. Hart is my type. And god, I need him. I'm getting hornier by the day. Maybe I can break away this weekend…

After reading, Lori uses her app to get us food delivered from the cafe across the street and begs me to stay for some cards. We end up playing an old family favorite, Crazy Eights, and reminiscing about Dad and his treacherous tactics at the game. He was never above cheating, much to our ongoing annoyance.

It's nearly the end of regular visiting hours by the time I stand up and stretch, my arms high over my head. "I gotta get going…."

"You're not driving home this late, are you?" Lori asks with that same overly worrying motherly concern. "I know your boss's driver has been taking you home. Is he still here?"

I sigh. "It's not even eight yet. I'm fine! Andrew went home, but I'm just going to grab an Uber."

Lori's eyes dart to Liam, but she doesn't say anything. Liam immediately stands up. "Neither of us wants you in an Uber on a Friday night. I'll take you home."

I open my mouth to protest and send him some sharp words, but Lori is very closely watching our interchange. And I promised to be a grownup.

Besides, in his fancy-ass sports car, he can get me across town faster than an Uber anyway. And maybe, alone and with Lori well out of danger, I'll have the chance to say what I really want to say to him.

"Yeah, okay," I say, pushing out a breath.

I say my goodbyes to Lori, kissing her on the forehead and promising to come back over the weekend.

Out in the parking lot, we find Liam's sleek, silver Maserati. Of course, he has the best set of wheels that money can buy. He took all my dad's money and bought himself houses, cars, and God only knows what else. Maybe he's not as blingy as your average wealthy guy, but he definitely has expensive taste. Meanwhile, until recently, every month was a struggle of penny-pinching and ramen-eating in order to make my rent.

Asshole.

As I slip into the passenger seat of his car, I prepare myself for the forty-five-minute ride home. I can do this. I can be in a car with him and not claw his eyes out, right? Yes. *It's not even an hour. I can be civil for that long.* I just keep repeating that inside my head.

Liam lowers himself into the driver's seat, then glances over at me, his gaze raking over my dress. It's one of the ones Hart's personal shopper bought for me at Exeter House that morning after I'd spent the night at his place. Last week, he'd had all the clothes she'd brought me delivered straight to my house.

Liam's gaze settles on my very prominent cleavage. "I like the dress. Is it new?"

I bristle immediately and snap, "Can we please just leave?"

Is he wondering how I could have bought such a dress since I'm so poor—the way he obviously prefers me to be? Thief of my inheritance.

His masculine scent pulls me under, and suddenly, I feel like I can't breathe. He's so fucking handsome, which is not helping my resolve. I have to remind myself over and over that he's an asshole. A selfish prick who only cares about himself.

He reaches over, placing his arm across the back of my seat. "Cass, can we just talk for a minute?"

Oh. My. God. "No, Liam. I've done what you asked. I've been grownup and civil for Lori. That doesn't mean we're going to be *chums* , okay? Those days are over, and too much water has passed under the bridge. I honestly just want to go home and go to sleep."

His finger finds a strand of my hair, and he toys with it absentmindedly. "Cass." His voice is low, pleading. "Please. Let's talk about this."

I pull away from him, flipping my hair over my shoulder and swivel to face him. "Okay, if you insist," I say, my voice dripping with anger. "Let's talk about it. What made you think it was okay to take *everything* away from me after Dad died?"

"Cass..."

My chest feels tight, and I'm flushed with rage. "You left me with nothing, Liam. *Nothing.*"

I'm saying all the things that I've been bursting to say to him since Dad died and I ended up with no inheritance to speak of. Liam and I never had a chance to speak face-to-face. He's been avoiding me almost the entire time, until he came back to town just over a month ago.

But now? Yeah, now, I'm ready to lay into him.

My anger lashes him, sharp and cutting, I can see it in the way he pulls back. "There are very good reasons for—"

"*Really?* And what reasons might those be? What could possibly justify taking every cent my dad left me?"

Pushing out a breath, he leans back against the headrest and closes his eyes briefly. "I've told you I'll pay your rent, Cass. Your tuition, your living expenses. Whatever you need."

I fold my arms tightly over my chest and narrow my eyes. I could strangle him. "Yeah, *you'll* pay it. But it's *my* money. I want to pay my own bills, Liam. Why is that so difficult for you to understand?" I glance out at the dark parking lot, anywhere but at Liam's face.

He doesn't even bother answering me or trying to explain. Pushing out a harsh breath, he starts the engine, and we pull out. Thank God. I literally can't wait to get home and text Hart. Right now, the thought of him is the only thing keeping me sane.

A little over a half hour later, because he mostly exceeded the speed limit and we rode in complete silence, Liam pulls up in front of Hill House. The second he cuts the engine, I reach out to open the door, but he quickly hits the auto-lock, preventing me from opening the door. I expel a breath and pound a fist once on the window in frustration.

He wraps a large hand around my elbow. "Wait, Cass. Don't do this. Let's clear the air between us once and for all."

I half-turn to face him, and before I can even say anything, he reaches up and threads his hand through my hair, cupping the back of my head. And then, shockingly, he pulls me into a kiss.

Everything in me screams out in protest, and yet my body...*fuck that treacherous bitch* . I sink against him and, in spite of the faint protest in my brain, just give into it. His tongue invades my mouth, taking absolute control. His grip on the back of my head tightens, pulling me closer, deepening the kiss.

This is the first time we've ever physically acted on the simmering sexual tension between us and...*wow*. I've been missing out. He tastes like the coffee he just drank after dinner, and it feels like we just meld together easily. I reach up and place my hands on his shoulders, my fingertips biting into the fabric of his shirt.

Heated flames of sexual energy lick at me from the inside, igniting a similar need to the one I've recently found with Hart. It's so crazy how similar the two men are—how they both feel, how they move, even how they kiss. I wonder if the reason I chose Hart is because he's so like Liam. Like, in some subconscious mind-fuck kind of way, I've played myself. Freud would have a field day with this.

Liam's hand finds my breast. He slips his hand down my low neckline, beneath my bra, to cup my naked breast. When he squeezes, I moan a little, moving my hand up to thread through his thick hair.

Fuck , he's a good kisser. And I'm being pulled over by an overwhelming wave of desire. Pressure builds in my core, and I feel like I might come just from him kissing and fondling me. I release a low moan against his mouth.

"God, Cass…I *need* to fuck you," he says against my lips, his voice husky and even a little frantic. I'm so used to hearing him cool, calm, and collected that it jars me a little—and I'm suddenly pulled into the present, aware of what's happening.

Ripping myself away from him, I press back against the passenger door and stare, wide-eyed, in shock as my breath comes hard. Still in shock, I straighten my dress as Liam stares at me with smoldering eyes, his own solid chest rising and falling. *Holy shit*. What just happened? What did I just *allow* to happen?

I hold my hand up to my mouth. "Oh, my God. *Oh, my God*."

He reaches out for me again, and I press my back flat against the door. "Unlock this door, Liam. Do it right now."

"Promise me, if I do, you won't run before we talk."

I swallow. "Yes, sure. Just unlock it." It's a lie, of course, and the minute he presses the button to unlock, I open the door and bolt.

"Cass, wait…"

But I do the exact opposite. I launch out of the car, promptly slamming the door shut, then sprint up the walkway to Hill House. I hear the car door open, but I don't look back, pushing through the front door and slamming it behind me.

Once I'm inside, I rest my back against the door, the breath heaving out of my lungs. I can't believe what just happened. His mouth, his hands, the unreleased sexual tension tightening in my core.

"Hey, Cassie," Haley says. She's sitting on the couch, open books and papers surrounding her. "Everything okay?"

I push off the door and head toward the staircase. "Yeah, I'm fine. *Thanks*."

But I'm *not* fine. Not even close.

CHAPTER 23

IN THE DARK

HERE'S A KNOCK ON THE BEDROOM DOOR.

"Cassie!" It's Sam. "Haley said you came in all flustered. I wanted to check on you."

"I'm fine," I call out, my heart still thudding violently against my ribs. I can't breathe, actually. And I'm feeling a bit lightheaded. Am I having a heart attack?

I'm trying to figure out what to do when my door pops open. I hadn't locked it. *Damn* .

"You don't sound fine," Sam says, hand on her hip. She stands in the doorway, looking me up and down. "What's going on?"

I rub my breastbone and take a deep breath. "I think I'm having a heart attack." My hand snakes up to the base of my neck, pressing two fingers to the base of my throat, feeling for my pulse. I try to count each heartbeat, but I can't stay focused.

"Racing heart? Shortness of breath? Light-headedness?" she asks flatly, not an ounce of concern in her voice.

"Yes, yes, and yes," I answer.

"Yeah, classic panic attack. I get them all the time. Okay, not *all* the time. But before I went on my anxiety meds."

I frown, pondering that. This feels way too visceral to be a simple panic attack. "You're sure? I could be dying."

Sam crosses the room and sinks onto my bed. Reaching out, she takes my hand in hers. "Breathe," she tells me. Then she counts, instructing me to take one deep breath in, then let it out slowly. She counts in a steady rhythm. Amazingly, after a few cycles, it actually helps.

Her eyes flick up to my face. "Now, tell me what happened."

I shake my head. I can't admit it. It's way too shameful. "Um. Nothing happened."

Her pale brows twitch up. "That's obviously *not* true. Avery saw the car pull up so she looked out the window to see who it was. She said she saw you…making out…with your brother. So…does it have something to do with that?"

Mortification burns my face. I want to sink into the floor this very minute. Someone *saw* us? I feel like I'm going to puke. "*Step* brother," I correct. "No blood relation."

"Okay, sure. Stepbrother." She couldn't sound more disinterested in my clarification.

I fall back against my pillows, pulling one up to cover my face. Then I proceed to scream into it for several seconds before pulling it back down. "Okay, so. There was a kiss. But that's it." I pause, remembering. "Wait, *and* a little bit of groping."

I watch Sam's face closely for any sign of revulsion. There isn't any, thankfully.

Sam just studies me for a few long, silent minutes. "So, ah, do you have feelings for him? Like, *deeper* than brother and sister?" she asks carefully.

"*No !*" I practically scream. "I hate him. He took everything from me and totally fucked me over when I was at my most vulnerable. Setting aside the brother-sister thing, how could I ever be with someone like that?"

She frowns. "Maybe he has a reason for doing what he did."

I lift my hands in exasperation. "Well, I wouldn't know. He won't share my dad's will with me, and he won't tell me who my dad's attorney was."

"If you're named in a will, you're legally eligible to receive a copy."

"I never got a copy of anything." I shake my head, at a loss.

She pulls one of my cactus-shaped throw pillows into her lap. "Wasn't Hart—I mean, *Lucien* —going to help you with that?"

I push out a breath. "He would if I had the relevant information, which I'm having trouble getting, and just when I was about to make some progress, Lori's accident happened. Now I feel like I'm back to square one. Lucien can't do anything until he sees what's laid out legally."

Avery sucks in a breath through her teeth. "Shit. Maybe you can take Liam to court to get the documents."

I laugh. "Yup, if I want to suck up all the money Hart has paid me…kinda weird, I guess, since I'd just be paying it back to him in lawyer fees. Ugh, it's *all* so impossible."

"Well, listen, how about you get some sleep tonight, and since it's Saturday tomorrow, I'll treat you to lunch? Maybe even hit the Huntington Library for high tea and a nice stroll around the gardens?"

I ponder that for a moment but it sounds unappealing. What I *really* want to do is see Hart. It's been weeks since I've seen him and I haven't had any contact or affection from him or any male, at least since this shit-show with Liam just now. That's probably what's made me more susceptible to Liam's advances. Seeing and being with Hart will get my head on straight and help me forget whatever this is with Liam.

"I'll get back to you in the morning about whether or not I'm feeling up to it," I hedge.

"Okay, sounds good." She slaps me on the knee and stands up. "I'll hold you to it!"

I watch as she leaves, and the second the door clicks closed, I pull my phone out and send a text to Hart.

Hey, just got home. Mom is getting released from the hospital next week and everything is fine. I know you said to wait until she's out of the hospital, but I really need to see you tonight. Can you come here?

Almost immediately, those three little dots pop up. I hold my breath, waiting for his reply.

Is everything okay?

I type out my reply.

Yeah, but it's been a rough day. Plus, it's been too long since I've seen you.

I wait for his reply, but after a few minutes, I switch over to check my social media accounts. He must be busy, though, doing what? It's late. Is he at Obscura?

A few minutes later, a notification pops up with Hart's reply.

I've reserved a room at a hotel in Pasadena. Meet me there in an hour.

When he sends me the address, I release a long, disbelieving breath. *Shit*…of course, it's the most expensive hotel in my area. And he just booked a room like it's nothing. Fuuuck. He gives me the room number, and of course, it's the penthouse suite. *Of course* .

I glance at the time—it's late, but fuck it. Although I'm the one who reached out to him, I only half-expected him to actually come out here. He's such a busy guy, and Malibu is a fair distance away from Pasadena. But just knowing I'll see him in an hour is such a relief. I imagine sinking into his hard chest, tucking myself into his warmth, and falling asleep…after some mind-blowing sex, of course.

I hop into a hot shower, then quickly shove all my makeup, toiletries, and clothes into a bag. After telling Avery and Haley where I'm going, I jump in my car and head over to the hotel. The person manning the front desk is already aware of who I am, and after handing me the keycard, she sends someone to help me take my *one little* bag upstairs to the penthouse. It's ridiculous actually, and I'm kind of self-conscious about my worn, threadbare bag.

When I swipe into the suite, it's empty—and absolutely gorgeous. It's like a large apartment with a living room, bar area, and dining area—as well as a short hallway that I'm guessing leads to the bedroom.

I turn to the bellboy and hand him the only two crumpled bills I have on hand. "Thank you."

With a quick nod, he smiles and leaves, leaving me alone in the penthouse. One second later, I get a text that sends my heart racing.

In the bedroom.

He's already here. My breathing speeds up, and my face immediately feels hot.

I head down the short hallway to the master bedroom. When I open the door, it's dark inside. Pitch black. I reach for the light switch when his voice emerges from the abyss.

"*Don't* ." On instinct, I pull my hand away. How can he see me? "No lights. Come in and close the door."

I suck in a deep breath and do as he asks. "Thank you for coming out here. I didn't really expect you to drop everything."

"Come here," he says in that thick British accent.

I kick my shoes off and carefully pick my way over to the bed, using his voice as my guide. I've obviously never seen this room in the light, so my advance isn't exactly graceful. Once my knee hits the side of the bed, I climb up onto the mattress. His large frame is in the middle of the bed, and my roving hands pick up on the fact that he's only wearing his underwear—nothing else.

"Did you lose your clothes?" I tease.

"This is what I sleep in," he answers. "You, on the other hand, are overdressed."

With a little laugh, I sit up and pull my dress off, flinging it into the darkness. Now, we're evenly matched. I'm in my bra and panties. "Better?"

His only answer is a deep rumble of approval that comes from somewhere deep in his chest. Scootching over to him, I find the crook of his arm and chest and nestle into it. His warmth calms me instantly, and I sink into it. His heartbeat is strong and steady and lulls me into a deep sense of contentment.

I press my cheek to his solid chest and close my eyes. "I missed you…" I whisper.

"You've had a difficult day. Talk to me, Little Fawn."

I shake my head. "Mom is getting better. Stronger. She should be released really soon."

"But there's something bothering you. I can hear it in your voice. In the way it catches a little when you speak."

How is it possible for a complete stranger to know me so intimately? I don't want to sound overly romantic, but is this what kismet is? Two people who were meant to come together?

I adjust my position a little, nestling even deeper into his arms. "My stepbrother. I've been trying to avoid him during this whole ordeal but tonight…he was there at the hospital. We don't talk much anymore. We were close at one time but not since he went off to college and now he's just become this cold, calculating jerk. Nothing like he used to be. I just—"

I cut myself off. How much should I really get into it with Hart? I'm sure he doesn't really care about my stepbrother drama. But to my surprise, he tugs me a little closer.

"Why does he upset you?" he asks.

I push out a breath. "Because…I don't know. Like I told you at your office, when my dad died, my stepbrother took my dad's business and left me with nothing."

There's a moment of silence before he says, "Definitely an asshole move. But he can't keep something from you that's rightfully yours."

I shrug, my hand finding his chest. I press my palm against the faint dusting of coarse chest hair. "And yet…that's exactly what he did. I don't know if I can ever forgive him for it."

He begins stroking my hair absentmindedly. "Life is too short to hold grudges, Little Fawn."

"Says the quillionare…" I laugh. The absurdity. "I mean, how you could possibly relate? No one would ever dare take anything valuable from you."

His muscles tighten beneath my hand. "Why would you say that? You don't know anything about me," he says stiffly.

I glance up at him, but I can't see anything. Just blackness. He doesn't sound angry per se, just…I don't know…defensive, maybe. "You're right…so tell me. What has the quillionare had stolen from him?" I keep my voice playful because I sense him building protective walls around himself.

How could he possibly relate to my dad's business being snatched away from me? People like Hart—or Lucien, or whoever he is—have everything handed to them. It's so easy for people like him—wealthy, attractive, and powerful. What could he possibly want for?

There's a long stretch of silence, and I wonder if he's fallen asleep. Finally, he releases a heavy breath and says, "There's a woman I've loved all my life, and recently, I've come to the realization that I'll never be able to truly have her, no matter how hard I try to convince myself otherwise."

Those words, spoken in the darkness, give me the impression of a long-held secret that he's confessing to me. My heart sinks. It's funny how I'd assumed I was someone special to him. I guess it's just a fantasy I built in my head. We've really only known each other a little over a month, after all.

"Who is she?" I ask, trying to keep my voice from cracking.

He places his hand on mine where it is pressed against his chest. "It doesn't really matter, does it? We'll never have a future together, and I'm trying to come to grips with that."

I swallow. "But...why can't you be together?" I know I'm prying, but maybe if I understand the reason he can't be with her, it'll make me feel better about Hart and me. Which, I have to remind myself *yet* again, has always been temporary.

"There's a part of me she can't accept. That she'll never be able to accept."

I rise up onto my elbow, and glance down at him—or where his face should be. "Never is a long time. I've found that people grow, and shift, and change." I don't know why I'm trying to convince him that the love of his life will eventually accept him. "Or, I don't know, maybe there's someone else waiting out there for you."

Like me .

No, not me.

I have to stop telling myself that Hart and I have anything beyond an incredible sexual connection. He can't even show me his face, for God's sake. If that doesn't scream "I've built a wall around myself," then I don't know what does. This man isn't available to anyone other than this mysterious woman he's in love with.

Hart rises up, forcing me back down flat on the mattress. I can feel his large body looming over me. "Right now, there's only you and me," he growls. "Right now, *you* are the center of my universe."

My blood pressure skyrockets. *Gulp* . Okay, well, that makes me feel better.

His large hand skims down my rib cage to the elastic of my panties. His hand dips inside, to the curls between my thighs. "You are like a drug, Little Fawn." The warmth of his breath brushes across my lips. "I've spent the last few weeks obsessed with the taste of you, haunted by the sound of your little moans when you climax. *You* are in my blood."

I lift my hips up off the bed. "Oh, really?" I say on breath.

One long finger pushes into me, and he chuckles a little. "You are already wet for me."

Honestly, I'm wet and ready the second I'm in the same room with him. My body is aware of him on the most basic, primal level.

He swirls his thumb around my clit, teasing the little pearl as his finger moves inside me. In the darkness, I can feel his face close to mine, his breath warm on my cheek. "I want to see your face," I say, my hips rising and falling with the rhythm of his thrusts.

"*No*," he says firmly.

"But why?" I ask, pouting a little. "I want to look into your eyes when I come."

"You will *not* see my face," is his only answer. No reason. No explanation.

I consider pushing the issue, but with his fingers inside me, I'm not feeling very adversarial. Heat swirls inside me, and all thoughts vanish—the worries about my mom, the stress about Liam, it's all gone. My head is spinning, and I feel myself careening off the edge.

"Do you trust me?" Hart whispers in my ear.

My eyes flutter closed.

I do…

CHAPTER 24
DIRTY LITTLE SECRET

I NOD IN THE DARK, ALL BREATH ESCAPING MY LIPS.

"Tell me, Little Fawn..."

My God, he wants me to *speak*? I can hardly concentrate. "*Yes*," I say in a rush. "Yes."

"Good." He removes his hand from me and places a quick kiss on my lips.

I whimper at the loss of him. "Why did you stop?"

Seconds later, I feel the mattress shift as he stands and walks somewhere in the room. I hear a drawer or cupboard open then close, then he comes back over to me—I can't see him, but I can hear his muted footsteps as he walks across the plush carpeting. I flinch as he reaches down and curls his hand around my upper arm, and he pulls me upright. He ties a piece of fabric around my eyes.

"If you remove this blindfold, it is over between us. Do you understand?"

Wow, talk about *dramatic*.

"Yes, I understand."

I'm desperate to see his face, but honestly, I'm more desperate to have his cock inside me. And I have no doubt that what he says is true. Men like Hart are all about control and trust. Break trust, and that's the end. All or nothing. Black or white. So, yeah, there's no way I'm peeking.

A minute later, dim light bleeds in through the corners of the blindfold. He wants the lights on...but why?

"Hold your wrists out."

Sucking in a breath, I do as he asks. I've seen him tie up Willow, so I have an idea about what's going to happen. I immediately feel butterflies in my stomach. A length of silky rope cinches tightly around my wrists.

"Get on the bed. Lie on your back," he commands.

With my wrists tied in front of me, I scramble onto the bed and try to position myself in the center, on my back. Once I'm positioned, he pulls my hands up over my head and ties the rope to something—the headboard, or a bedpost, I'm guessing. Then he ties down each one of my ankles, pulling my legs apart. I'm still wearing my underwear, but I can't help but feel exposed nonetheless.

He leaves me like that for a minute, and anxiety trickles through me. I lick my bottom lip, waiting. I've never been tied up before, and the level of trust this takes is unreal. He can do anything to me right now, and there would be no way for me to stop him. Even if I scream...we're in the penthouse. Who's going to hear me?

Seconds later, I tense as an ice-cold blade presses against my shoulder. Oh. *Shit* . I suck in a sharp breath, my heart racing, wondering what he'll do next. But before I can utter a sound, he jerks the knife up and cuts my bra strap. It falls limply to the side, then he moves to the other and does the same thing.

I suppress a whimper. It was such a beautiful bra—and brand-new. But he bought it, so I guess he's allowed to ruin it. Still, it's a shame. With one last swift cut, he severs the front seam between the two cups, then lays the knife against my belly while he pulls the ruins of the bra off of me.

With swift efficiency, he picks up the knife and proceeds to do the same thing to my matching lacy thong with swift, confident strokes of his very sharp knife. In seconds, that's gone, too.

Now, I'm naked, tied to the bed, my arms over my head and legs spread wide. I'm the most vulnerable I've ever been with a man. My body is trembling with excitement, anticipation, and more than a little fear. I can't believe I'm letting him do this, but if I'm being honest with myself, I want it. I want the sting of pain. I want the uncertainty of what he's going to do next. I want Hart to dominate me, use me as he wants, and bring me to the very brink of pain and pleasure.

"Are you cold?" he asks in a gruff voice.

"No."

"*Fuck* . You are so damn perfect," he says, palming one of my breasts.

I know that can't be true. My breasts are too big, my hips too wide. I have dimples and blemishes everywhere. How could he possibly find that beautiful?

As though reading my thoughts, his hand slides up my thigh, to my hips. With one hand, he grabs the fat of my hip and squeezes. "*Fuck* , yes."

I squirm a little, more embarrassed than anything, but I can't move much.

"You're going to need to remember you trust me," he says, a darkness in his voice.

I nod, my entire body on fire. What's he going to do?

Suddenly, the knife is back. The sting of cold steel slides down my sternum, all the way down to my stomach. I swallow a gasp. He's not hurting me. *Not yet*.

He's taking it slow, like he's savoring my fear and anticipation. "I crave the thought of putting my mark on you. Something permanent."

Under my blindfold, I blink in shock and fight to keep from tensing up, holding perfectly still.

He continues. "A tattoo perhaps, or maybe a scar. Or even..." The icy blade presses flat against my lower stomach. "My child growing inside your belly."

I suck in a trembling breath. That's not likely to ever happen, but that makes me hot regardless, for some reason.

"There's just something about the thought of laying permanent claim on you..." The tip of his knife suddenly bites into my flesh, a sharp and painful pin prick near my hip. "Marking you as *mine* so that no other man will ever touch you. *Ever*." Slowly, he presses the edge of the blade to bite into my skin, and I suck in a breath, pain slicing through me.

"What are you doing?" I ask, my voice breathless with fear.

I feel the puff of his warm breath against my lips. "I'm marking what's mine, Little Fawn. Hold very still and give in to the pain. Release yourself to it and allow me this indulgence. It's making me so painfully hard. It's making me want to take you with a violence I've only fantasized about."

I suck in a deep breath and force myself to remember that I'm supposed to trust him. But it's no easy feat.

A hand briefly caresses my cheek. "That's a good girl," he whispers in my ear. He continues to drag the blade against my hip, drawing more pain, though I can't tell if it's a deep scratch or if the cut is actually breaking the skin. In spite of the pain, my head swirls with a strange sort of giddiness and liquid heat wends its way through my limbs. My nipples are aching, hard, tight points.

He removes the knife for a moment, runs a fingertip over the wound, then briefly places that finger on my bottom lip. My tongue darts out to detect the coppery taste of my own blood. Prickles of arousal blossom all over my skin, and the tension in my core tightens impossibly, sending spasms of heightened arousal through my muscles.

I should be horrified that he's wounding me, cutting me. But I'm not. It makes me feel...wanted, cherished. Owned. Those feelings are strong and heady, like an intoxicating brew of controlled substances swirling in my blood, my brain. I *want* to be possessed by this man. I want him to use me for his pleasure.

A wave of almost intense relaxation settles over me as if I've already had an orgasm or two. An overpowering desire to surrender to his every whim takes hold. I sink against the mattress, intensely attuned to him.

The ice of his blade continues to scratch and cut my skin. "I mean to take you in every way possible tonight. Possess you in all the ways I possibly can. And you'll give yourself to it, won't you, my precious little fawn? You want to please me, I can sense it. And these marks I'm putting on you will always remind you of this night. This night when even now, before it even begins, I know I won't be able to get enough of you."

The mattress suddenly shifts as he changes position, and the flat of his blade suddenly presses against my throat. Fear streaks through me like lightning. "Take me into your mouth. Take me deep."

Without a word, I open my mouth wide for him, and he presses his stiff, hard cock between my lips. The knife never moves away from my throat, and he lets out a groan as he thrusts his hips forward, plunging the length of his cock far back into my mouth until it touches the back of my throat.

"Use your tongue, Fawn. Taste me."

For several long minutes, he slowly thrusts himself into my mouth and pulls back again, panting with mounting excitement as I roll my tongue along the underside of his cock, savoring his earthy taste. Each time, he plunges in a little deeper until he's pushing into my throat, stretching me there. I get the sense from the way he's breathing that he might come when suddenly he pulls out of me and takes the knife away from my throat.

"Fuck, that feels too good. But I don't want to come yet." He's breathing heavily as he speaks, and the mattress shifts again. "This is going to last all night, Fawn. I won't get enough of you, but fuck if I'm not going to try."

He bends to feather kisses across my breasts, down to my ribs, then I feel his tongue on my hip, swirling around the tender spot he'd just marked. It stings, and I know he's tasting me.

"Mmmm," I moan, shifting my hips a little. "That feels good."

He chuckles under his breath. "You like that, do you?"

Prowling up my body, he kisses along my stomach, then my rib cage, until he reaches my breast. He sucks my nipple into his mouth and bites down—hard. Oh, fuck. Then he swallows my scream with a deep kiss, pinching my nipple to draw out the pain, intensify it, and make it last.

He breaks the kiss and whispers against my lips, "That's it, Little Fawn. That's it. Ride the wave of adrenaline."

The scent of him, the feel of his warm body hovering above mine, his hand on my nipple, pinching, has me writhing. Heat builds inside me, slithering through my veins like a living thing. It's *consuming* me from the inside out. There is no world outside this hotel room, this bed where Hart is owning every inch of my body, commanding it to pleasure him.

"Please," I say, pulling against my restraints. If I could reach down and touch myself, I would. "Please, Hart."

"Please, what?" I can hear the amusement in his voice, and it frustrates me. He's playing with me.

"I need to feel you inside me," I beg. He hasn't even touched my sex, but it's already flooded, tingling with hot need. This is already too much. I'm wound too tight.

"Oh, I *will* fuck you. But first, I want to push you to the very edge." His lips are on my breast again, his warm breath washing over me. "I crave your tears of surrender."

Moving down my body, he sinks his teeth into my skin along the way—*hard.* He starts once again at my breast, then moves down my ribs to my stomach, biting me everywhere. His head moves toward my inner thighs. With every bite, I yelp each time, rocked by the pain of his teeth cutting into my skin. I'm almost certain he's drawn more blood.

Then, without warning, his tongue snakes out against my sex. My hips jump off the mattress, and if I weren't tied down, I would have been launched into the stratosphere. My body jerks, tense, anticipating the sting of his teeth there in the tenderest of places. When that doesn't come, I relax a little, my muscles unclenching slowly. His tongue tests the seam of my entrance, and I groan. He's right where I need him.

"*Yes*," I hiss. "Oh, my God."

Like the expert he is, he rotates between sucking on my clit and thrusting his tongue inside me. In seconds, he has my body wound up so tight I actually forget to breathe for a second. Balling my hands into fists, I throw my head back. It's the only range of movement I have. I squirm a little, but he reaches up and holds my hips down with both hands.

I'm his captive. A slave to his whim, his need.

Once he has me on the very edge of the precipice, seconds from climaxing, he pulls away abruptly, denying me that final release. My heart is racing and the breath sawing from my lungs when he pushes himself off the bed, but as the blindfold is still on, I can't see where he's going or what he's doing.

I can hear his muted footsteps as he crosses the room and unzips something, his bag maybe?

"I brought several things to toy with you," he says cryptically. "So far you've liked my surprises and I think you'll like this next one, too."

A few seconds later, I feel something soft, like strips of leather, against my thighs. I recognize the feel of it immediately—a leather flail. I saw one in his cabinet at Obscura.

My anxiety kicks up a notch. Will it be too much for me? Pain can be fun, but too much...my mind is immediately cast back to that moment in Obscura, when he was spanking me, hard. Too hard, too much, too fast. But he pulled back the second I'd told him to, and when I said I trust him, it was the truth.

Lightly, he brushes the strips across my thighs. Back and forth, back and forth, a little harder each time. "Relax your muscles," he says gruffly. "Trust that I know your body. I know what you need."

Swallowing, I nod. Taking a deep breath, I force my muscles to relax—*again* . I feel like I'm always doing that, but I'm new to this, so I guess it's natural that I'd be a little apprehensive at first.

He pauses, brings the flail up, then back down on my inner thigh with a heavy *slap* . I cry out as pain slices through me, starting at the point of contact, then radiating throughout my body. I can feel it all the way to my fingertips. Then, just as another blow comes down on the same thigh, I feel his fingers push inside me again. With every thrust of his hand, there's a bite of his flail on my flesh. Thrust, *slap.* Thrust, *slap.* Pretty soon, there's no discernible difference between pleasure and pain. They're entwined together, setting my blood on fire, pushing me toward climax.

"You are so fucking tight," he growls. "I need to feel this sweet cunt milking my cock."

I'm so lost in sensation that I'm beyond speaking, completely lost to the pleasure and pain he's inflicting on my body. I close my eyes and inhale, so close to my climax. I bite my bottom lip to hold out as long as I can.

Then, all of a sudden, his hand is gone. The flail is gone. I hear the rustle of fabric, and the bottom of the mattress dip as he settles himself between my spread thighs. He brushes the tip of his huge cock along the seam of my entrance, toying with my wetness, and I practically come out of my skin. The sensations swirling inside me are going to drive me insane if he doesn't do something about it soon.

"*Please,* " I beg shamelessly. "I need you to fuck me."

"Do you want my come inside you, Little Fawn?"

God. Fuck. He knows I do. This is a sick game. "Yes," I croak, twisting against my restraints.

"Tell me a secret," he whispers. "Something no one else knows. Do that, and I'll give you my cock."

My mind scrambles for something, anything, to throw out at him. But I must be too slow because he says, "You kissed your stepbrother tonight."

I stiffen in shock.

How does he know that?

He chuckles. "I'm *always* watching, Little Fawn." He leans over me, and I can feel his large body hovering above mine. "But what I want to know is…did you enjoy it?"

"*No* ," I say quickly.

I can feel him pull away from me as if looking into my face, and I want to cry out.

"Don't lie to me," he says firmly. "I know when you're lying."

I swallow. I've never admitted this to anyone but myself, and saying it out loud feels wrong somehow. But…*God* , he's going to pull away if I'm not honest. "Yes," I say. "I enjoyed it."

Fuck. Now he knows how depraved I really am. And I've also violated our agreement to be exclusive to him for the months we're together. Is he angry with me?

I feel the tip of his cock at my entrance again. "You let him touch you, fondle you. Did you want his cock?"

"Yes," I say quietly. A tear rolls down my cheek. I don't know why I'm crying. Maybe it's just the realization of how fucked up I really am inside. Because this lust I've felt for Liam didn't just start tonight.

With a violent thrust, he's inside me, sliding his full length in balls deep. I gasp, arching my back as he settles his hips between my spread legs. Will I ever get used to the size of him?

"Breathe," he grumbles in that beautiful accent. "*Breathe* , Little Fawn."

I suck in a breath, then exhale slowly. He waits for me, holding himself completely still, until my muscles relax a little. Then he rocks his pelvis against mine, slowly thrusting, pulling out of me, almost entirely, then plunging back in. With the blindfold on, all I see is darkness, and it just heightens the myriad sensations flooding through my body. It's incredible.

"Ah, yes. Good girl," he soothes, and I swear, for a second, he sounds exactly like Liam. No wonder, though. Ever since that kiss in the car, my stepbrother is at the forefront of my mind. And, God help me, I can see his beautiful face in my mind's eye, right now. That pull of his lips when he smiles. In my fantasy, it's *him* inside me right now, pushing his cock into me forcefully—and *fuck* , that thought just catapults my desire into a whole new level. Every sensation is heightened, more intense.

I moan at how good he feels inside me. It's been a few weeks but feels more like forever since I've been fucked. I lift my hips, rocking against him in a silent demand for him to fuck me deeper, harder.

I don't even have to say anything. Hart knows my body more than I know it myself. He slides his hands under my ass, lifting me up a little to give him a better angle. The head of his cock slams into my cervix, hard. Violent. With an urgency that matches my own. He dips his head and captures my mouth in a kiss.

"*Fuck* . I can't get enough of you," he says, pulling out of the kiss slightly, his deep baritone vibrating against my lips.

The bed rocks forward and back, hitting the wall in a steady rhythm as he thrusts into me forcefully. I ball my hands into fists, clenching so tightly, my nails bite into my palms. The pain centers me somehow and helps me control the riot of desire swirling through me.

I can't stand it. I pull against the restraints until my wrists feel raw. I need release, and I need it now. The urgency inside me has gathered into a violent storm on the verge of breaking. I'm losing control, can't breathe, can't think. All I can do is *feel* as the sensations wash over me.

Euphoria is within my reach. I can feel it gathering in my veins.

"Breathe, baby," he grinds out through gritted teeth. "Breathe."

I don't. I can't. I'm beyond help at this point.

"Oh, *fuck*," he growls. "Fuck. I'm going to come in your sweet pussy."

With one final thrust, he stills. His cock swells and stiffens, pumping everything into me. At the same moment, I feel the cold bite of steel against my breast. The sharp blade licks my skin, leaving a trail of pain in its wake. The most delicious kind of pain that pushes me right over the edge.

The most delicious climax slams into me, quick and violent. I arch my back and just give in to it, allowing it to completely devour me. Wave after wave of hot, undulating energy overtakes me, rushing through me like liquid fire. It lasts for a long time, and Hart rocks himself against me, prolonging the delicious waves of ecstasy, stealing the breath from my lungs.

With shallow thrusts, he continues to draw out my orgasm— milking me for every last moan and gasp, before my body finally goes slack.

And the entire time he's inside me, I'm imagining it's Liam.

CHAPTER 25
CONNECTION

As I come down from my orgasm high, I feel Hart pull away from me. A second later, I hear the faucet in the bathroom, then there's a warm washcloth between my thighs as he cleans me up. He's gentle, which I find oddly endearing. For such a strong, powerful man to take care of me this way...it almost seems impossible. I've never been cared for like this, and it makes me feel safe. Valued. *Wanted.*

When he's done, he tends to the areas his knife touched, cleaning them, then gently rubbing a salve into the cuts. "It won't scar," he says. "I know how deep to cut."

I blink under the blindfold. When he cut me...it had heightened the pleasure, and that realization both thrills and horrifies me. I would have never guessed I was someone who got off on pain, but Hart is awakening new parts of me, and I'm not sure how to feel about that.

He unties my wrists first, and my arms relax against my sides. Then he moves to my ankles, freeing each one. As the ropes fall away from my wrists, I instinctively reach for my blindfold.

"*Don't*," he warns darkly.

My hands fall to the bed, and I push out a breath. "I already know what you look like when I was at your office." I've told him this before, but it bears repeating. "Tell me why you won't let me see your face. We're not even at Obscura."

"I just can't. Do not ask me again."

I hear him rustle through his bag, then he returns to the bed and unties my blindfold. As it falls away from my face, my breath catches—is he letting me see his face, after all? But no, as I blink, I see the light is on but very dim, coming from the hallway beyond the doorway. But his mask is firmly in place.

"The mask again?" I ask.

Lord. How long are we going to do this? We're halfway through our three months we plan to be together, and he's still not allowing me to see his face, unless I'm meeting him at his office as my lawyer. I don't understand it, but then, I guess I don't have to. He's not asking me to understand it, is he?

I glance down at my body and see the areas where he used the knife. The cuts are superficial, glistening from the liquid bandage he used to seal them. The ones on my hip are where he drew blood. It's a heart he decided mark on me. I smile to myself. I know it should upset me, that he's marked me like this. But it doesn't. I like it.

And I believe him, that it won't scar. But for the short time I have it, it will be my reminder of Hart.

Swinging my legs over the bed, I try to stand up, but the second my feet are on the floor and I stand, my legs begin to shake. He's right beside me, catching me before I fall. I lean against his muscular frame, and he pulls me close.

"That's how I know I've done my job well," he chuckles. "When you have trouble walking."

"Hardy-har," I say, straightening. I glance up at him. "And how do I know if I've done my job well?"

Beneath the edge of his mask, his lips curl up into a devilish smile. "Oh, I think you know."

A wave of heat flows through me. Lord. How does he do that? I just had an epic orgasm. How can he ignite my desire all over again, after only five minutes? His skills are seriously impressive.

I rub my hands over my face. Now that I've had my release, I'm bone-tired. It's been such a long, emotionally taxing day. "I'm taking a shower." When he steps toward me, I point a finger at him. "Alone, unless that means you're taking off that mask."

He falls back, his beautiful mouth dissolving into a frown. "If I want to shower," he says defiantly, "I'll shower, Little Fawn. If I want to fuck you in the shower, then I'll fuck you in the shower." He hesitates, standing straight and tall, his large arms folded across his hard chest. But he must see how tired I am, because he relents a little. "Come on, I'll start the water for you."

We head into the bathroom with only the dim light from the hallway. He tells me to keep my hand away from the light switch, which I obey. Then, he does exactly as he says, adjusting the water to the perfect temperature, then he opens the shower door to let me step in. And then—*my God*— he steps in behind me, mask and all. But the shower head is so low, the water doesn't come anywhere near his face.

To my surprise, he doesn't make a move on me. He unwraps a bar of soap, grabs a washcloth off a shelf in the gigantic shower and begins lathering the soap. The smell is *amazing*. It's that really classy, gardenia smell, and I drink it in.

"Turn around," he says.

I do as he asks, turning my back to him. He begins washing my shoulders, my arms, smoothing his way down my body. I'm so sore and so tired, I just stand there absently as he washes me.

He's so gentle, skimming over my stomach, to the tender space between my thighs, to the light flail marks he left on the insides of my legs and the cuts on my hip. So gentle. It's incredible how he can be two things at once—powerful, violent, and commanding...but also gentle and so considerate.

He washes my entire body, then grabs a new washcloth and washes himself. After rinsing us both with the handheld shower head, he turns the water off and opens the shower. I step out onto the plush bath mat as he grabs a towel and begins drying me off.

I laugh, grabbing at the towel. "I'm tired, but I'm not that tired. I can dry myself."

He ignores me, continuing to dry me off while water drips off of him. It strikes me, suddenly, that he's such a good caretaker. Funny, because I don't think of guys as being particularly good at taking care of other people. I guess it's just because the guys I usually date are all about themselves. Even my orgasms are happy accidents in their worlds. If I have one, great. If not, it's no skin off their backs.

Hart is different.

And he's not mine to keep. He'll *never* be mine.

Once he's done drying me off, he towels himself off, then presses his hand against the small of my back, guiding me back into the bedroom. I crawl onto the bed, and he lowers himself next to me, pulling me against him. The little hairs on his chest are damp, and I rub my cheek against them.

This is heaven. This is what happiness is. A man who comes to see me when I ask him to, lavishes me with attention, and gives me brain-frying orgasms on command? I can't help but feel like this is a fantasy. Maybe I'm sitting in a padded room somewhere, out of my mind, imagining all this…

"What are you thinking about?" he asks.

I nestle even deeper into his embrace. "I'm just thinking how unreal this all is."

"All of what?"

I shrug one shoulder. "Me. You. Everything. It feels too good to be true. I mean, I guess it's temporary, anyway."

"It is," he says flatly.

I rise up a little, so I can twist and look up at him. "But does it have to be? You could stay. Or maybe I could transfer to a school in London. I don't know…we could be together?"

I feel his entire body tense up. Oh, fuck. I've done that thing that I always do. I've said something wrong, and now he's not going to bolt. Will he ghost me like all the other guys?

"Cassandra," he says, and I know he must be pissed because he uses my name, which he hardly ever does. "There is a lot you don't know about me, and if you did…" his words trail off.

I tense immediately. "What? If I knew *what?*" I ask.

Talking to this guy is like chasing my tail. Nothing ever makes any sense, and of course, why would it? He never explains anything. Everything is secret, even his face.

Maybe in his real life, and in his business life, he never has to explain himself. He just barks out orders, and people trip over themselves to follow his commands. But I'm asking him to do it now.

The silence stretches between us, and I know he's already dug his heels in and refuses to pursue this. So if he feels that I don't know him, I decide to get him talking about himself.

"Tell me about you, then. Something I might find surprising."

He clears his throat, and I can already sense him opening up a little. Just a tiny fraction. But it's something. "I'm a cat person."

I gasp in mock horror. Actually, that is surprising. I would have pegged him as a dog guy, for sure. "Dogs are the *best* , though. Cats couldn't care less if you died, but a dog..." I shake my head. "They are forever loyal."

"I was bit by a dog as a teen," he says. "I'd bent down to pet it, and it just latched on to my hand without warning."

I nod, listening. "That same thing happened to my brother." I pause, then correct myself, "I mean my stepbrother. It was our neighbor's dog. Though, honestly, my brother is the idiot in this scenario. The neighbor warned him, said the dog wasn't friendly. *I* tried to pull him back, but he's always been so fucking stubborn and he stuck his hand through the fence anyway." I laugh a little. "He never did *that* again."

A pause. "Do you hate your brother so much that you'd wish him hurt?" His voice is tight, like he's siding with Liam.

"No. Of course not," I say lightly. "And he really wasn't injured. Not like what happened to you. It was just a little scratch on his hand. But it freaked him the fuck out." I can't help but laugh inwardly. "If he'd listened to me...but he never does. I don't have value where he's concerned. Not worth listening to, not worth my dad's inheritance. Nothing."

Hart pushes out a breath. "Earlier you said you kissed your brother," he says calmly. "Why would you do that if you dislike him so much?"

It's my turn to tense up. "Okay, first of all, *he* kissed *me.* It was completely out of the blue. And I blame my reaction on *you.*"

He belts out a laugh. "Why me?"

I reach up and brush my fingers over the dusting of hair on his chest. The slow, rhythmic *thud* of his heart is heavy against my ear. "Because you've awakened something inside me, something I've never felt before. It's like…you've lit a fire in my chest."

There's a tightness in his voice—the first sign of jealousy I've heard since he mentioned the kiss earlier. "So that makes you just…kiss random guys now?"

"He's not a random guy," I say, pinching his nipple a little, just for fun. "But, I have to admit that there's always been something between Liam and me, ever since we were teenagers."

"Then why aren't you with him?"

I glance up at Hart, my gaze roving over the details of his stag mask. "It's complicated."

He shifts next to me. "I like complicated. Tell me."

It occurs to me that I've opened up to Hart way more than he's opened up to me. And here he's turned the conversation back on me again. Still tucked against him, I shake my head. "First, you tell me—how was your Obscura persona born?"

What I'd rather know is who the woman is who hurt him, the one he wants but can't have. But I know he won't tell me that. Not yet, at least. We have to build up trust first, and I get that.

He smooths his hand up and down my arm absentmindedly, stroking me gently, sending tingles all the way to my fingertips. "A group of us from university came together and founded Exeter House. Obscura was Domino's brainchild, his dark creation. He often spoke to me about the freedom and release the anonymity of Obscura offers." He pauses for a minute, and I wonder if that's all he's going to say, but he continues with a hint of emotion in his deep voice. "About a year ago, I went through something…difficult. I'd lost control of my life, my direction, desires, everything. Obscura offered me control. It offered me the illusion of what I really wanted in my life but couldn't have."

I swallow, my cheeks flushing. "Of *who* you really wanted…" I correct for him.

I half-hope my comment will lead to a conversation about the woman who broke his stone-cold heart, but it doesn't. He's silent. When he finally does speak a few seconds later, all the emotion from a moment ago is completely gone. "Why aren't you with Liam?" he asks stiffly, steering me back to the original topic.

"Because he betrayed me," I say simply. "In the most horrible way."

"How so?"

God, do I really want to get into this with Hart? I'm just afraid it makes me sound bitter. Or pathetic, because I allowed Liam to do this to me.

"Well, it's mostly everything I've already told you. My dad always told me I'd have a stake in his company when he passed. Of course, we didn't think that would be for a long, long time, but when it happened last year, my brother wouldn't allow me to have anything to do with the business. My dad had been paying my way through college and there was a hope that I'd eventually take a position at his company. My brother left me completely destitute."

Hart shifts his position a little, pulling me a little tighter against him. "You seem to be doing okay."

I snort. "Yeah, now. Thanks to you." I glance up at him. "I do appreciate the money, by the way. That was really nice of you, considering I'm not really working for you anymore."

"Money can be corrosive, and it can attract the wrong kind of people if you're not careful," he says. "Maybe your brother was trying to protect you from that."

"Shouldn't that be my decision?" I pause, frowning. "Whose side are you on anyway?" I ask playfully, not really mad.

He pushes out a laugh. "Devil's advocate. I'd like to see you repair things with your brother. Family is all we have sometimes. And we never know how long it will last…"

I push out a heavy breath. "Well, we'll see. If he stops being an arrogant asshole, then maybe we'll talk. What about you? Are you close with your family?"

He shrugs one shoulder. "My parents were divorced when I was quite young. I've always had a good relationship with my mum. My relationship with my bio dad is dodgy. I had to spend part of the summer with him as a kid. We don't speak much nowadays."

Well, he's close with his mom, and that's a good sign. "Siblings?"

That tightness in his body reappears. He takes in a long breath and releases it. "No."

Hmm. Maybe he always wanted siblings? I can understand that. When the sibling relationship is good, it can be *really* good. But when it's bad…God, it can be devastatingly painful. I should know. I've experienced both.

"That's probably for the best. You're *really* annoying," I say with a laugh, trying to lighten the mood.

His deep chuckle vibrates against my cheek, and I'm filled with a sense of contentment. Is this what being in a fulfilling relationship is like? I've honestly never gotten this far—the place where we cuddle and share secrets. It's weird because I feel like I know Hart on a deeper level than the short time we've spent with each other should reflect. Or maybe it's just my imagination or wishful thinking.

"What is your deepest fear?" I ask him. Because it's nothing about his past, necessarily, I'm hopeful he'll answer it.

He's silent, considering, then he says, "Of never really being loved for who I am."

I smile against his chest. It's such a painfully sweet answer, and it makes my heart ache. I rise up onto one elbow and look down at him. "You're intelligent, successful, devastatingly handsome…what's not to love?" I'm teasing him, but it's true.

He sighs like he's being weighed down by regret. "I've made decisions that have pushed away the ones I love."

Is he talking about that woman again? I swallow back the acrid taste of jealousy. "I have no idea what you've done, or not done, but almost anything can be forgiven," I say.

"Oh, really? So you would forgive your stepbrother?" he asks.

I think about it for a second. Liam has done some pretty shitty things in the name of greed, but… "Honestly, if he were truly contrite and worked to improve things between us, then I might consider it. It's the trust that's difficult to restore."

Hart nods, deep in thought.

I'm desperate to ask him what he did to make so many enemies within his family, but I don't dare. He'll tell me if and when he wants to.

He rolls onto his side, half on top of me. His hand slides down my thigh, slipping to the heat between my thighs. "I don't want to talk about past regrets." His mouth hovers inches above mine, his breath bathing my lips in warmth. "All that matters is me and you, and this moment."

I smile up at him, gazing deep into his brown eyes in the very dim light. He wants a distraction from the pain our conversation has unearthed, and I'm here for it. It's well after midnight and we just got done fucking for hours, but I'm happy to be the only distraction he will ever need.

I know I shouldn't think that way. I know this thing between us is temporary, but I can't help it. I feel a connection with Hart that I've never felt with anyone before.

Correction, I've never *allowed* myself to feel with anyone before.

CHAPTER 26
TANGLED WEB

I STARE UP INTO HIS MASKED FACE, AND HIS BEAUTIFUL LIPS pull up into a smile. "Spread your legs for me."

Delicious heat wends its way through my body. Just the sound of his deep, accented baritone sets my pulse racing. I'm already putty in his hands. Swiftly, I spread my thighs, eager to find out what he has planned for me.

His long finger dips inside me. "You're already wet," he says, amused.

"Yes." The word catches in my throat. I'm so keyed up already that I find it hard to speak.

"That pleases me, Little Fawn. So beautiful. So ready to fuck."

With that, he pushes up off the bed and walks across the room, bends over his bag, takes something out, then returns to me. I can't see what he has in his hand until he places something cold on my stomach, but not the knife. I reach up to feel it, looking down. It's heavy and metallic, with pearl-sized orbs linked together on a string.

He also has a tube in his hand and squeezes a dollop of something onto the tip of his fingers. "Remain very still," he commands. "This will feel strange at first."

"Wha—"

Before I can even get the question out, his fingers slide down to my asshole, and his finger teases the rim before he boldly slides his forefinger deep inside. I nearly come out of my skin, my hips launching off the mattress, but he holds me down with his free hand. "Shhh, shhh," he soothes. "The pressure and heaviness will fade."

It doesn't hurt. It just feels strange. Awkward.

Once I'm settled again, Hart takes the string of metal pearls and slides them into me. Honestly, it feels more comfortable than his finger, so I relax a little.

"These are beginner beads," he says. "They'll heighten your pleasure. Has a man ever taken you there?" He touches my asshole again.

I swallow heavily and shake my head.

"Mmm. I'll enjoy being your first then."

I swallow. Never in my life did I think I would ever have beads up my ass, but you only live once, right? Also, I'm coming to learn that, when it involves pleasure, Hart is usually right.

"Okay, if you say so," I answer, my hips twisting as he threads the entire string of cold beads into me.

When he's done, he lowers himself onto the mattress, his large body hovering above mine. I can't see his cock, but I can feel it heavy and hard against my inner thigh. My core is wet again, my clit buzzing with energy, and combined with the heaviness of the beads inside me, I feel like I might spontaneously combust.

I lift my hips and tilt my head back. "Please, Hart."

He lowers his head and brushes his lips lightly against mine, then reaches between us and teases my entrance with the tip of his finger. He lowers his head and whispers in my ear, his mask cold and hard against my cheek. "I'm going to pump another load into this sweet pussy. Then, the next time, I'm going to take your asshole. I can't get enough, Little Fawn. You are my obsession."

"Yes," I say on a breath, arching my hips up.

My eyes flutter closed, and I can't help it—I hear Liam's voice, not Hart's. It's *Liam* talking dirty to me. It's *his* large body hovering above me. *His* cock that's poised to push inside me. Hart is just a vessel—a vehicle for the fantasy that's evolving in my head.

Shifting his hips slightly, he slides his cock into me. I groan, relishing the feeling of him fully seated inside me once more. The metal beads create a delicious kind of pressure that just add to the onslaught of sensations engulfing me.

Grabbing his shoulders, I hold on for dear life as he thrusts into me—hard and fast—and I cry out in sheer bliss. He feels so damn good, and I've learned in the last few weeks that I like it rough. *Really* rough. The way he gives it to me. His thumb finds my nipple, and he flicks the sensitive peak as he plows into me. My body comes alive beneath him, igniting an ember of passion that soon becomes a wildfire.

"You are so fucking perfect for me," he growls into my ear. "You feel so good. So hot and so fucking tight."

His thrusts become longer, harder, and more focused. I writhe beneath him as his pelvis slams against my clit, stimulating it to the point of agony. Passionate agony that's amplified by the anal beads. Within a few strokes, I can already feel my climax building. It's like a ball of energy, starting in my clit, moving outward, and growing in intensity.

I moan and dig my nails into the skin on his back. Liam's face flashes in my mind as pure, undiluted bliss explodes inside me, pulsing through my entire body. Enraptured, I call out hoarsely, "Liam. Oh, fuck yes. Fuck me, Liam." I scream his name until my throat stings. My channel tightens around Hart's shaft, and he lets out a loud, primal groan, then stiffens—filling me with his come and subsequently coaxing yet another, smaller orgasm from my exhausted body.

When we're both completely spent, Hart pulls out of me, quickly reaches down, and tugs on the string of anal beads, pulling those out. Then, without any word at all, he pushes up from the bed, turns, and walks to the bathroom.

Holy shit.

Now that I'm in my right mind, I'm *mortified* . I called out another man's name in the middle of sex. *Fuckkkkk* . That is literally the worst thing I could have done.

And to make it worse? The man I called out for is my stepbrother. What the hell could have led me to do such a stupid thing? Liam and I have never even... I swallow, my heart racing. What does this mean? Does it mean anything at all or is the worse possible Freudian slip at the worst possible time?

Hart is gone for nearly ten minutes, and when he returns, he's fully dressed, wearing black slacks and a white, unbuttoned dress shirt. But of course, he's still masked. He gently tosses me a warm washcloth and it lands on my stomach.

I grab the washcloth and sit up. "Thanks. Um, Hart, I, uh—"

He interrupts me before I can apologize. "I'm going to head down to the coffee shop downstairs. I have work I need to do."

His tone is stiff and cold. He's definitely pissed. And I can't blame him. When he marked me with his knife earlier, he said I was his—and now I've fucked everything up by calling out Liam's name. I can only imagine how I'd feel if he'd said Willow or some other woman's name—maybe even his mystery love—while he'd been inside of me. I swallow.

And he's going down to the coffee shop in the middle of the night? But when I glance at the clock, I see that it's after 5 a.m. Shit. We never even slept, and yet, I'm so keyed up there's no way I'll sleep, even though my entire body aches from fatigue and all the rough sex.

"Sure," I say, sheepishly. "Maybe when you get back, we can talk."

With a terse nod, he finishes getting dressed, then takes his computer bag and leaves the room. I imagine he'll remove his mask as soon as he gets in the elevator, and I half wonder if I should follow him, just so I can finally get a glimpse of his face as Hart, and not as Lucien. But I quickly dismiss that idea. I'm already in enough shit as it is. I don't need yet *another* reason for him to be pissed at me.

Using the washcloth, I clean myself up. Then I get up and open the curtains, allowing the brightening pre-dawn morning light to flood the room. We managed to fuck all night. How am I *not* surprised? Hart has amazing stamina. And he still didn't need to sleep after all that, either.

I dig out my T-shirt and curl up in the bed, suddenly giving in to the fatigue seeping through my limbs. Hart may not need to recharge but I sure do. I close my eyes, determined to think through this clusterfuck when I'm better rested.

My phone pings from somewhere across the room, and my eyes crack open to sunlight flooding the room. It's still morning, mid-morning from the looks of it, and with a glance at the clock, sure enough, I see that I've been asleep a little over three hours. I stretch and get up from the bed and pad across to my bag. The phone reads almost 8:30 a.m., and I'm momentarily frozen in fear, wondering if Hart is ordering me to leave. Or worse, tell me he never wants to see me again?

I unlock my phone, but instead of Hart's name, I see that it's a text from Liam.

I can't stop thinking about you. I need to see you.

Butterflies riot in my stomach, and I push out a breath, seized by a feeling I can't really define, even to myself. I might have just told on myself, imagining him during sex, but that doesn't mean I forgive him for all the shit he's put me through since Dad's death.

Something cold and painful twists in my heart. This is all so fucked up. I type out my response.

I can't. We can't do this. What happened last night in your car was a mistake.

Seconds later, he replies.

We need to talk before I leave town.

Dear God, he's staying at Lori's house, so avoiding him over the next few days, when she's due to be discharged, is going to be difficult. I'll need to go over and prep her house, do a little cleaning up, and stock her fridge and cupboards with some groceries. I also need to make arrangements with a temporary part-time caregiver, so once Lori is released from the hospital, we're ready. Even though Liam could do some of that, or have his assistant do it, I know there are details he's likely to miss. Because, men.

But the absolute *last* thing I need is to see Liam's beautiful face, which at this point, is just a reminder of what happened between us in the car. And worst of all, how it led to me fantasizing about him while another man was inside me.

With a bit of time and distance, I'll forget about this. Right? It's just a passing thing. It doesn't mean anything—God, how I hope it doesn't.

Just email me with whatever you need to say, I reply.

The dots appear that show he's typing out a response. It's probably an infuriating response, though. Because, knowing him, he's going to push the issue. I don't have the emotional energy to deal with him right now, so I turn my phone off and shove it back into my purse. I need to leave this hotel room ASAP. I need to go home and sort out these feelings, if possible—because, right now, I'm tangled in a web of confused emotions.

I take a quick shower, then throw on my clothes. In the living room area, next to the phone, there's a notepad and a pen. I write out a quick note to Hart, telling him I've gone home and that I'll call him later. No explanation, because I don't even know what to say. I could just text him all this, but I don't want to turn on my phone again and see Liam's reply. And I don't trust myself not to look.

Once I'm back at Hill House, I run into a few of my roomies fixing breakfast in the kitchen. They ask me for an update on my stepmom, but I just make some vague comments and go straight upstairs. I'm still bone-tired from the draining day, the events of last night, *and* all the vigorous fucking I did with Hart. I fall into bed without even changing my clothes.

The second my head hits the pillow, my mind wanders to Hart and Liam, but I force those thoughts away. I just need to get some sleep, and then I'll be able to think through this whole situation with a clear head. But one thing I won't do when I wake up—I won't go to the hospital. I'll just call Lori on the phone instead.

The following day, I just go through my usual routine: wake up, grab breakfast, and attend class. The familiar rhythm gives me an odd sense of control, even as my life spirals into a dark, bottomless pit of chaos.

When I finally turn my phone back on, I'm disappointed to see that Hart hasn't texted me since I left him the note. On the other hand, Liam won't stop blowing up my phone.

And I don't know how to feel about any of it.

Hart was always meant to be a temporary thing, right? So why am I so upset about him ghosting me? And Liam...*God* , I don't even know where to start with him. He's fucked me over so badly in the past, I just don't know if I can ever forgive him. And yet...my heart thuds in excitement whenever he's near or even when I get a notification on my phone with his name on it.

After class, I drive myself over to the hospital to see Lori. It just doesn't seem right to call Hart's driver, Andrew, when whatever this is, is still hanging between us.

It's just before noon, so my chances of running into Liam are slim. He's never at the hospital at this hour and I'll be long gone before he can break free from his work for his usual time with her. The man is always working, it seems—or at least, that's what Lori tells me. And thank God for that, because running into him right now would be awkward as fuck and I'm positive Lori would detect it immediately.

When I walk into Lori's hospital room, she's sitting up in bed, finishing her lunch, spoon poised over a cup of vanilla pudding. The TV is blaring a rerun of some old sitcom. She looks like her normal self—rested, hearty, and no longer so pale. I'm flooded with relief. Although, she has a learning curve ahead of her with this special hypoglycemic diet she'll have to maintain, she's going to be alright.

"Hey, Lori," I say with a smile. "You're looking fantastic today!"

Her eyes light up when she sees me. "Oh, honey. I didn't know you'd be coming by. Liam just left. It's a shame you missed him."

I frown. He just left? How weird. He's never here at this hour. "Ah, that's too bad," I lie.

She glances toward the door as if he'd just walked out through it and frowns. Her voice takes on a conspiratorial tone. "I'm really worried about him. He's exhausted. I can tell he isn't sleeping, and he's stressed about something, distracted."

I fight to keep my face completely neutral. "Hmm. That's weird. Maybe it's just him worrying about you. I mean…you gave us a big scare, and after losing Dad, well…" I suck in a quick breath and let it go.

She reaches out and takes my hand. Her skin is cold, so I hold her hand against my stomach. "If something *had* happened to me," she says in a small voice. "I'd like to think you two could put aside your differences and take care of each other. Aside from me, you are the only family each other has that either of you can count on."

I shake my head and release her hand. I don't want to get into this with her, especially now. "Okay, but *nothing* happened to you. You're here, and you're going to be taking better care of yourself from now on, right? Because we both need you."

But she doesn't appear to be listening. Her face is still intent on the point she wants to push across. Good ol' Lori. Stubborn as ever. "He's a good man, Cassie. I know he can appear cold, but that's just his way. Things weren't good for us when we lived in England, and when I left his father, he was so young and...I leaned heavily on him, probably too heavily. He was my little man, just ten years old. He promised he'd be the one to take care of me and told me I didn't need anyone else. In spite of that, he accepted your dad readily as his own when we got married. That serious little boy who'd seen way too much for his age never left him. Not even now, at twenty-five. But Liam always has a rational reason for doing the things he does. He's not trying to be cruel."

I walk over to a beautiful fresh bouquet of roses on her side table and bend to smell them. They're from Liam, of course. "I know. We'll work our differences out given some time. Don't worry so much."

I don't know if I really believe that, but at this point, I'm willing to say anything to get her out of this dark mood she's in. She should be excited about getting released and getting back to her normal life, working with her charity again, puttering about her house, and starting some new craft project.

I turn back toward her and change the subject abruptly. "So did the doctor give you your discharge date yet?"

Before she can even respond, I hear Liam's voice as he enters the room. "Hey, Mom, I forgot my—" He stops cold when he sees me, stiffening his posture. Our gazes meet and lock. I swallow, and he blinks. "Cass."

CHAPTER 27
COMPLICATIONS

The second Liam steps through the door, my heart leaps into my throat. God. *Dayum.* How is he so beautiful? He's wearing a pair of navy-blue slacks with a white button-down shirt, sleeves rolled up to expose his muscular forearms. His hair is neatly combed back, and his chiseled jaw is freshly shaven. He looks perfectly coifed and put together—like a model who's just stepped off the pages of a fashion magazine.

It's such a cruel twist of fate; the man I hate most is the same man who makes my heart race and my knees go weak. If there is a God, then He's up there laughing at me right now.

I push out a breath and glance up at the ceiling. Of course, he would be here at the exact moment I stopped by to visit Lori. My bad luck has been *unbelievable* lately. My God.

I gather every ounce of patience I have, which isn't much, and meet Liam's steady gaze with a tight smile. "Hello." Then I deliberately turn my attention back to Lori. "As I was asking…what did the doctor say?"

Lori is oblivious to the tension crackling between Liam and me—or, at least, she *acts* oblivious. I know she's secretly thrilled that Liam and I are together in the same room again. If I didn't know better, I'd suspect she'd somehow arranged it.

"They took some blood this morning. If everything comes back clear, then I go home tomorrow."

"Oh! That's great," I say. "I have classes in the morning, but I could pick you up in the afternoon and take you home."

"I'm free all morning tomorrow," Liam interjects. "I'll take her home and get her all set up. I'll probably have to duck out for a little work in the afternoon, though."

I don't even look at him. "Okay, then I'll come to check on you later in the day, make sure you have everything you need." I glance up at Liam pointedly. "I'm sure Liam is headed home *any day now.*"

Thank God for that, too. If I have to suffer his presence much longer, I can't be held responsible for what happens between us— I'm either going to kill him or fuck him. And neither one of those outcomes is ideal.

He thrusts his balled fists into his pockets. "I head back to the East Coast Thursday morning," he supplies stiffly.

Perfect. I can manage to avoid him for two days, right?

"I'll pop over to check on you after you get home, Lori. But call me if you think of anything you need." I lean over and kiss her on the forehead, then make a beeline for the door.

Liam follows me out. *Dammit*.

"Cass, wait." He trails me down the hallway.

I ignore him, dodging empty gurneys and laundry bins as I head toward the elevator.

"Cass, *fuck* , wait," he says again, catching up to me. From behind, he grabs my elbow, and pulls me to a stop, turning me around to face him.

"What is it, Liam? I'm not really in the mood to talk right now," I say, jerking my elbow out of his hand. I'm successful, but only because he releases his grip. I press the down button for the elevator, and it lights up.

His gaze rakes over me, and I suddenly feel self-conscious. "You look pale. Are you getting enough sleep?"

I push out a frustrated breath. "Is that why you chased after me? To discuss my sleeping habits?"

He straightens and shoves his hands into his pockets, which makes him look every bit the business shark I know he is. He's so tall that he's looming over me. "We need to talk about what happened in my car."

"Uh, *no* . Actually, we *don't* ," I say. "That's the great thing about free will—we can both just go about our lives and pretend nothing happened."

He takes a step toward me, and I swallow. "Cass. We can't ignore this thing between us. God knows I've tried over the years, but something is pulling at us both and we owe ourselves the chance to find out where it leads."

I shake my head. "That might have been true before you took *everything* from me, Liam." I swallow, suddenly feeling nauseous. Must be all the stress of the last couple of days. "I really can't deal with this right now. I have enough on my plate."

His dark brows are drawn together in concern. "What's going on?"

I ignore his question. The elevator pings and the doors slide open. Saved by the bell. Literally. Two or three people file out, then I step inside. "I think it'd be better if we just stay out of each other's way until you leave."

Thankfully, Liam doesn't follow me into the elevator. In an uncharacteristic act of mercy, he allows me to leave, his eyes locked on mine until the moment the doors block him from view. As soon as they slide closed, I release a relieved breath.

That evening, I'm sitting on the couch in the living room, half-watching a sitcom while staring at my phone when Haley walks in with a bowl of nachos. She plops down on the couch next to me and shoves the bowl at me. "Want some?"

The smell hits me like a Mack truck, and I pull away like she's just offered me a platter of steaming cat poop. Bile claws up my esophagus once more. "Ugh, what do you have on those? They smell horrifying."

She looks at me with some serious side-eye. "It's regular nacho cheese, Cassie. You love my nachos."

"No, they smell different. Are you sure the cheese hasn't gone bad?"

She takes a chip that's dripping with cheese and pops it in her mouth. She crunches loudly and appears to be analyzing the taste. "Nope, they're fine."

I shake my head and grimace, my stomach clenching. "*Yuck* ."

Haley puts her nachos down and twists her body to face me. "What's going on with you lately?"

I stiffen under her scrutiny. "What do you mean?"

Her gaze flicks over me. "You're more tired than usual. You're not eating. I mean, *nachos* gross you out, for God's sake. That's weird."

I shrug one shoulder and look away. I'm not comfortable being the subject of her concern—even though she's right on all counts. But it's probably because I'm so torn up over this Hart and Liam situation.

I glance back at her. "I'm just going through some stuff right now. I'll be fine."

Her eyes narrow. "Is this about the guy dressed up like a deer?"

"*Stag* ," I correct. "And…kinda. It's complicated."

"Well, whatever it is, I just want you to know you can talk to me about it." Then she scooches close and pulls me into a tight hug.

The pressure on my breasts makes me flinch. "Oh, ow," I cry out.

She lets go immediately and looks at me with renewed concern. "What's wrong? Are you okay?"

"Yeah, it's just my boobs," I say, cupping them gingerly. "They've been so sensitive lately. Just the slightest touch is *excruciating* ."

She leans back and studies me again. "Tired. Grossed out by nachos. Painful breasts." She points at me. "You need to take a pregnancy test."

"*What* ? No! I'm not pregnant. I've been taking my pill"—when I remember, but I don't say that last part. "I'm just depressed or something. It's nothing to worry about."

She shakes her head. "If it were just the tiredness, and loss of appetite, then maybe. But sore boobs are a sure sign that something else is going on. My aunt had the same thing happen to her, and it turned out she was pregnant with *twins.* "

Oh, *Jezus* .

I lift my hands in surrender. "Fine, I'll take a test tomorrow if that gets you off my case about it."

Haley stands up and grabs my hand. "Oh, no, we don't have to wait until tomorrow." She pulls me up the stairs to Sam's room. She knocks on the door once, then opens it. Sam is sitting on her bed, doing homework. "Hey, Sam, do you have that extra pregnancy test? Cassie needs it."

"I don't actually need it," I rush to clarify. "Haley just *thinks* I need it."

Sam's face lights up. "Oh! Sure. Let me grab it."

She leaves the room and returns with a pink box, then hands it to me. "There were two in the box, but I just needed one. It was negative, thank God," she laughs.

I glance down at the box, my stomach pitching. Even though I know it's highly unlikely that I'm pregnant, it's still possible, I guess. The first time I was intimate with Hart was several weeks ago, and I'm not sure when my last period was. I don't really keep track of that sort of stuff. But I do remember checking my pill pack after that first time with Hart and I was three days behind on the pack. But Haley had said doubling up would do the trick so that's what I'd done to catch up.

I take the box into the bathroom and pee on the stick with Haley and Sam standing just outside the door. By the time I clean up and set the pregnancy test on the counter, the *entire* house—Sam, Haley, Avery, and our new roomie, Skye—is bent over the stick, watching the moisture creep across the test window.

I sit on the toilet and try to breathe through the dizziness that popped up out of nowhere. Even if the test ends up being negative—this entire ordeal is stressful.

"Oh!" one of my roommates says. I don't even know which one it is.

I can't see the test from where I'm sitting, but I straighten and try to peer through the gap between Haley and Sam. "What? What does it say?" Was that a good *oh*, or a bad *oh*?

"We have to wait the full five minutes!" Avery chides the group and glances at the timer on her phone that's counting down.

An excruciating few minutes pass, and I almost get up and demand a look at the test, when the timer beeps. My heart stops.

"Uh, ok," Haley says. "Should we have her take another one? Just to be safe?"

I stand up. "Tell me what it says!"

My roommates part like the Red Sea, and Haley picks it up, then hands it to me. I stare down at the plastic stick and blink. "Who has the instructions? What do two lines mean? Is that negative?"

Sam throws a concerned look at me, then passes me the instructions. "It's, um, it's positive, Cassie."

Positive?

No.

"That's...it's wrong. Does anyone have another test I can use?"

Everyone just kind of looks at each other, like they're in as much shock as I am.

"I'll go down to the pharmacy and grab another one," Avery says.

"Good idea, Avery," Haley says, turning to me. "I'm sure it's faulty. I've heard these things can report false positives."

I just nod numbly. Thank God for friends. At least I'm not trying to figure this out alone.

One hour and six tests later, it's confirmed.... I'm definitely, 100 percent pregnant.

With Hart's baby.

The guy who won't respond to my texts.

Fuck.

How did my life get so complicated so quickly?

CHAPTER 28
GHOSTED

OKAY. SO. *CRISIS.*

I'm pregnant, and I have no idea what I'm going to do. My roomies assure me that everything is going to be okay, but honestly, none of us know that. That vague statement isn't the least bit comforting.

"I can, um, make an appointment at a clinic, if you want," Haley says.

"Good idea," Skye chimes in. "I know one close by that my cousin used. And if we act fast, all you have to do is get the pill to take care of things."

"Perfect. If you make an early morning appointment, I can go with her," Sam says. "She might be able to skip her first class. Is that okay, Cassie?"

I just nod numbly, but I don't say anything. What *can* I say? This can't be real. There's no way *any* of this is real. I'm walking and breathing, but everything around me feels strange.

I suck in a breath. "I'm, uh….going to go grab some chicken. Do you guys want some?"

My roomies give me their orders, and once we're agreed, I get in my car and head down to Colorado Boulevard. I park in front of the chicken place, shut off my engine, and tilt my head back against the headrest. After a few minutes of silence, which I *desperately* need, I pull my phone out of my purse and dial Hart's number. It rings several times, then eventually goes to voicemail.

Frustrated, I hang the phone up and type out a text.

Please call me when you get this. It's urgent.

I stare at the text window for…I don't even know how long, before giving up and tossing my phone into my purse. Hart used to text me back immediately. The fact that he hasn't means he must still be pissed about what happened at the hotel.

Fuck. My. Life. How would he even react to this news? I can't even guess at what he's going to say, or how he's going to feel about this.

I grab the food order and head back to Hill House. We eat in the living room, while everyone tries to make me feel better about my situation. I smile and laugh in all the right places, but my heart just isn't in it.

After eating a little chicken and half a buttermilk roll, I head up to bed. It's hours before my actual bedtime, but if I stay up, I'm just going to stare at my phone, waiting for Hart to text me back. And I'm just so bone-tired anyway. Maybe when I wake up, things will feel a little less apocalyptic. One can hope, anyway.

By the next afternoon, it's clear Hart has no intention of texting me back, so I decide to go looking for him instead. I try calling Exeter House and am told that I wouldn't be allowed admittance to his penthouse unless he's in residence. Is he out of town? He didn't mention anything to me about leaving. So I then decide to head to Obscura instead. I still have my stag necklace and throw on my little "uniform"—the black dress—pull my hair up, and do minimal makeup before driving the hour from Pasadena to Malibu.

Before I hand off my battered Honda to the valet, I grab my fawn mask from the back seat. Ms. Lawrence is at the door, as usual, and greets me with a smile.

"Welcome back, Fawn. Nice to see you again."

I swallow, suddenly nervous. "Thanks. Is Hart here tonight?"

She presses her lips together and shakes her head. "I'm afraid I don't know. It's been a busy evening. If he's here, he'll be in the founders' area."

"Great, thanks. I'll go check."

I drop my phone off at the check area, then go in search of Hart—which turns out to be no easy task. For a random evening during the week, it's bumping here at the club. I make my way down the entry staircase, across the main floor then over to the lounge and bar area, which is overflowing with scantily clad, masked people. I scan the faces, looking for Hart's distinct stag mask, but I don't see him.

As I move toward the dance floor, I feel a slight bump on my shoulder. I turn to apologize to whoever I just collided with, and I see Willow's bunny face staring back at me wide-eyed. I stand there frozen for a second, not sure what to say. The last time I saw her was at Hart's penthouse, and she was *not* happy to see me, was weeping on Hart's shoulder and begging him to take her back.

Awkward.

"*Fawn ,*" Willow says loudly, so her voice carries over the music. She's no longer wearing her dark-haired wig and has her natural sandy-blond hair down around her shoulders instead. "You're back." And she doesn't seem happy about it, either.

Cold fear grips me, and I wonder if she's back with Hart now. Perhaps in his anger, he opted to go back to the sub who is less problematic. Someone who obeys him automatically. Someone who knows her place. Someone who doesn't call out another man's name during sex.

"Hey, Willow." I force a smile. It's with no small relief that I notice she's no longer wearing the stag necklace like mine. It's a half-faced phantom mask instead. I remember the dark and handsome stranger at the bar, the man Hart chased away from me. He'd been called Phantom and had a similar mask to Willow's necklace. She's with him now? It didn't take that long for her to move on to a new Dom after all. "How are you doing?"

She narrows her eyes. "I'm better now, no thanks to you. Are you here to steal another Dom for yourself now that Hart's no longer coming around?"

I blink and frown, but make a show of fingering my necklace. Her eyes sink to it and she scowls, but she gets the message.

She tosses her chin up haughtily and scans the room as if she's looking for Hart to appear at my shoulder. "Well, he did me a favor by letting me go. It's hard not to catch feelings for him. But, whatever, it's just as well. No one is ever going to live up to the memory of *her* ." She shrugs but doesn't quite pull off that she doesn't care. "Once I had that lightbulb moment, it made everything easier to accept. He moved on to you because you're a novelty. But he'll tire of you, too. He'll never be satisfied because he can never have what he really wants. *Her.* She's the ghost that will haunt every relationship he has."

Her. The woman Hart told me about in that quiet, resigned voice when we were at the hotel. That woman he loves, but can never have.

Willow takes a step toward me and lifts a strand of my dark hair. "I see why he wants you. Dark hair, beautiful curves…a good substitute so he can pretend. And I don't even mean that in a cruel way. But you shouldn't get any ideas about him. His heart isn't free. Trust me."

I swallow. Willow is obviously still pissed at me, but there's also a valid warning in her words. She has no reason to lie now, and my heart sinks at her honesty. I could chalk up her attitude to bitterness, but she's not angry, not trying to claw my eyes out. Salty, yes. But she seems to want to warn me.

I nod. "Yeah, you're probably right. I don't think we're destined for more than a hot fling, anyway."

And maybe having a baby together. But people who aren't a couple do the co-parenting thing all the time, don't they? We can be amicable, do the best thing for the baby…

I can't believe I'm even considering going through with the pregnancy. But it's all my thoughts gravitate to, and I don't want to make a decision one way or the other until Hart knows everything. If I could only find him to tell him.

Willow shrugs again. "What I don't understand is how much and how quickly he changed things when he brought you into the mix."

I frown. "What do you mean? What did he change?"

Her eyes roll behind her mask. "Before you popped up, he had a slim partial mask that he switched out for a full mask. He rarely even wore one—when we were alone, anyway."

I narrow my eyes at her. "You mean, when you were with him, he didn't have the mask on? You—you've seen his face?"

Her pale brows furrow. "Of course, I have. Haven't you?"

I swallow and refuse to answer, suddenly devastated and furious at the same time, thinking about all the times I asked him to take off his mask and all the times he staunchly—even angrily—refused. "What else did he change?" I ask.

"Well, that British accent is the biggest one."

I blink. "*What?*"

"That only started when you were brought in to watch us. He had an American accent before that. I thought maybe it was some fetish of yours, so he did it for you?"

"No," I shake my head. "I didn't ask him to change anything."

How strange that he had an American accent before I arrived at Obscura. I suddenly remember my roommate, Gwen, telling me the same thing weeks ago when I first told her about Hart. But why would he change his accent for me? Even when I met Lucien at his office in Beverly Hills, he had that accent.

I'd confront him about it, but he's ghosting me right now. And for that matter, we have more important things to discuss than his accent, which brings me back to the reason I'm here.

"Is he here tonight?" I ask. "Have you seen him?"

She huffs. "I haven't seen him in weeks. Besides, I've kind of got my own thing going on, now." She touches her Phantom necklace. "I'm not looking for him."

In spite of her saltiness, I do empathize with her. At least she's given me some valuable information. She could have just told me to fuck off.

"I understand. I'm happy for you." It's the truth. I'm glad she's been able to move on from Hart.

We say a cool goodbye to one another, and I head home, completely deflated. The reason Hart is ghosting me is my own fault, so I can't even be angry about it, which is the worst part. I just want to scream, cry, and rail at him.

When I get home, Haley is in the living room, watching something on television. She turns toward me as I walk in. "Oh, hey, Cassie. How are you feeling?"

I shrug one shoulder and put my purse down. "Emotionally exhausted."

Her gaze flicks over my dress. "Did you go somewhere fancy?"

I kick off my heels and plop down on the couch. "I went to Obscura to try to find Hart. He isn't there. I've texted him. Called him. I'm not sure what else I can do."

"You know where he works. You could call him there—or just show up."

It's true, I could call his office. He never really seemed keen on mixing his Hart persona with his real life, but this is an emergency. What he wants or doesn't want is irrelevant.

"True. I'll try calling his office tomorrow." I sigh. "And after that, I don't know. I guess I'll just have to deal with this whole situation on my own."

"Oh, speaking of which, I made an appointment for you at the clinic for next Monday. Is that going to be okay? Sam said she'd go with you."

I nod, numbly. Honestly, I'm not even sure that's what I want. I just don't know. My feelings about it are all over the place.

"Thanks, Haley. You've been a good friend."

She smiles, and as though she read my mind, she says, "Anything for my girl. And, listen, if you don't want to go through with it, that's okay, too. We can figure it out either way."

Her absolute acceptance of my decision, regardless of what it is, makes me burst into tears. I hadn't even known it was coming, but all of a sudden, I'm blubbering nonsense about how fucking crazy the last few weeks have been and how thankful I am for my roomies. Haley leans over and pulls me into her arms, hugging me tightly.

"Shhhhh," she says, rocking me gently. "It's going to be okay, Cassie. Everything will work out."

I pull back, tears still streaming down my face. My eyes feel swollen, and my nose is dripping so badly I can barely breathe. "But you don't know that. You can't possibly know that."

"Hey, Cassie." She tilts my chin up, so I'm looking at her. "It's going to be okay because we're going to *make it* okay."

I nod, sniffing loudly. "I'm sorry, I'm not usually this emotional."

She pulls me back into another hug. "It's the hormones. I've heard they're brutal during pregnancy."

Great . Perfect. Only nine more months of being a complete emotional wreck.

"I think I'm going to head up to bed. I'm exhausted," I say.

Minutes later, I'm in bed, curled under the covers. I don't even take off my dress, brush my teeth, or remove my makeup. I'm just too tired to deal with any of it. Hart *completely* ignoring me is absolute agony.

But as I drift off to sleep, it's not Hart I dream about...it's Liam.

CHAPTER 29
BETRAYED

THE NEXT AFTERNOON, WHEN I GET HOME FROM CLASS, I find a private spot on the patio at Hill House and call Lucien's office. I feel a little guilty invading his personal life like this, but I knew him as Lucien before I ever knew him as Hart. It's not like I've *never* interacted with him as Lucien in the real world.

Besides, this is important.

Lucien's assistant answers the phone on the second ring.

"Hey, Sara," I say. "This is Cassie Fitzgerald. Can I please speak with Lucien? It's really important."

She hesitates on the other end of the line. "Cassie, hi. I'm sorry, he's still out of the country. How important are we talking? Because his reception is spotty at best. It's been days since he's even checked in with me."

I blink. Is she talking in code? Still out of the country? I spent the night with him three days ago…

"Uh, um. *What?*"

"Yeah, he's in Nepal. Hiking in the Himalayas for the past two weeks. But I can take a message. He'll be back in the office next Monday."

My brain stutters to a halt. What? Is that the story he's given his office, so he could escape to Pasadena guilt-free? "Hiking in the Himalayas," I repeat like an idiot.

She laughs. "I know, right? It's this crazy thing he does every year. Picks a different mountain range. If you can find his social media accounts, he posts some amazing photos. Well, when he can get reception. Some of them are *unreal.*"

I frown. Posting actual pictures sounds a bit too elaborate for a lie.

"W-when did you say he left town?"

Before she can even answer me, I'm on my phone, hunting down his social media, and sure enough, there are dozens of pictures of him hiking in a country that's on the other side of the planet from me. All dated and *definitely* real.

"He left two weeks ago," she says. "Do you want me to—"

"Great, thank you," I interrupt, hanging up.

I stare at my phone, completely mystified. How could Lucien be in the Himalayas for two weeks and *also* in a hotel room with me just a few days ago?

My heart starts to thud in my chest, and I feel a panic attack coming. Bile burns at the back of my throat.

A dark realization starts creeping in. Could it be that the man I *thought* I'd been fucking is someone else entirely? It would explain how oddly formal and confused Lucien was when I met him that day at his office.

And now I'm pregnant with his baby…whoever *he* is!

I'm on the verge of throwing up, and I rush into the house, grabbing my purse from the foyer.

"Hey, Cassie," Skye says brightly. But as soon as she catches sight of my face her tone changes. "Is everything okay?"

"*No* ," I say, fishing my keys out of my purse. "Everything is definitely *not* okay. I need to go see my stepmom. I'll be back."

Her hand flies to her chest. "O-okay."

I fly out the door and get into my car. I just need some advice. Someone who can tell me what to do. And Lori loves me like a daughter. She just got home from the hospital this morning, but I know she'll help me figure this out.

Since Lori's house is in Malibu, it's a full forty-five minutes later before I'm pulling into her driveway. I blast my music loudly to drown out my thoughts, and prevent me from freaking out.

When I arrive, I enter through the back door, which the family uses almost exclusively. The door's unlocked, so I push it open and call out Lori's name.

"I'm in the den, hon!" she replies.

Oh, thank God. Just hearing her motherly voice fills me with a sense of relief and comfort. I move through the kitchen, and into the den. Lori is sitting in her recliner, wrapped in her favorite fleece robe, watching a game show.

"Hi, honey," she says, glancing over at me.

I walk up and give her a hug. "Are you excited to sleep in your own bed tonight?"

She grins up at me. "Yes, thank God!"

Just then, her phone beeps, and she asks me to bring her a bottle of water so she can take her medication, which I do.

When I pull the bottle out of the fridge, I walk by the little landing area that has the hooks on the wall where we all used to hang our car keys. Lori's car keys are there and just beside her is *another* set of keys. One of the fobs on the key chain has a red stylized trident on it. I've seen that symbol before—on Liam's car.

His spare set, hopefully?

I walk back in and hand her the bottle. "Liam's here?" I ask, my heart suddenly thudding. He's the last person I want to see right now. And I definitely don't want him around when I ask Lori for advice about my predicament.

"Oh, yes. He canceled his afternoon meetings. He wanted to stick close to home to make sure I was doing okay."

I frown. "But he knew I was coming…"

She shrugs and opens her water bottle, knocking back her pills. "He's out for a run on the beach. He said he'd be gone for a while. Said something about needing to clear his head."

Relief washes over me, and my muscles immediately unclench.

"Oh, but he mentioned that paperwork you were looking for. You can probably go grab it now if you want."

I shake my head. "What papers? He didn't say anything to me the other day."

"Your dad's will, and a copy of the trust, is what I think he said."

I blink. Oh! *Finally*. Something I said at the hospital the other day must have gotten through to him. "Where did he leave them? In the dining room?"

"Upstairs, in the guestroom."

The guestroom is what Lori calls Liam's old bedroom that she has mostly left decorated with his high school athletic memorabilia, some kind of empty-nester shrine to the ghost of kid past. Liam is most likely staying in his old room while he's been here.

Well, it's not his room anymore and I'll be quick about getting what I want. I can shove them in the car, make sure Lori's comfortable, then be gone by the time he gets back from his run. No harm, no foul.

"Okay, let me run up and grab those before I forget, then."

I'm still swimming in confusion and emotion about the Hart thing, but there's no way I can pour my soul out to Lori knowing Liam could walk in at any second. I'll just have to talk to her tomorrow, I guess.

As I climb up the stairs, I ball my fists in frustration. Fuck. Liam. My God. Why is he always getting in my way?

Butterflies are at war in my stomach as I move down the hallway and push Liam's bedroom door open. As I step inside, I suck in a breath and immediately wish I hadn't. It smells like him in here—his expensive cologne, his musky male scent. I moan inwardly.

The papers are lying in a neat pile of manila envelopes on the desk, so I scurry across the room and scoop them up. Just as I'm turning, I catch sight of the doorway just beyond that leads to the adjacent bathroom. It's ajar, mostly open to the bedroom and the shower door has just opened.

I freeze. Either Lori has a very cleanliness-fixated intruder in her house or Liam came home a lot sooner than she thought. But instead of ducking out before I'm noticed, I freeze, completely shocked by what I see.

Liam is standing naked on the bathmat, drying himself with a towel. He's turned away from me, and my gaze lands on his deliciously toned ass. I'm momentarily mesmerized, my gaze climbing from the dimpled muscles of his lower back up to his tapered waist and then to his broad shoulders.

I'm backing slowly away as Liam wraps the towel around his waist and then turns to reach for another towel for his hair. As he does so, he turns partially toward me and exposes the massive tattoo covering his shoulder.

I freeze, my gut diving to the ground. It's a stag, with antlers and a head formed from stylized Celtic knotwork. It's…

It's *exactly* like Hart's tattoo.

In the exact same spot.

My blood freezes. What the *actual* fuck?

I almost drop the bundle of envelopes I'm holding. *No.* This isn't possible. My brain refuses to accept what's right in front of me. Hart isn't Lucian. He was never Lucian.

Hart is Liam.

Liam is Hart.

Oh my fucking god. Hart, the man who I let dominate my body, whose cock I begged for…all those things we did. All those things I let him do. Hart is…*my stepbrother*. The bundle of papers drops to the floor and scatters at my feet. Liam turns, and our eyes lock.

One heartbeat. Two. His mouth opens.

"*You* ," is the only word I can choke out. "You're *him* —" I shake my head.

"*Fuck* ." He's still dripping wet with only a towel around his waist. "Cass, wait—" He steps toward me and holds out his hand as I back away.

I just shake my head, unable to speak.

"Cass, this isn't how I wanted you to find out."

I blink. *Yeah, no shit.*

He advances on me, and I take a step back. "You've done some horrible things in your life," I say on the verge of hyperventilation, tears forming. "But *this?* My God. This is next-level cruel, Liam."

He's only a few feet away and about to reply when I do the only thing I can think to do. I turn on my heel and run. As fast as I possibly can.

I can't breathe. The air is clogged in my throat, and sucking in a full breath is nearly impossible. What's worse, my heart is racing so fast, I'm afraid I might pass out.

I rush out the back door without even saying goodbye to Lori. I just jump in my car and peel out of there so fast I lay down half the rubber on my tires right in front of our old house.

It's minutes later and I'm at the stoplight before I can even formulate a plan. I can't trust myself to drive all the way back to Pasadena like this. So I head to one of my favorite places in the area—Zuma Beach.

I manage to still the zillion thoughts racing through my head long enough to get there safely. When I pull up and park, I'm relieved to find the beach empty. It's the middle of a weekday on a chilly, breezy day, so of course, it would be.

With tears streaming down my face, I kick my shoes off and walk out to the edge of the water and cross my arms over my chest, hugging myself tight. How could Liam do this to me? In my mind, I go back and replay every interaction I had with Hart.

The mask.

The accent.

The insanely crazy chemistry we had.

How could I have *not* known Hart was my stepbrother? I'm such an idiot. But even as I admonish myself, I wonder—did I really miss the signs, or did I simply ignore them? If I'm being honest with myself, something about Hart always felt familiar, but I chose not to question my own intuition. I chose not to look too deeply into his eyes, probably because I was afraid of what I'd find in my own heart.

I sink down onto the sand and look out over the water. The ocean breeze whips through my hair, and I take in a lungful of briny air. It calms me instantly. Just a little.

When I was younger, this stretch of beach always made me feel better, somehow. There's nothing really extraordinary about it. There are definitely prettier beaches in Malibu, but my dad brought me here often as a kid, and when I'm here, I feel close to him.

Inside, I feel heavy and on the very edge of panic. God, what am I going to do? In the past month, my life has gone from normal and boring to an absolute flaming shit-show. Like, epic soap opera-level. That's when you know it's bad. When it's something the writers of a soap opera might dream up.

And here I am at the end of it all, pregnant, carrying my stepbrother's baby.

Fresh tears spring up, and I don't even try to stop them.

"Cass!"

I push to my feet and spin around. Liam is a little distance away from me and striding purposefully toward me. He's wearing jeans and a gray hoodie, shoes dangling at his side. It's the most casual I've seen him since we were teenagers, and it makes him look so much younger.

"Leave me *the fuck alone*," I yell, still sobbing.

He's already within a few hundred feet of me, his long legs eating up the space between us. "You left without letting me explain."

Explain. Yeah, explain this, you asshole. Rage seethes through me, stiffening my limbs. "Oh, I'm sorry. Should I have pulled out a book or magazine to skim while you dressed yourself?"

"Cass." He reaches out and grabs my arm to prevent me from walking away. "It wasn't supposed to happen like this."

"Yeah, no kidding," I say, twisting my arm out of his grasp. "How did you even find me here?"

He glances at the nearby stand. "Lifeguard station seven. It's been your favorite spot since we were kids."

I wipe my face with the back of my hand. "So what you're saying is that I'm utterly predictable. Did I behave in every other way you predicted?"

He reaches for me again, but this time I don't pull away. "It's because I *know* you, Cass. And, listen, because I need to tell you this finally. It's been killing me for far too long because...Cass, I've loved you for as long as I can remember."

I scoff at that. "Loved me? *Loved* me? And what is your definition of love, exactly? Ghosting me after Dad died—the man who treated you like a son? Taking *everything* from me and keeping me in poverty? Dressing up in disguise so that you could fuck me?"

"It wasn't meant to be that—I just wanted to...Cass, I've been fighting this for so long. I devised ways to cope because I knew I could never have you. You were only meant to watch me with Willow. I hoped that having you there would be enough to satisfy the fantasy. But...I should have known. This thing between us wasn't something I could harness or control. It's too powerful. But in my arrogance, I tried...and I failed. I'm sorry, Cass. I want—"

I yank my arm out of his grip. "You *want*. It's all about what *you* want. Without consequences. What did you think would happen when I found out it was you? What the fuck did you think this would all lead to? You have no idea of even the smallest consequences that have come from this. How much this has ripped our lives apart—this family, everything. And now—" I cut myself off, unable to get it out. I look at him, horrified once again at the realization.

I turn and start to walk away.

He's right on my heels, grabbing for my arm. "And now...what?"

I spin on him, eyes burning, hands balled into fists. "And now...now, I'm *pregnant*."

For exactly two seconds, he has no reaction. Almost as though he doesn't understand what I just said, but then his eyes dart down to my stomach and his brows knit together. "Pregnant?"

I push out a violent breath and roll my eyes skyward, throwing my hands up. "Yes, *pregnant*, Liam. As in I'm going to have a baby. *Your* baby." The last bit comes out strangled, choked by new tears rising up.

A muscle in his jaw ticks. "When were you going to say something?"

"You're fucking joking, right? I've spent the past two days trying to find Hart to tell *him,* but he fucking ghosted me. Figures, since he never existed in the first place."

"Hart exists. *I* am Hart, Cass. He's the man I've been afraid to show you for all these years. But please believe me when I say...everything that happened between us these past few weeks was real."

I glance out at the ocean, watching as the waves crash, then recede. Seagulls circle and squawk overhead. "I don't—I *can't* believe that. This is just another instance of you taking what you want no matter the costs. Like what you did with Dad's company. You wanted it and you took it—consequences be damned." I ball up a fist and swing, pounding him on his chest once. It's like hitting a boulder. He makes no move in reaction. "You *selfish fuck* , Liam. I honestly don't know what's real anymore."

I'm just so confused. And I'm tired. So fucking tired. I want to go home, crawl under the covers, and just…disappear into myself.

Reaching out, he brushes the side of his thumb along the line of my jaw. I lean into it, momentarily forgetting how much I hate him. When he speaks his voice is low, intent. "What I feel for you is real, Cass. And the baby—*our* baby—he or she is real, too. We can make this work."

Our baby. What right does he have to talk about our baby?

Shaking my head, I step back from him, staring at him with narrowed eyes. "No. *No.* You've betrayed me in the worst possible way. I can't forgive what you've done, not now. Maybe not *ever* ."

The look on his face is pure pain, and I wish I could feel good about inflicting it. But there's a heaviness in my chest that makes it hard to breathe.

"Tell me what I can do, Cass." It's the first time in our lives that I've ever heard real fear in his voice, and it shakes me a little. "Whatever it is, I'll do it. If it's money, I'll transfer my whole fucking account to you right now—everything I have. It's yours. Just…don't walk away from this. From us."

I swallow. "Money isn't going to fix this."

A year ago, it might have. If only he'd just given me what I was owed from my dad's estate, then things wouldn't have been so strained between us. But now, God, so much has happened—and coming back from it…I just don't think it's possible.

"I love you, Cass," he says again. There's anguish in his voice, unshed tears in his eyes. His bare sincerity guts me.

I swallow. How I wish things could have been different. But as my dad would say, you can't unring a bell. What's done is done.

"If you love me, Liam, then you can prove it by walking away right now and leaving me alone."

CHAPTER 30
CONFESSIONS IN THE DARK

"I FEEL LIKE I'M DYING," I BLURT OUT FROM UNDERNEATH the covers.

Avery is sitting next to me on my bed, peering under the comforter where I've spent the last two weeks, since that confrontation with Liam on the beach. "You need to get out of bed, Cassie. Get some fresh air."

"I don't feel well."

Which is the truth. The first trimester of pregnancy is proving to be brutal, as it turns out. I never went to the clinic appointment Haley set up for me. I decided to keep the baby, come what may. But in all honesty, it's not the near-constant nausea that's keeping me in bed. It's the heavy ache in my chest. I miss Hart. Or Liam. Or whoever he is. I miss the warmth and intimacy I'd found with him. The connection. I've never felt that with anyone before, and now that it's gone...I feel lost.

Sam pokes her head in from the doorway. "We're worried about you, Cassie. What about your classes?"

"I've emailed my professors, and I have people recording my classes. I'll get caught up." Eventually. Maybe. Right now, none of that seems to matter. If my grades plummet, then they plummet. I can't summon the energy to care.

Avery pushes a lock of my uncombed hair behind my ear. "What about your mom?"

"She texted me. My stepbrother delayed his trip back east." I fight back the tears that form whenever I think about him. At first, it was anger, but over the last week or so, the anger has dissolved into a deep, soul-crushing feeling of loss and sadness that I just can't seem to shake.

"Well, you're not eating, and we're really worried," Avery says. "Think of the baby," she adds almost under her breath.

The baby is making me sick as hell with a complete loss of appetite so I'm not feeling guilty.

Avery and Sam share a long look. "Well, sweetie, you have to take care of yourself. At least have some of the juice I brought up."

To shut them up, I grab the glass, take a sip of the sickly sweet apple juice, battle a wave of nausea, then set it aside. Fighting a shudder, I settle back into my blankets. "I just need to sleep. Please?"

Avery frowns. "That's pretty much all you've been doing. How 'bout you get up and take a nice hot shower? You'll feel like a brand-new person afterward."

I eye my perpetually optimistic roommate. Will that new person she promises I'll be still be knocked up?

The girls soon get the hint and leave me alone again, thank God. Haley just moved into one of the empty bedrooms, and

Avery, I think, has been sharing with her temporarily to allow me privacy in my wallowing.

I only get up to use the bathroom. And that's all too frequent, thanks to my condition. The girls have brought me plates of food that they've had to return to the kitchen hours later, untouched. I know they're worried about me. I can hear the conspiratorial whispers just outside the door.

I'm too weak and tired to care. I wish I was too dehydrated to make tears. I've been crying way too much. I'd say 50 percent of my waking hours are spent crying and sniffling. I don't even have the strength to read or watch something on my laptop. I just lie here and stare at the ceiling.

It's nighttime and the room is dark when there's a tap at my door again. I can only imagine what they've plated up for me tonight in order to coax me to eat.

"Whatever it is, I don't want any!" I call out. "But...thanks anyway."

The door cracks open regardless, and I squint at the bright light backlighting the person standing there holding a grocery bag in hand. It's a tall figure—much taller than any of my roommates. And much bigger, too.

A man . I recognize him immediately and respond by throwing my covers over my head. "Get out," I bark.

The door closes but I know he's not gone. Footsteps approach my bed and I hear the rustle of the bag.

"Is something wrong with your hearing? I said *get the fuck out.*"

"Your roommates are worried about you." Liam's quiet but firm baritone seeps through the layers of my blankets and sheets. "I am, too."

"You lost the right to worry about me," I snap. "Go away."

Of course, being Liam, he completely ignores me. He sinks down on Avery's bed, rustling in the bag. "I've stayed away for two weeks hoping this would get to the point where we could talk, but those two weeks have been torture. Because you asked, I've stayed away as long as I possibly could."

I huff and flip the blanket off me long enough to glower at him in the dark. "Wrong. You were gone an entire year, remember? Two weeks should be a cakewalk."

He ignores my saltiness and reaches into the bag, pulling out a plastic container. "Have one of these. They're dried ginger slices. It will help your stomach. There's also some ginger ale and dry crackers in the bag. When you're feeling up to it, I put some of Mom's meatballs and rice in your fridge."

I immediately tense. "Does she know?"

He hesitates and then slowly shakes his head. "She's worried about you. Wondering why you haven't come to see her."

I'm silent at his gentle reproach. If he thinks he's going to use Lori to get to me, then he has another thing coming.

"She's going to find out eventually, Cass. You're her stepdaughter and this is her grandchild."

I blow out a breath. "Reminding me of how fucked up this situation is isn't going to get you anywhere."

He sucks in a deep breath and lets it go. "Do you want me to tell her? Is that what you want? Because it would probably be best coming from both of us."

"I want you to tell her. I want you to admit to her how you purposely kept me in poverty, then offered me a job in a moment of desperation so you could take advantage of me and take everything you possibly could away from me, including my dignity."

He's silent for a long moment, and I stare into the shadows, making out just the outline of his beautiful face in the darkness. God, why does he have to be so perfect on the outside and so rotten on the inside?

"It wasn't supposed to be this way. I tried to tell you on the beach. But you wouldn't listen. All I'm asking for is that you hear me out now. Hear everything but also *listen* to me. Don't try to put a twisted spin on it because I know it's easy to do. It's easy to do because I've kept myself hidden from you all these years."

I frown. "All these years? What are you talking about?"

He reaches up and rubs his jaw, then blows out a breath as if coming to a decision. "I've loved you for as long as I can remember, Cass. Since the night I first met you when our parents were dating."

I shake my head. "We were kids."

He shrugs his broad shoulders. "I didn't do it consciously, Cass. Deep down, I always knew it was wrong. We may not be blood-related, but our entire family still considers me your big brother, and because of that, I always kept my feelings for you secret. But sometime around when I left for university, I realized it was getting harder to hold back. God, Cass, if you only knew the torment I felt then. Living with you, loving you, *wanting* you...I vowed to get away. So I decided to go back to the UK for university, as far away as I could get. And tried to forget."

I blink, remembering how stiff and distant he was that first Christmas back from college. That was the beginning of everything changing between us. It was the deterioration of our friendship. A pang of sorrow pierces my heart when I remember the sadness and confusion I felt back then.

If I'm being honest with myself, it was more than friendship for me, too. But damned if I'm going to admit that to him now. Not after every horrible thing he's done since.

"You weren't pining away for me, Liam. You were dating all kinds of women in college and afterward. And in the last year, you've had your regular round of models *and* Willow, so don't try to—"

"Try to *what*?" he says, his tone growing a little defensive, a little impatient. "What on earth could I possibly be trying to gain by confessing all of this to you?"

My mind races to find an answer to that question, but I come up blank.

He holds out the container of ginger. "Please at least chew on one of these, and I can tell you the rest. If you want nothing to do with me after you've heard me out, I promise you I won't bother you again."

I blink, thinking. Well, this could answer some questions I've had. "Only if you also answer every question I have—*honestly*."

"Deal." He shakes the container of dried crystallized ginger, and I take one.

The taste is sharp, with a little spicy kick to it, but also sweet. I suck on it for a few seconds and follow his directions to chew on it slowly.

He sets aside the container and lets out a long, resigned sigh. "I was at Oxford, and yes, I dated. I had relationships. Nothing lasted very long. I didn't want it that way. It was hard when every woman I dated I compared to you and they always fell short."

I blink, listening carefully to the tone of his voice, trying to detect the obvious lie or manipulation there. But I can't. He sounds exhausted and resigned, like he's decided to lay everything out on the table, then allow me to decide his fate. Hopefully, he can accept the outcome when it comes to that.

"By the time I finished University, you'd already started school out here so I opted to go to the East Coast—"

"—to work for Dad's company and plot its takeover, right?"

I throw that accusation out there because the raw honesty in his voice is already starting to get to me. He seems to have an explanation for everything, and for some reason, that scares me more than anything, because I *need* the anger. I *need* the resentment. Without them, I'm afraid of what feelings might creep into my heart for Liam. And I can't allow that. The last several weeks have proven just how dangerous Liam is to my heart.

I fold my arms tightly over my chest and refuse to look at him, staring at the darkened ceiling instead.

He's been silent while I seethe, but suddenly he moves and my eyes dart to him. He dips his head, his face falling into his hands, and he rubs his eyes.

When he speaks, his deep baritone cracks with emotion. "He wasn't my biological father, Cass, but I couldn't have loved him any more if he was. Patrick Fitzgerald was the best man I've ever known."

None of this is news. I was always aware of the special bond between my dad and his stepson. Those feelings were mutual, and yes, sometimes I resented him for that, feeling like sometimes Liam stole the spotlight from me. They were close, and now that I think about it, I can't tell whether I resented Liam for that closeness with my dad or resented my dad for his closeness with Liam. I blink, my mind swirling with confusion.

"And that's why telling you this secret is the hardest thing I'll ever have to do. It means breaking a promise I made to Dad before he died—something I'd always intended to take to my grave..." His voice fades, and a cold silence stretches between us.

Secret? I swallow past the dryness in my throat. My dad wouldn't have kept secrets from me. No way. I wasn't as close to him as Liam was, but that doesn't mean we weren't open and honest with each other. Still, by the way Liam is talking, I can tell he's telling the truth. Whatever Dad told him, it was something heavy.

I sit up slowly, my heart in my throat. "What secret, Liam? Tell me."

CHAPTER 31
THE ENTIRE TRUTH

LIAM PICKS UP THE CONTAINER OF GINGER SLICES AND, without a word, offers it to me as if that's the price I have to pay to keep him talking.

Not wanting to stop and argue about it, I take another ginger slice and chew on it. Besides, they're tasty, and I can already feel the queasiness start to fade.

Liam sets the container down and rubs his forehead. "The business was failing, Cass. When he died, he was in reorganization. I was working with the trustees for chapter eleven—"

"*What?* No. That can't be true."

He heaves a sigh. "I wish it wasn't. I wish I didn't have to tell you this. He was deeply ashamed and swore me to secrecy. He said it would kill him if you or Mom found out. Despite the stranglehold in cash flow, he struggled to keep you two in the lifestyle to which you'd been accustomed—one he couldn't afford anymore. I tried to talk sense into him, tried to convince him that both of you were strong enough to understand, but the man had his pride. And he flat out refused when I offered to help him."

I shake my head, confused. "You are one of the wealthiest people in the country, Liam. Articles have been written about your success, for God's sake. How is that possible if Dad's business was bankrupt?"

"I had an inheritance, as you already know, from my grandmother. It was held in trust because she didn't have a good relationship with my biological father and she didn't want him touching it. I came into the money when I turned twenty-one…" He shrugs. "And I've invested it wisely."

I blink. "So that money…is all yours? What about Dad's company?"

"It still exists. When Dad died, I paid off his debts, purchased the company and bailed it out. But it hasn't been profitable for a while."

I swallow. "So what does Lori live on, then?"

"I set up trusts for both her and for you. She lives off her trust and…" His voice fades again, and my eyebrow arches.

"You set up a trust for me out of your own money?"

"Yes. To cover your college and living expenses for the first few years out of college."

"Why am I only hearing about this now?"

I can practically hear him swallow, and I tense, suddenly aware that he's about to serve me another tough pill to swallow.

"Part of the reason was you wouldn't take it if you knew it came from me and…part was to keep the predators at bay."

I frown into the darkness. "What predators?"

He pushes a breath out, as though he doesn't want to tell me but knows he has to. "Ever since you started dating, I've managed to…keep you free from any entanglements you might regret later."

I frown. "What does that mean? You chased off my boyfriends?"

Another long, tense beat passes before he answers. "Yes."

I blink. "Why? If you decided you couldn't be with me, you didn't want anyone else to be with me, either? You wanted me to be alone?"

"No, that's not what I wanted. You're smart, beautiful…sexy. What man wouldn't want to be with you? But I'm your brother, Cass, and after Dad died, I felt responsible for you. So, if you started dating someone, I'd…have them investigated. And…" He shakes his head. "…they weren't good men, Cass."

That makes me bristle. "According to who? *You*?"

"When Dad's company was doing well, you were an heiress of a considerable fortune, Cass. The wrong kind of men can sniff that out like bloodhounds. It's not something I'm proud of, but honestly, I'd do anything to protect you."

I blink. "I had a full-on complex about my boyfriends ghosting me."

"Believe me when I say—if there was any other way I could have protected you from them, I would have. But I couldn't just sit back and allow them to bleed you dry while living off you like parasites."

I frown, thinking back to the incidents that align with what he's telling me. One of my high school boyfriends had "borrowed" my credit card and gone on a spree, promised to pay me back, then broke up with me. Weeks later, I'd received a check with no note in the amount to cover the bill. I'm now wondering if that check came from Liam and not my ex-boyfriend.

I clear my throat. "You were hardly ever around. How did you know to…"

"I was around more than you think. But yes, I did stay away from you. It was…easier, though admittedly painful. So I kept my distance."

"Until the mystery job at Obscura…"

"As I told you on the beach, I devised ways to cope. They probably weren't the healthiest ways. I partied a little too hard in college and drank a lot. I dated women who looked like you. I explored the darker side of my sexuality, hoping that would distract me enough from the empty feeling I had inside when I realized I could never have the woman I truly wanted."

I swallow my mangled piece of ginger, then bend and dig into the bag he left on the floor. I pull out a can of soda and pop the tab, sipping the chilled ginger ale. But I have no words. It's all one hell of a strange, convoluted tale and yet…it's explaining so much. So much I'd wondered about for so long.

"When I saw you again at Lexi's engagement party, it all came rushing back, that yearning, that emptiness. Then you lost your job and needed money. I tried to get it to you through Mom, but you wouldn't speak to me, so I devised a plan that would help us both."

I scowl into the darkness. "How? By turning me into your prostitute?"

"You were only meant to sit in the chair and watch us. That's all. I wasn't going to touch you. I hid my identity as best I could. The mask, my accent. It was all to give you deniability. A few weeks at a job that paid insanely well, then you could walk away and you wouldn't have to come to me for the money. And for me, well, I'd hoped it would exorcise my demons by indulging at least in part, in the fantasy. I was never going to—"

He cuts himself off and sucks in a long, shaky breath. "Believe me, Cass, I never intended to touch you. But that just proves what an arrogant asshole I am. I thought I could resist you. I thought I could control this thing between us. That's on me."

I'm stunned silent for a moment. Yes, he'd told me this at the beach, but I was so shocked and overwhelmed, I hadn't listened. But really, what is there to say? Everything he did to me in that room at Obscura...*I'd wanted it*. I'd begged him for it. And it was the hottest, most intense sex I've ever had in my life.

"There it is, Cass. The entire truth. I haven't held anything back."

I'm silent for a long moment, just sipping my soda.

"Ask me anything," he says, eager to break the silence.

"I don't have anything to say. I've just heard a big long story about how you've lied to me for over a decade about...*everything*. How should I react when my entire world has been upended—*yet again?*"

Silence falls between us again. He's staring at me in the darkness, but my eyes are fixed on a distant point of the wall instead. I set aside the empty can of soda.

"I'm sorry, Cass. I haven't said that yet. For all of it. But I can't apologize for loving you. And now that I know how good it can be between us...I can't give you up."

"That's not your choice to make," I snap back.

"We can move past this. For the sake of our family. If not for me, then for Mom, and the baby?"

I rub my forehead when a sudden throbbing starts at my temples. I've been weak for days, and the sudden rush of sugar has probably brought on the headache. I'm so tired, and I feel so hollow inside. I'd cry again if I had any more tears left.

What a mess.

What a *fucking* mess he's gotten us into—and all because he claims to be in love with me. And if I'm being honest with myself, I think I've been in love with him, too. But I didn't dare examine that feeling until this moment.

I fall back on the mattress with a loud sigh. It's too much. And it's too complicated. And I just don't have the energy to deal with this right now.

"Are you alright? Do you need anything?"

"I need to be alone. I need time to think."

"Cass, please. I'm begging you for another chance."

The irony. Liam Force doesn't beg for anything.

"Another chance for what? I don't think I could escape you now, even if I wanted to. We share Lori, and now, we share a child. I acknowledge that you have rights, as the father."

He stands and approaches the bed, then reaches out to stroke my cheek with his thumb. "And us? What about—" He cuts himself off when I shrink away from his touch and plaster myself against the wall.

Slowly, he lets his hand drop to his side. Silence. When he speaks again, it's in a low, hoarse voice. "I'm not sure what I can ever do to make this up to you. But until I broke that promise to Dad and told you everything, I've been a man of my word. And I will be. I'll take care of you and the baby. For the rest of your lives, you'll want for nothing. You'll have everything you ever need."

"And if I need you to back off and stay away?"

A deep, shaky sigh. "I'll give you that, too."

Not another word is said between us, and when he turns to go to the door, I feel the heartache split my chest like a physical blow. Tears immediately spring to my eyes, and any words I might say choke in my throat.

Then he's gone.

And I'm here, in the dark. Alone.

I close my eyes and remember Willow's words at the club. *He'll never be satisfied because he can never have what he really wants. Her. She's the ghost that will haunt every relationship he has.*

When he took Willow as his sub, he asked her to dress like me and wear a wig to match my hair. A full year before I ever showed up there. He told her about me…

He even told *me* about me. *There's a woman I've loved all my life, and recently, I've come to the realization that I'll never truly have her.*

I suck in my breath, remembering how I treated him then, as Liam. I'd made my feelings crystal clear, and he'd known then that I hated him. Or that I told myself to hate him…*We'll never have a future together, and I'm trying to come to grips with that*.

Even then, when he was with me as Hart, he knew that it could only be temporary. But the pain in his voice when he'd told me about her. That was real.

There's a part of me she can't accept. That she'll never be able to accept.

I search my memories for other incidents in our past that are suddenly so clear now, in light of what he's told me.

I wanted to think the worst of him. I wanted to hate him. Because hating him was so much easier than the alternative. So much easier than realizing that I loved him and that no other man would ever compare.

Fuck .

Seconds later, before I even realize what I'm doing, I'm out of bed. The head-rush takes a moment to get over, but I make it to the doorway on relatively steady legs.

The hallway light is on, and I'm at the top of the stairs, vowing to take them slowly. Haley's standing at the bottom of the stairs talking in a low voice to Sam, and they're giggling. They stop and stare, wide-eyed when they notice me.

"Is he gone?" I ask shakily.

"Your brother? Yeah, he just took off without even saying goodbye. He looked upset. I'm guessing he's going to go find Hart and beat the shit out of him for you?"

My stomach does a nosedive. *Ugh.* No need to give them all the sordid details now. I don't even think I could if I wanted to.

"I need to..." I start down the stairs, leaning heavily on the railing. Sam jumps up to help me like I'm an invalid.

"Be careful, in your condition..."

Haley is staring at me. "I'm so glad you're up. Can I make you something to eat? Then I'm going to need to dish on your brother. He's so damn hot."

She's rambling, and I'm ignoring both her and Sam. By the time I reach the door, I'm feeling much more steady. I'm lightheaded from the lack of eating, but I whip open the front door.

"Hey, where are you going?" Sam asks.

"Be right back, I have to tell him something."

"Oh, he's gone by now. He left a couple of minutes—" Haley's remarks are cut off when I slam the door closed after me in my rush to the street. I'm hoping on the off chance he hasn't pulled out yet.

Sometime during the evening, it started drizzling and the rain is coming down at a fairly steady pace. I'm barefoot and in my pajamas, but I run across the cold, wet sidewalk regardless. Just before I reach the curb, I hear an engine start and headlights come on. My head jerks toward the car pulling away from the curb. It's a silver Maserati, and it's heading straight past the house.

"Hey!" I call out, waving my arm, but Liam doesn't see me. His eyes are glued to the road.

It's a quiet neighborhood road so in an act of desperation I dart out to the center of the lane and stand in his path, my arms held out, hands splayed to stop him.

Immediately, the brakes squeal against the wet street and he stares at me through the windshield in shock while the wipers beat at a steady pace. Without even pulling over, he yanks back the parking brake and jumps out of the car.

"What the fuck, Cass? I could have hit you."

I'm hyperventilating now, feeling a rush of adrenaline hit me. "You didn't see me. I had to stop you."

He slams the car door shut, leaving it sitting in the middle of the road. The headlights catch the light fall of the rain.

"Cass, it's wet and cold. You don't have shoes on—"

"Shhh. Shut up. I need to tell you this before I change my mind. I need to—just don't say anything."

He approaches as I'm talking and stops just a few steps away. "Let's go inside–"

"*No.* Stop bossing me around and listen, alright? I love you. I've always loved you, and when your actions hurt me it was easier to tell myself that I hated you." My sentence ends on a sob and soon the rain is mingling with my own tears and my eyes are blurry. "You were my best friend when we were kids. All through school. When you left, it was like I lost a part of myself. I just—I don't want it to happen again. I love—"

And the next thing I know, Liam's arms are wrapped around me and he's kissing me. On my face, on my lips, my neck. My face is between his big hands.

"God, Cass, is this real? It seems too good to be true."

"You fucked up big time. *Big time*. But I wasn't making it easy on you. I get that now. It was too hard. Too complicated. I didn't..." I shake my head.

"Shhh. Shhh. It's okay. I'll work every day of the rest of my life until you can forgive me."

Those words...I'm not sure why, but they make me cry even harder. He's pulling me close against his body and then...then...

He does the most stunning thing of all. While still holding me, he falls to his knees, hugging me around my waist tight, he presses his face to my belly. I can't tell whether he's laughing or crying. My hands go into his now-damp hair, threading through the thick locks. I hold him like that when he suddenly turns his head and kisses the center of my stomach.

"I love you, Cass. With everything that I am, I've always loved you. I don't deserve you, but you bet that I'm going to thank my luck every damn day. I love you, and I love our baby. I know it wasn't what either of us planned, but I'm so fucking happy right now I can barely believe this is real."

I hug him tighter to my stomach, then bend to kiss the top of his wet head. But I have no words for this. My heart is full to bursting with every beat, and I'm sobbing.

Suddenly, whoops and hollers come from the direction of the house, and we both turn quickly to see all my roommates—Sam, Skye, and Haley—standing on the porch, cheering for us.

By the time Liam gets up off the wet street, we're both soaked like drowned rats, but his grin is as wide as mine and my cheeks hurt.

He takes my face in his hands and places a kiss on the tip of my nose. "I love you, Cassandra Fitzgerald," he says again.

I pull back and gaze into his eyes. It's like I'm *truly* seeing him for the first time. How could I have been so blind, for so long? I smile up at him, my heart swelling. "I love you, too, William Force."

His lips curl into a half smile. "Never call me that again."

I lift a brow.

He dips his head, his lips hovering above mine. "Never mind. Call me whatever you want. Just promise you won't leave me ever again."

We're still in the middle of the road, and a car honks at us. We both ignore it.

"As long as you tell me the truth, I'll never have reason to leave," I say.

His lips touch mine. "Deal," he says, his warm breath brushing across my lips. "I've definitely learned my lesson."

"Good," I say, pushing my lips against his in a quick kiss. "Now, let's go inside. We have some catching up to do."

CHAPTER 32

UNCONVENTIONAL FAMILY

BREATHLESS, I FALL BACK AGAINST LIAM THE MOMENT HE pulls out of me. Our sweat-soaked skin sticks together. And our chests are rising and falling fast. He tugs me against him and kisses me on the forehead. I squirm against the itchy carpet beneath us.

"That would have been much more comfortable on a bed than on the floor," he chides, laughing.

I roll my head over and kiss his broad, solid chest. "It's your fault."

He blows out an amused breath, staring up at the ceiling while stroking my arm. "How on earth was it my fault? *You* attacked *me.*"

I bat my eyelashes a couple of times and flash him a grin. "Because you were the one looking insanely sexy putting that crib together. I had no choice but to attack you."

"Well, as your punishment, I may just leave you lying on the floor. I doubt you're getting up from here by yourself." He runs his large palm over my swollen belly. I'm just about to finish my second trimester, and my sex drive has been ridiculously high for the past few months.

Liam has had no complaints and has been happy to comply—when he's here. But since he's been hopping from coast to coast every few weeks while he makes the transition of moving his company headquarters to the West Coast, it's been a little dicey fitting in all the extra sex while he's here.

But there is a hard deadline for the company move. He's promised me there will be no traveling in the last six weeks just in case the baby comes early.

"So you're going to keep me on the floor, barefoot, naked, and pregnant?"

He stretches his thick, muscled arms over his head and then turns on his side to face me. "Now *that* is a delicious thought." This line he quips in his British accent and punctuates with a wicked grin.

He does that sometimes. Pops the accent on me just to mix it up a little and make me hot. He knows I like it.

I snicker at him, and he reaches up, palming my cheek and staring at me with an adoring look in his eyes. "You are so fucking beautiful that sometimes it hurts to look at you."

"And *you* are a very accomplished liar. I'm a beached whale. Especially on the floor. What was I thinking? Sex on the floor of the nursery? I mean even *not* pregnant, carpet burns are hell."

Since I've been showing, the sex has gotten a lot more vanilla than what we started out doing, but that's because Liam has been far too protective to go rough. Though he's made it quite clear several times that he's enjoying himself all the same.

"Besides, there'll be plenty of time to get back to the creative stuff once the baby's here," he reassured me.

Liam pushes off the floor and steps out of the room to grab some washcloths. He returns to hand me one and as he cleans up, he looks down on me with mock offense. "The dirty things you just made me do to you on the floor of our baby's room!"

I laugh. "Oh, yes, you sure acted like you hated every second of it. Besides, this is the last room of the house we haven't 'christened.'"

The side of his mouth turns up cockily as he reaches his hand down, waiting for me to grab on so he can pull me up off the floor. "Then my work here is done."

I point to the pieces of the still unfinished crib. "Hardly!"

I'm still mostly clothed, though my large mommy panties got flung across the room somewhere. I straighten the skirt of my casual cotton maternity dress across my legs and take his hand.

With one quick tug, I'm on my feet. He plants a kiss on my lips and takes the used washcloth from me. I point to them in his hand. "Make sure those make it inside the hamper. We don't have a clean-up crew here."

It's been months since we've visited Obscura together. We've been too busy house hunting for an adorable bungalow in the quiet Pasadena neighborhood adjacent to Caltech so that I can finish attending school next year while we raise the baby. I'm sure our Obscura visits will resume after we become parents and once we're over the sleep deprivation.

"Ooof." I rub my belly. It's been weeks since I felt the first kicks, but since then, the baby hasn't let up.

"Something wrong?"

I smirk at him. "Your son won't stop kicking me."

Immediately, he presses his hand to my belly, and in less than a minute, another kick lands near his palm. I reposition Liam's hand on my stomach, and he grins when he feels it.

He rubs his hand over the spot. "Be a good boy, Patrick. Mommy needs to keep her energy up."

I quirk a brow at him and am about to make another suggestive comment when his phone chimes. It's sitting across the room on the brand-new changing table.

He moves to scoop it up and walks to the bathroom with the washcloths while he reads it. I go over to the changing table to inspect the folded baby clothes on top, all still with their tags. They need to be washed, but that's a project for next week.

I turn back to look at the remains of the crib, trying to figure out how I'm going to talk him into finishing the job when he comes back.

"Mom wants to know if we can get together for dinner tonight. Are you okay with that?" he calls to me.

I nod and smile. "Of course. She hasn't seen you since you got back to town." He's back in the room typing out a quick response. Then sets his phone back on the changing table and returns to assembling the crib, picking up the screwdriver and the assembly instructions.

I take a deep breath, happy that we'll see Lori tonight. She's been amazingly supportive through all of this. And, of course, she's over the moon about the baby—her first grandson. When we'd told her that he was a boy and that we'd decided to name him after Dad, she'd cried for an hour straight. We'd all cried, actually, huddled in a group hug.

That isn't to say that she wasn't shocked when we first told her about us. When we'd sat her down to tell her that we were a couple—and then on the heels of that announced that we were going to have a baby, she'd stared at us, wide-eyed and pale, and said, "Oh…I'm, ah, I'm going to need to take some time to absorb that."

It had been an awkward first few days, but she'd rebounded.

I couldn't help but laugh at the irony. All that time she'd spent trying to throw us together, so we could be one big happy family again. She'd had no idea that it would come about in the way it did.

We're unconventional, our little family. But we are definitely happy.

My eyes wander back to Liam as he successfully screws two more pieces of the crib together and looks about as satisfied with himself as if he'd just completed open-heart surgery. I can't help but smile.

"See? You're doing great, and here you wanted to hire someone to do all this. I knew it would be special for the two of us to do it ourselves."

"The *two* of us?" he says with a teasing smile. "I don't see you helping much with this mind-boggler."

"You're putting it together, and I'm admiring your ridiculously hot body while you do it. Win, win."

I toss him a little blue onesie, and he catches it against his chest.

"Now that the crib is done, we can put the dresser together," I say.

He tosses the onesie aside and walks up to me. Then reaches out and brushes the tip of his finger down my arm. "I have an idea. Why don't we skip the dresser, Little Fawn, and head to our bedroom instead?"

Mmm, I love it when he calls me that. We *just* had sex, but I know when he calls me by my Obscura name, he has something *extra* fun in mind. We obviously can't be as adventurous as we once were, but Hart never fails to disappoint.

I lift my shoulder and look at him through my lashes, playfully feigning innocence. "Yes, Hart. Whatever you say. I'm here to obey."

Just as I turn to leave and head to our bedroom, he slaps my ass. When he speaks, I can hear the smile in his voice. "Good girl."

CHAPTER 33
HALEY

"I FUCKED THE HOTTEST GUY *ALL* MORNING," I SAY TO MY wide-eyed roommates clustered around me. "I met him last night at the hotel bar, and this morning I woke up next to him. I'm telling you, it was the hottest thing I've ever done—with the hottest dude I've ever done!"

It's parents' week at Caltech, and my housemates—Cassie, Sam, and Avery—and I are all sitting at our table, while we wait for our parents to arrive at the Institute-sponsored luncheon. Since none of the parents have arrived yet, I'm regaling my roomies with the story of the *ah* -mazing hookup I experienced this morning. Each one of them is leaning in, drinking in every sordid detail.

"So, wait, what does this guy look like?" Sam asks.

I purse my lips. "Tall, muscular, angular jaw. *So* handsome...and older. *A lot* older."

Avery angles her head. She's the most innocent of all of us, and she's been wide-eyed for my entire sexcapade story. "How old are we talking?" she asks.

I shrug. "Umm, I think he said he was forty-three." I rush on, speaking quickly in the wake of their shocked expressions. "Listen, it doesn't matter. As they say, age ain't nothing but a number, right? Especially when the guy is tall and muscular—*so* damn hot. And perfect, because I was just looking for a one-time thing."

"*Forty-three* ." Avery gasps incredulously. "You can*not* be serious."

Sam busts out laughing. "Oh, my God, that's my *dad's* age, girl. Are you scanning the AARP membership list for dates now?"

I hold up my hand as if taking an oath. "Hey, don't knock it 'til you've tried it," I say defensively. "This guy *really* knew what he was doing. He was *miles* better than the guys our age who haven't met a clit in their entire lives."

My thoughts are cast back to the way my sexy stranger stepped out of that shower, completely naked with droplets clinging to his abs. His hot gaze was fixed on me as if he wanted to eat me up. I'd snuck into the bathroom and caught him stroking himself while the water cascaded over his chiseled frame. That image will be forever branded in my mind as—*handsdown*— the most erotic thing I've ever seen. And the sex that followed...*dayum* . I gulp as my inner temperature rises by several degrees just from the memory of it. *Whew.*

Sam glances down at her phone, then curses under her breath.

"What's up?" Cassie asks. "Everything okay?"

"My dad is here," she answers as she types out a text to him.

I laugh. "Uh, yeah, duh. It's parents' week. That's why we're all here."

"Yeah, I was hoping he'd opt out. My dad is a complete asshole. But hey, he pays the tuition so I guess he gets to come to the events, whether I want him here or not." She's still glancing down at her phone. "He's parking," she says, tucking the phone into the back pocket of her jeans with a roll of her eyes.

"He forks over a fortune to you every month," Avery says. "So he can't be *that* bad."

It's true. I've heard through the grapevine that Sam's dad is a self-made billionaire, though I'm not sure how he made his fortune. She doesn't really talk about it. I think it embarrasses her. But she never wants for anything. Everything is paid for—tuition, housing, car, *and* her dad gives her a generous clothing allowance. We all benefit from those last two, sometimes borrowing her car or her clothes.

Sam sighs. "Yeah, but it's his guilt money. He pays to make up for basically ghosting me after the divorce—the divorce *he* caused by cheating on my mom. I'm telling you, the guy's an asshole. He's probably only here today to save face."

I push out a breath. "Well, all we have to do is smile through the next few days, then we're off the hook until next year."

Cassie pushes out of her chair—she's seven months pregnant and not moving too elegantly, but she's still quick on her feet, striding a few feet away to wave down her stepmom and her stepbrother-slash-baby daddy in order to direct them to our table. Not long after that, I spot my parents arriving. I pop up and wave them over to our table, too.

At that same moment, I catch sight of someone else approaching from the corner of my eye. He's tall. That's what I notice first. A tall, bearded Viking who moves with confidence in his long stride. And he's walking straight for our table.

I turn my head to get a better look at this new gorgeous specimen when my heart stops.

I blink.

What?

No.

It's the guy from this morning. The one who fucked me so hard I'm still sore. I didn't even catch his name, but he's walking straight toward me. His blond hair is combed back, and his blue eyes are just as vivid and sharp as I remember from hours ago. He's wearing khakis, a navy sweater over a white dress shirt, and a long, tailored coat. *Dayum.* He looks wealthy and polished today, like he just stepped away from his yacht club to attend this shitty luncheon.

I frown. Is he stalking me? What the hell is he doing *here?* Did he actually hunt me down? Dude, time and place. And with my parents here, now is *definitely* not the time *or* the place. Shit.

I take a step forward and open my mouth to say something when he catches sight of me. His gaze collides with mine, and his step falters—only slightly—as confusion dawns on his face.

Confusion? Okay, so…clearly he's not here for me, then? Or… What the fuck is going on here?

That answer comes almost immediately.

Sam walks up to him and says, "Hey, Dad. Our table is right over here."

I don't know what she says after that because the floor instantly tilts beneath my feet. I feel nauseous, and it's hard to breathe. My parents are awkwardly greeting my roommates, and I'm standing here, dumbstruck. I blink rapidly, but that doesn't help. My chest feels tight and I think I see spots as I watch Sam and her dad.

Her dad.

He bends to kiss her on the cheek then returns his gaze in my direction, studying me as he lowers himself into one of the empty seats at our table. The one right across from me.

"Hey, all, this is my dad, Logan Kirk," Sam says with a slight eye-roll when he's not looking.

Shit, shit, shit—shit. *Shit*.

I arrange my place setting for a minute, barely hearing whatever it was my mom just asked me. Avery is taking charge of the introductions of everyone, and I'm hearing everything as if it's coming from a long way away, down a mile-long tunnel.

Come to think of it, there's some blackness at the edge of my vision, too, like looking down said long tunnel. Is this what passing out feels like right before it happens?

Placing my hands flat on the table, I push out of my chair so quickly it flies back, almost toppling over. I mumble something to my parents and excuse myself. Then I make a beeline for the only place I can think of—the women's restroom, which is on the far, *far* side of the banquet area. Hopefully, I won't pass out and take a header into the floor before I get there.

As soon as the bathroom door shuts behind me, I sag against the wall—oblivious to the people in the restroom with me. There must be a half dozen or so.

Oh, my God. *Ohmygod.*

What just happened?

I squeeze my eyes shut and pray I'm just hallucinating.

Sam is my bestie. We live together at Hill House, and over the last few months, we've become *super* close. Like, confess-our-darkest-secrets kind of close. And, and…wow…this is all so surreal.

The door opens, and Cassie waddles through it. Her eyes lock on me, her eyebrows pinched in concern. "Hey, are you okay? You look pale, and you rushed away from the table pretty abruptly. I mean, I'm not moving very fast these days, but I did have to hit the bathroom anyway since this kid loves sitting right on my bladder. I thought I'd take the opportunity to check on you."

Pressing a hand to my churning stomach, I release a long breath. "I...um, I think I fucked up, Cassie. Like, *really* fucked up."

The concern in her eyes shifts to borderline panic. "*What? What happened?*"

"That man in there—the gorgeous Viking who just showed up. Um, I've seen him before," I say.

She blinks, confused. "You mean Sam's dad?"

Oh, dear God. Hearing her say it out loud just makes it worse.

"Yeah." I can taste bile rising in the back of my throat. "He's the guy I was talking about earlier, before all the parents started showing up."

She's still confused, and I don't blame her. What are the odds of this happening? "The hookup guy at the hotel? Last night and, uh, this morning?" she asks.

I nod. "Yeah," I say on a whimper. "I can't believe this. I fucked my best friend's dad. What the hell am I going to do?"

BIOGRAPHY

Evelyn has been telling stories in her head for as long as she can remember. She lives on the west coast with her family, and a menagerie of pets. She loves lattes, all things Disney, gaming, and writing dark, wildly sexy stories that give readers all the feels.

Sign up for news and updates:
evelynaustinbooks.wixsite.com/my-site/newsletter